WHAT WOULD SCOTLAND YARD DO WITHOUT DEAR MRS. JEFFRIES?

Even Inspector Wi... ...use his secret weapon is as... ...fries—the charming detec... ...series. Enjoy them... ...mystery

The Inspector an...
When a doctor is found dead in his own office, Mrs. Jeffries must scour the premises to find the prescription for murder.

Mrs. Jeffries Dusts for Clues
One case is solved and another is opened when the inspector finds a missing brooch—pinned to a dead woman's gown. But Mrs. Jeffries never gives up on a case before every loose end is tightly tied.

The Ghost and Mrs. Jeffries
Mrs. Jeffries may not be able to see the future—but when the murder of Mrs. Hodges is foreseen at a spooky séance, she can look into the past to solve this haunting crime.

Mrs. Jeffries Takes Stock
A businessman has been murdered—and it could be because he cheated his stockholders. Luckily, when it comes to catching killers, the smart money's on Mrs. Jeffries.

Mrs. Jeffries on the Ball
A festive Jubilee celebration turns into a fatal affair—and Mrs. Jeffries must find the guilty party.

Mrs. Jeffries on the Trail
Who killed Annie Shields while she was out selling flowers so late on a foggy night? It's up to Mrs. Jeffries to sniff out the clues.

Mrs. Jeffries Plays the Cook
Mrs. Jeffries finds herself doing double duty: cooking for the inspector's household and trying to cook a killer's goose.

continued
AUG 2017

Mrs. Jeffries Pinches the Post
Harrison Nye had dubious business dealings, but no one expected him to be murdered. Now Mrs. Jeffries and her staff must root through the sins of his past to discover which one caught up with him.

Mrs. Jeffries Pleads Her Case
Harlan Westover's death was deemed a suicide, but the inspector is determined to prove otherwise. Mrs. Jeffries must ensure the good inspector remains afloat.

Mrs. Jeffries Sweeps the Chimney
A dead vicar has been found, propped against a church wall. And Inspector Witherspoon's only prayer is to seek the divinations of Mrs. Jeffries.

Mrs. Jeffries Stalks the Hunter
Puppy love turns to obsession, which leads to murder. Who better to get to the heart of the matter than Inspector Witherspoon's indomitable companion, Mrs. Jeffries?

Mrs. Jeffries and the Silent Knight
The yuletide murder of an elderly man is complicated by several suspects—none of whom were in the Christmas spirit.

Mrs. Jeffries Appeals the Verdict
Mrs. Jeffries and her belowstairs cohorts have their work cut out for them if they want to save an innocent man from the gallows.

Mrs. Jeffries and the Best Laid Plans
Banker Lawrence Boyd had a list of enemies including just about everyone that he ever met. It will take Mrs. Jeffries' shrewd eye to find who killed him.

Mrs. Jeffries and the Feast of St. Stephen
'Tis the season for sleuthing when wealthy Stephen Whitfield is murdered during his holiday dinner party. It's up to Mrs. Jeffries to solve the case in time for Christmas.

continued . . .

Mrs. Jeffries Holds the Trump
A very well-liked but very dead magnate is found floating down the river. Now Mrs. Jeffries and company will have to dive into a mystery that only grows more complex.

Mrs. Jeffries in the Nick of Time
Mrs. Jeffries lends her downstairs common sense to this upstairs murder mystery—and tries not to get derailed in the case of a rich uncle-cum-model-train-enthusiast.

Mrs. Jeffries and the Yuletide Weddings
Wedding bells will make this season all the more jolly. Until one humbug sings a carol of murder.

Mrs. Jeffries Speaks Her Mind
When an eccentric old woman suspects she's going to be murdered, everyone thinks she's just being peculiar—until the prediction comes true.

Mrs. Jeffries Forges Ahead
A free-spirited bride is poisoned at a society ball, and it's up to Mrs. Jeffries to discover who wanted to make the modern young woman into a postmortem.

Mrs. Jeffries and the Mistletoe Mix-Up
There's murder going on under the mistletoe as Mrs. Jeffries and Inspector Witherspoon hurry to solve the case before the Christmas Eve eggnog is ladled out.

Mrs. Jeffries Defends Her Own
When an unwelcome visitor from her past needs help, Mrs. Jeffries steps into the fray to stop a terrible miscarriage of justice.

Mrs. Jeffries Turns the Tide
When Mrs. Jeffries doubts a suspect's guilt, she must turn the tide of the investigation to save an innocent man.

Mrs. Jeffries and the Merry Gentlemen
When a successful stockbroker is murdered just days before Christmas, Mrs. Jeffries won't rest until justice is served for the holidays . . .

Mrs. Jeffries and the One Who Got Away
When a woman is found strangled with an old newspaper clipping in her hand, Inspector Witherspoon will need Mrs. Jeffries' help to get to the bottom of the story.

MRS. JEFFRIES
WINS THE PRIZE

EMILY BRIGHTWELL

BERKLEY PRIME CRIME, NEW YORK

BERKLEY PRIME CRIME

An imprint of Penguin Random House LLC
375 Hudson Street, New York, New York 10014

MRS. JEFFRIES WINS THE PRIZE

A Berkley Prime Crime Book / published by arrangement with the author

ISBN: 978-0-425-26811-7

PUBLISHING HISTORY
Berkley Prime Crime mass-market edition / March 2016

PRINTED IN THE UNITED STATES OF AMERICA

10   9   8   7   6   5   4

Cover illustration by Jeff Walker.
Interior text design by Kristin del Rosario.

Penguin
Random
House

For Ella and Ethan Mauer—the next generation of readers

CHAPTER 1

———◆———

"Thank goodness that tiresome woman finally left. Some people simply have no sense of appropriate behavior. I invited her to luncheon, not to waste my whole afternoon." Helena Rayburn glared at the double oak doors and crossed her arms over her chest. Although she was well into middle age, what gray she had blended easily with her blonde hair, making her appear younger than her years unless one were close enough to see the crow's feet around her blue eyes and the disapproving lines bracketing her thin mouth. She was tall and her ramrod-straight posture made her look even taller.

"Now, Helena, she didn't stay that long. It's only half past two. Besides, we're all still here. Do you want us to leave?" Althea Stanway, known as "Thea" to her friends, rose to her feet and put the delicate gold and white teacup on the trolley. A petite woman, she'd retained her girlish figure and privately hinted that she wore only the lightest of corsets. But the gray threaded through her curly brown hair and the slight sag beneath her chin betrayed the fact that she was no longer a young woman.

"Don't be ridiculous, the two of you are old friends and you're always welcome, you know that. But she's an entirely different matter. Your problem, Thea, is that you're too kind," Helena said. "You've always been that way, even out in India. As I recall, you were the one that encouraged the rest of us to befriend that woman even though she was nothing more than a governess."

"She's hardly a governess now." Isabelle Martell, who'd been sitting on the settee, got up and began pulling on her beige kid gloves. Slightly chubby but smart enough to pay the finest dressmaker in London to help her conceal her unfortunate shape, Isabelle was also a blue-eyed blonde. Her face was round as a pie plate and her features unremarkable, yet she carried herself with a confidence that convinced people she was not only attractive, but also witty and poised. "From what I hear, she paid cash for that huge house in Mayfair and she's buying a country estate as well."

Helena snorted. "Just because she's rich now doesn't mean we have to accept her as an equal. As far as I'm concerned, she's no better than a jumped-up little shopgirl."

"Then why did you invite her to luncheon?" Thea asked.

"I wanted to determine how serious she is about orchids," Helena said. "Unfortunately, she is very serious indeed. It was bad enough that she used her money to worm her way into the Royal Horticultural Society, and because of that, we've had no choice but to let her into our club."

"We didn't have to let her in," Thea laughed. "We may all be members of the Royal Horticultural Society, but our local group has no official affiliation with them. The Mayfair Orchid and Exotic Plant Society is completely independent."

"Lady Prentiss asked me to approve her application for membership," Helena argued. "I had no choice. Her husband is one of the governors of the Horticultural Society."

Isabelle picked a piece of lint off the cuff of her sleeve. "So you acceded to Lady Prentiss' wishes because you want her to use her influence with Lord Prentiss to get you that spot on the Narcissus Committee."

"Don't be ridiculous, I did what she asked because I didn't dare refuse. If you'll remember, she and Lord Prentiss are both judges in our orchid show next month and we don't want to offend them," Helena retorted. "And because we've had to let Chloe Attwater in, none of us will have a hope of winning this year. You heard her bragging about what a beautiful conservatory she has and how she already has her gardener working on acquiring the best specimens possible so she can enter them."

"There's nothing wrong with a bit of healthy competition," Thea pointed out.

Helena snorted. "It's nothing of the sort. None of us can compete with the financial resources she has at her disposal."

"Speak for yourself, Helena." Isabelle grinned broadly. "I certainly intend to give all of you a good run for your money. This year my orchids are superb and I fully expect to take home a ribbon."

"Mine are excellent as well," Thea added. "And I, too, fully expect to take home a prize."

The drawing room doors opened. Mrs. Clemment, the housekeeper, hurried into the room. "Mrs. Rayburn, you'd best come. There's something terribly wrong in the conservatory."

Helena sighed irritably as she got up. "Whatever are you talking about, Mrs. Clemment? I've still got guests."

But for once, Mrs. Clemment wasn't going to be bullied by her employer. "I'm aware of that, ma'am, but it doesn't matter. This is urgent. You'll see when you get there, ma'am, it's difficult to explain, but you'd best come right away. There's big trouble."

Taken aback, Helena blinked in surprise. Her servants *never* talked back to her. But then she noticed that Mrs. Clemment's hands were clasped together tightly and her face was white as a sheet. "Very well."

Mrs. Clemment turned and charged back through the still open doorway.

"Perhaps I'd better come with you." Isabelle quickened her step to catch up with Helena, who was already heading for the hall. "Mrs. Clemment isn't one to exaggerate or get upset."

"I'll come as well," Thea offered.

Mrs. Clemment didn't wait for any of them. She raced down the long corridor so fast the other three had to almost run to catch up with her, and they were out of breath as they reached the end of it.

The cook, the scullery maid, and the upstairs maid stood by the open door of the conservatory. Their eyes were wide, glassy with shock, and their faces fearful. Mrs. Clemment stopped, pressed her hand against her heart, took a deep breath, and pointed inside. "There, it's in there."

"For goodness' sakes, Mrs. Clemment, what's in there? What's going on?" Helena demanded. Despite trying to sound authorative, there was a tremor in her voice.

"It's not for me to say, ma'am." Mrs. Clemment took another breath, lifted her chin, and met her employer's gaze. "You'll see for yourself when you go inside."

The housekeeper stepped back so the mistress could enter and then turned to the staff. "Everyone, get back downstairs and wait for me. I'll be down soon."

Huddled together, they scurried down the narrow hall that led from the main corridor to the back stairs.

Helena was now deathly afraid but determined not to show it. She straightened her spine and stepped through the open door into the conservatory. Isabelle and Thea followed behind her. As soon as the ladies were inside, Mrs. Clemment stationed herself against the doorjamb again.

Built of glass, the conservatory was connected to the first floor, not the ground floor of the house. The space was almost as wide as the house itself. To the right of the door stood a series of tall cupboards filled with gardening tools, pots, vining wire, and everything else needed for growing plants. In the two corners opposite the cupboards dwarf fruit trees were planted in huge pots. Along one glass wall stood a trellis covered with exotic-looking climbing plants, some of which had brightly colored yellow, orange, and red blooms. On the opposite side of the room, a long black tarpaulin hung suspended from the glass ceiling. A center aisle bisected the conservatory and ended at a door that led out to the back garden. Four long rows of tables, two on each side of the aisle, filled the remainder of the space. They were covered with trays of seedlings, exotic cacti, and blooming plants in every imaginable color. Outside, the sun went behind the clouds, plunging the normally bright room into a temporary gloom.

Seeing nothing alarming, Helena relaxed and moved farther down the aisle toward the door. "I don't see anything," she muttered.

"What's behind that?" Thea nodded at the tarpaulin.

"Nothing of importance," Helena said quickly. "There's a plant bed behind there, that's all."

She started to turn so she could ask Mrs. Clemment what was going on when suddenly Isabelle said, "Look, what's that?" She pointed to the end of the closest aisle where a large brown mound of something suddenly shifted into view. Isabelle had poor eyesight, and in the dim light, the details were very difficult to see.

"I've no idea." Helena moved toward it and the other two were right on her heels. Her vision wasn't that much better than Isabelle's and both women were too vain to wear spectacles. "It looks as if Tufts hasn't cleared away . . ." Her voice trailed off as she got closer and she realized the heap wasn't a sack of dirt, but a person in a brown coat. He was slumped over with his head resting on his chest. A bowler hat was lying on the floor.

"Oh my good Lord," Helena exclaimed. "It's Mr. Filmore. What on earth is he doing sitting in my conservatory? Mr. Filmore, Mr. Filmore, explain yourself please. Are you drunk?"

Thea, who had the best eyesight of the three, spoke up. "I don't think he's going to answer you, Helena. Something is wrong."

Helena and Isabelle both craned their necks forward

and squinted into the quickly darkening gloom. Neither woman moved and it was little Thea who stepped around them toward the very silent Mr. Filmore.

"Don't get too close," Isabelle ordered.

Thea ignored her and pointed toward Mr. Filmore's chest. "Oh dear, you'd best come take a good look, Helena. There's blood. Lots of it." She shifted her gaze to her friend. "If I were you, I'd send for the police."

"The police, but why? Shouldn't we just get him a doctor? He's had some sort of accident."

Thea was now standing directly in front of the mound that was Mr. Filmore. "He hasn't had an accident."

"How on earth do you know?" Helena demanded. "He obviously came in here and . . . and . . ."

Thea ignored her and kept on speaking. "Not unless you accidentally stab yourself in the heart."

Mrs. Jeffries, housekeeper to Inspector Gerald Witherspoon of the Metropolitan Police Department, took her place at the head of the kitchen table. She inhaled deeply, filling her nose with the fragrant scent of freshly baked bread. "That smells wonderful, Mrs. Goodge." She smiled at the portly, gray-haired cook.

"Let's hope it tastes good as well." The cook put the loaf on the table next to the teapot. Four pieces of the lovely brown bread were already sliced off the end. There was only the two of them for afternoon tea today so she'd not bothered with anything elaborate. Wiggins, the household footman, was having his afternoon out, and Smythe, the coachman, had gone to the stables. The maid, Phyllis, was out on a household errand.

The housekeeper was an auburn-haired woman of late middle age. Short and slightly plump, she had a ready smile, brown eyes, and a kindly disposition. She hadn't been a housekeeper all her life, but had come into service in London after the death of her husband, a Yorkshire policeman. Reaching for the teapot, Mrs. Jeffries poured two cups of the steaming brew while Mrs. Goodge arranged the bread on their individual plates. She slid one of them toward the housekeeper. "I do hope that Phyllis will get here while this is still warm."

"She should be back any moment. I only sent her to the draper's to pick up the curtain rings I ordered last week." She reached for the cut glass jar of gooseberry jam, took the lid off, and slathered a spoonful on her bread.

A strand of white hair slipped out from beneath the cook's cap as she bobbed her head. "Too bad Wiggins won't be back while this bread is still warm. You know how he loves warm bread. He's a good lad. Mind you, he's not really a lad anymore, he's a fully grown man now." Over their years together in the household, she and the footman had become quite close.

She'd spent her life in service and had once felt that taking a position with a policeman was a terrible way to end her career as a cook. After all, she'd reigned supreme over some of the finest kitchens in England, and when she'd come to London, her food had graced the tables of cabinet ministers, captains of industry, and a fair number of aristocrats. But when she'd been sacked from her previous position for being "too old," she'd had no choice but to accept a position in the Witherspoon household, and it had changed her life. She had a family of sorts now, and when she wasn't cooking, she and the others in their circle were busy doing the most important work possible—serving justice.

"I know." The housekeeper grinned. "He gets a bit stroppy when we treat him like he's sixteen. But then again, to us, he'll always be just a young lad." She turned her head as Fred, the household dog, got up from his rug by the cooker. Tail wagging, he trotted out into the hall, his nails tapping merrily on the wooden floor as he headed for the back door.

"Goodness, that can't be Wiggins, he never comes home this early from his day out," Mrs. Goodge muttered.

"Hello, old fellow," Wiggins' voice came a second before they heard the door shut. "I'm glad to see you, too. Come on then, let's go to the kitchen, I've got news, important news."

Both women went still as they heard that special tone in the footman's voice.

A second later, Wiggins, with Fred bouncing along beside him, came into the kitchen. He whipped off his blue tweed cap as he moved, revealing a headful of thick, dark brown hair that had a tendency to curl. His eyes were blue, his skin fair, and his cheeks still as ruddy as when he was a wee one, but his face was now narrower, manlier, and less like a young boy. His lanky frame had filled out as well.

"What kind of news?" Mrs. Goodge demanded.

Wiggins tossed his hat on an empty peg of the coat tree, hurried to the table, and sat down. Fred flopped down next to him. "Give us a minute." He took a deep breath. "I've run like the very devil was on me 'eels." He reached down and petted the dog's head.

Mrs. Jeffries had already poured his tea. She slid his mug toward him as the cook put a slice of bread on an empty plate and shoved it under Wiggins' nose. "Catch your breath and have your tea, the news will keep a moment or two."

"Ta." He took a quick drink of tea and smiled his thanks. "Cor blimey, that tastes good. I was parched and I've 'ad a good two pints to drink, but when ya run as fast as I did, ya run it off. But I do 'ave news."

"Yes, we know." Mrs. Jeffries tried not to sound as impatient as she felt.

"As you can see, I've come home a bit early. Generally, I 'ang about with Mickey Deals on my day out, and we usually go to the pub over by Shepherds Bush Station, The Bedford Arms, and 'ave a pint and talk football. But 'e didn't want to go there today. He insisted we go to the Admiral Nelson on Ladbroke Terrace, which is just 'round the corner from the inspector's station. Mickey's sweet on one of the barmaids that works there."

Mrs. Jeffries nodded. Inspector Witherspoon was assigned to the Ladbroke Road Police Station. "Yes, we all know where that pub is located." She tried to keep her spirits dampened, but it was impossible.

"Go on, Wiggins." Mrs. Goodge leaned toward him. "Stop keepin' us in suspense." Like the housekeeper, she, too, was trying to keep her hopes in check.

"After lunchtime, the place began to clear out and the barmaid come over to 'ave a chat and I'm not thick or anything, so I knew that Mickey wanted to have a chance to talk to 'er without me sittin' there gawkin' at the two of 'em, so I left. But it was still early so I decided to go over to the Golden Goose and see if Tom Whittle was there, that's 'is favorite pub and 'e's generally there in the afternoons. 'E's a bit of a blowhard, but 'e knows ever so much about football."

"Yes, yes, I'm sure he knows an enormous amount about the subject," Mrs. Jeffries agreed quickly.

"I'm only tellin' you about Tom so you'll understand why I was walkin' by the police station, it's the fastest way to the Golden Goose. I'd just gone past the station when Constable Griffiths come barreling past me so fast he didn't see me. He skidded to a halt when I yelled his name but said he had to hurry, they'd got a call for more constables at a house on Bellwood Place. The inspector and Constable Barnes was already there and had sent back to the station for more men. They was goin' to do a 'ouse to 'ouse." He paused dramatically. "And we all know what that means."

"It means we have a murder," Mrs. Jeffries said.

"Murder is never nice, but this one seems particularly gruesome," Inspector Gerald Witherspoon said to Constable Barnes. They were standing just inside the open door of the conservatory. The inspector was deliberately looking toward the garden instead of in at the corpse being examined by Dr. Procash, the police surgeon for this district. Witherspoon's normally pale complexion was so white it came close to being greenish in tone. His thin lips were compressed together, he'd run his hand through his thin brown hair and it now stood in tufts round his head, and his deep-set hazel eyes were troubled.

"It's an ugly one," Barnes agreed. The constable was a

tall man with the posture of a battlefield general, curly iron
gray hair under his policeman's helmet, and a natural ruddy
complexion. He and the inspector worked together on murders, but unlike Witherspoon, he'd been on the force and
on the streets longer and wasn't as upset by blood and gore
as his superior. "He was coshed on the head first, then he
was stabbed. This killer really wanted the poor man dead.
He or she used a fancy pair of garden shears as the murder
weapon."

They'd examined the corpse upon arriving and Barnes
had watched the inspector valiantly do his duty. Witherspoon was known to have his "methods" in solving murders, and one of those methods was to carefully examine
both the death wounds and the way the body lay in relation
to the immediate environment. At least that was how the
inspector had explained it when he was giving a training
class to new recruits. The constable was one of the few
people who knew that, in reality, Gerald Witherspoon was
squeamish and hated the sight of blood. Which was one
of the reasons the constable admired him—no matter how
distasteful or awful a corpse might be, Witherspoon put
duty and justice before his own feelings. He'd carried out
a thorough examination of both the body and the scene
before allowing the police surgeon or anyone else near the
body.

Witherspoon took a gulp of air and then glanced over
his shoulder into the conservatory. The police surgeon stood
up and waved at the constable standing across the room by
the door leading into the house. "Send the lads here with
the stretcher," he ordered. "Have them come around the

side of the house. It'll be easier to get the body out the garden door."

"Let's move out of the way." Witherspoon turned and moved outside onto the staircase. He took a deep breath before heading down to the back garden.

"Should we go into the house, sir?" Barnes went after him. "The ladies who found the body are waiting for us."

"They're the ones that identified him?" Witherspoon's voice trailed off as he reached the bottom step. He stopped and stared at the row of ferns lining the far side of the herringbone walkway. "I wonder what that is?" He pointed to a patch of red visible beneath the overhanging fronds of the largest fern. "And look, see, there's a trail of dirt across the walkway." He studied the thin line of soil and saw that it didn't end at the bottom step, but continued up to the conservatory door. Annoyed, because he should have noticed it earlier, he made a mental note to be more observant. "Someone carried something down these steps."

Barnes shoved past him, bent down, and moved the fronds back far enough for them to get a good look. A squashed bulb and the scattered crimson blossoms of a flowering plant lay on a mound of fresh dirt which spilled out of a crumpled burlap bag. "This must have been it. They brought down a plant, the kind you buy at a florist or a proper nursery. It looks like someone's just smashed it and then chucked it under here."

Witherspoon thought for a moment. "You're a keen gardener, Constable, do you know what kind it is?" He'd no idea why that was important, but the question had popped into his head.

"No, sir, I just know the common ones, but I've not seen one like this before in an English garden. Though it does look a bit like some of the exotic ones the missus and I saw at Kew last summer." He stood up and dusted off his hands. "Should we ask the lady of the house if she can identify it before we take it into evidence?"

"That's a good idea. Surely she'll know what sort of plants she has in her greenhouse." He turned as the gate squeaked and two constables with an empty stretcher slung between them rounded the corner of the house. "Let's go and have a word with the ladies." He moved out of the way to let the constables pass. "Then we'll come back and do a proper search of the entire place, including the mews. Let's walk around to the front door; it'll give us a chance to have a closer look at the property."

"And a nice piece of property it is, sir." Barnes surveyed the area with a practiced eye as the two men started for the gate.

"Indeed it is," the inspector agreed.

Leafy ferns and shrubs stood in a row along the walkway that curved to the tall wood fencing surrounding the property. Flowerbeds brimming with brilliant pink azaleas, red and purple rhododendrons, lilacs, and roses in every hue imaginable were planted along the two sides of the long garden between which was a perfect emerald green lawn. A white painted wrought iron table and chairs stood in the middle of the garden, and at the far end, a wide bed of ivy ran along the back fencing which separated the property from the mews. Barnes, who was a few feet ahead of Witherspoon, stopped suddenly. "They take their gardening seriously here, sir. The lawn is perfect and the conservatory is twice the size you generally see attached to a private house. The only jarring note is that." He pointed back the way they'd just come, to the staircase. The space under the conservatory was open to the elements and dim, but there was enough light getting in to see all the wooden supports holding up the conservatory. Piles of old wood, mounds of dirt, broken bricks, and crumbling stoneware pots were scattered haphazardly along the uneven dirt surface. Along the wall of the original structure, a stack of lumber, a wheelbarrow, and extra bags of peat and soil were propped up for storage.

"Yes, that's odd, isn't it," Witherspoon agreed. "But perhaps the owners are so used to the sight, they don't realize how much of an eyesore it is."

"Or perhaps they've put off doing anything about it until the weather gets cooler. That stack of wood in there by the wheelbarrow might be for a trellis."

"How very clever of you to think of that, Constable."

"Not so clever, sir." Barnes grinned. "I've got a stack of lumber just like it in my back garden and Mrs. Barnes is fit to be tied that I've not put it up. She wants to do some sort of climbing vine but it's been so warm lately that I've put it off until the weather cools down."

They continued around the house to the entrance, where a police constable stood guard. He nodded respectfully as he opened the door. "I'm glad you've come, sir. The mistress of the house is getting very upset. She's been out here twice demanding to see you. She's in the drawing room with the other ladies."

"Where are the servants?" Barnes asked as he stepped inside.

"Downstairs in the kitchen, sir. The housekeeper's made them tea."

"Thank you, Constable," Witherspoon murmured. "Go around to the back, please. There's a smashed plant under a shrub by the walkway and we'll need it. It's evidence so keep it in your possession here until we call for it."

"Yes, sir." He nodded smartly and hurried off.

Witherspoon stepped over the threshold and came to a full stop. He blinked as his senses were overwhelmed by the colorful and exotic décor. The walls were papered in a brilliant crimson with a pattern of golden interlocking curlicues. A gold statue of an Indian dancer sat atop a green, red, and blue silk tablecloth on the table next to the staircase. An oriental carpet of maroon, cream, and cobalt blue covered the floor and continued up the stairs. The room was unnaturally bright and it took the inspector a moment to understand why: Two mirrors, both with ornate frames of carved gold leaf, were on the wall behind the table and angled so they'd catch the light from the overhead transom. "This is a most unusual entryway," the inspector murmured.

"Of course it is." A woman stepped out of the first door in the corridor and came toward them. "These things are from India, and the wallpaper, carpet, and statue were gifts from the maharaja to my late husband. But you're not here to evaluate my décor, sir, but to take care of that nuisance in my conservatory."

"By 'nuisance,' I assume you mean the dead man." Barnes didn't crack a smile as he spoke.

The woman didn't even bother to acknowledge his presence; she kept her attention on the inspector. "I'm Helena

Rayburn and I take it you're in charge of this investigation?"

"That is correct, ma'am. I'm Inspector Witherspoon and this is my colleague, Constable Barnes."

She barely nodded in the constable's direction before turning on her heel and stalking back toward the open door. "We're in here," she snapped. "Do be quick about it, please, I need to get back into my conservatory and have a good look around to see if anything of value is missing."

They followed her into the drawing room, where two other women sat on a sofa. The smaller of the two gave them a shy smile while the other merely stared at them.

Witherspoon glanced around the large room and noted the influence of India was even more prevalent here. Two bronze elephants the size of Saint Bernards flanked the green marble fireplace; every table, cabinet, and bookcase was covered with brilliantly colored cloths and runners. A collection of brass figurines, all in the same or similar shapes as the big one on the foyer table, filled three shelves of a huge armoire. Exotic flowers, none of which the inspector could identify, filled half a dozen large blue and white ceramic pots along the wall facing the windows.

"Please sit down," Helena ordered.

Barnes fixed her with the stare that had sent more than one criminal running for cover when he was patrolling the streets. "I need to interview your servants. I understand they're in the kitchen."

She visibly drew back at his tone and then caught herself. "The back stairs are at the end of the corridor."

Barnes nodded politely to Witherspoon, who'd just sat down, and then left.

"I take it all of you were here when the body was discovered?" Witherspoon waved his hand to include all three of them.

"We were. This is Mrs. Stanway"—Helena pointed to the small, curly-haired woman perched on the edge of the seat and then to the other woman—"and this is Mrs. Martell."

"Who discovered the body?" the inspector asked.

"My housekeeper, Mrs. Clemments," Helena continued. "Luncheon was over, and we were having coffee when Mrs. Clemments came and said there was a problem in the conservatory. We went out to have a look."

"Who is 'we'?" he interrupted. He'd learned it was very important to keep the sequence of events straight in his own mind.

"All of us. Mrs. Stanway and Mrs. Martell accompanied me. When we got to the door of the conservatory, the rest of the servants were standing there, but Mrs. Clemments shooed them down to the kitchen. The three of us went inside and found Mr. Filmore. I sent one of the maids for the police."

"Mr. Filmore?"

"Hiram Filmore," she replied. "He has a shop in Hammersmith and sometimes supplies me with plants."

"What did you do once you'd sent for help?" he asked.

"We closed the door and came back up here and waited, Inspector," Helena replied.

"That's not quite true, Helena." Isabelle Martell spoke for the first time. "You looked around the conservatory to see if any of your plants were missing, remember."

"And I went to the lavatory to wash my hands," Thea Stanway added.

"So you were in the conservatory for some time after you'd found the body?" He watched Helena Rayburn's face as he spoke. He wasn't particularly adept at reading expressions, especially from women, but he could occasionally tell if someone was lying.

Helena arched her eyebrow. "I would hardly put it that way, Inspector. I took a quick survey to see if anything had been taken. Some of my orchids are highly valuable."

"Was anything missing?"

"I didn't have time for a thorough search." She slanted a quick look toward the other two women. "Isabelle, Mrs. Martell, kept insisting we leave, and Mrs. Stanway claimed she was feeling ill. So we left."

"Did you lock the conservatory door when you closed it?"

"No, I didn't."

"You must have been very upset about finding the body," Witherspoon said kindly. "I'm sure you didn't realize that locking the door might have been prudent."

"Oh no, that's not why," Thea Stanway interjected. "Mrs. Rayburn said she wished she could lock the door, but the key is lost. It's been lost for a week now."

Downstairs, Barnes and Mrs. Clemments were settled at the rickety table in the servants' dining hall, a narrow room at the back of the kitchen on the lower ground floor. The walls were painted a dull gray and the floors covered with a straw mat. Shelves filled with thick crockery, mugs, old tins, and mismatched china lined the walls.

Barnes noticed that Mrs. Clemments' hand shook as

she took a sip of tea. "Take your time, ma'am, and just tell me what happened."

"I don't know where to begin." She put the mug down and clasped her hands together. "Oh dear Lord, I'm acting like a silly ninny. I'm sorry. I've seen death before but never such a violent one."

"Perhaps it would be easier if I asked you questions," he suggested. "Why did you go to the conservatory?"

"Amy, one of the maids, said she heard something. I was going to ignore her as she tends to exaggerate just a bit, but she insisted this wasn't the first time today she'd heard a noise so I thought I'd better go have a look."

"Why didn't you go the first time she mentioned it?" Barnes wondered if the maid might have heard the actual murder.

"As I said, Constable, Amy hears things all the time. She's a bit of a nervous Nellie if you get my meaning. Add to that, when she first made the claim, we were rushing about getting ready for the luncheon and I simply didn't have time."

"Why didn't you send her to check?"

"She's not allowed in the conservatory. None of the staff is except for Mr. Tufts, he's the gardener, and me. So when Amy insisted she heard something again, I went to see if anything was wrong."

Barnes looked up from his notebook. "The other servants aren't allowed in the conservatory?" That might be a very important point and he wanted to ensure he'd heard it correctly.

"That's right," Mrs. Clemments replied. "Mrs. Rayburn is very particular about her plants and flowers—she grows orchids. She always keeps both doors to the conservatory locked, at least she did until last week—that's when both the keys went missing." She leaned toward him. "At first she tried to blame one of us, but I soon set her straight about that. I told her none of the servants would risk losing their positions by bothering her keys. It was right upsetting, Constable. None of us care about her silly old plants." She glanced over her shoulder at the closed door.

"Feel free to speak your mind. I won't repeat anything to your mistress," Barnes said quickly. He didn't want her shutting up now because she was afraid.

"No, but you might have to swear to it in court," she shot back. "Look, just because I'm a housekeeper doesn't mean I'm stupid. I know that police constables often have to testify to what they've been told by witnesses and that's what I am, a witness."

"Believe me, ma'am, one of the most intelligent people I've ever met is a housekeeper." Barnes grinned broadly as he thought of Mrs. Jeffries and the number of murders her powers of deduction had helped solve. "And you're right, of course, but I promise you, I'll do my best to keep whatever you say between myself and the inspector. Now, why don't you tell me about these missing keys."

She said nothing for a brief moment, and then something in his expression must have convinced her she could trust him. "Right then, the keys were kept on a hook in Mrs. Rayburn's day room. The only time any of the servants go in there is to give it a good clean once a week. Mrs. Rayburn keeps her correspondence and all her legal papers in there in her desk."

"Were the keys on a hook in the desk?"

"No, they were just inside the door. There's a series of hooks and Mrs. Rayburn kept the conservatory keys there as well as the keys to all of her trunks."

"Have the trunk keys gone missing?"

"No, they're still there."

"There were two conservatory keys?" Barnes clarified. "One for each door?"

"That's right, a big one for the outside door, that's the one the gardeners and tradesmen use, and a smaller one for the door at the end of the first-floor hall. That's the one the mistress uses."

"When was the first time someone noticed the keys were gone?"

"A week ago last Monday. That's when Peggy always does the day room. She went in to do the cleaning, and she generally finishes up by dusting the little table by the door that's just underneath where the keys would have been hanging. She noticed they were gone but she thought Mrs. Rayburn had them with her. But Peggy did mention to me that the keys were gone when she came downstairs for lunch, and I thought that the mistress probably had them as well. Sometimes she took them with her when she and the other ladies of the Orchid Club went out. She often came home with specimens that she took directly to the conservatory by the back door."

"Why would she have taken both keys then?" Barnes wasn't sure he understood.

"Because she was peculiar." Again Mrs. Clemments looked over her shoulder. "She was terrified someone was going to get into that wretched greenhouse and steal one of them ruddy orchids, so it was quite in keeping with her character that she'd take both keys. Especially as the other ladies had been sniffing about trying to get a peek inside the place."

At the inspector's home at Upper Edmonton Gardens, a number of other people were now at the kitchen table. Smythe was back from the stables and sitting next to his pretty blonde wife, Betsy. The coachman was a big, heavily muscled man with harsh features and plenty of gray in his dark hair. Betsy was the household's former maid but now spent her days taking care of their daughter, Amanda Belle. The child was now sitting on her godmother, Mrs. Goodge's lap and watching the proceedings out of eyes as blue as her mother's.

Phyllis, the household's current maid, sat farther down the table, and next to her was Lady Ruth Cannonberry, one of their neighbors as well as the inspector's "special friend."

"Are Luty Belle and Hatchet coming?" Ruth asked. She was an attractive middle-aged blonde with blue eyes, a smooth complexion, and a slender frame that housed a spine of steel. She was the widow of a peer and had loved her late husband dearly, but hadn't been unduly influenced by him or his class attitudes. The daughter of a country vicar and a free-thinking mother, she sincerely believed in Christ's instructions to love thy neighbor as thyself and that all souls are equal before God. Her ideas hadn't made her very popular with Lord Cannonberry's relatives, and they still complained that she embarrassed them greatly by her active membership in women's suffrage groups. Nonetheless, Ruth didn't let their opinion stop her.

"No, they're in the country visiting friends and won't be back until late this evening," Wiggins said. "But I wrote a note tellin' them what's what and left it with the butler."

"Good, then they'll be here for our morning meeting," Mrs. Jeffries commented. "Now, since most of us are here, Wiggins, tell us what you know."

"It's not fair," Phyllis protested. "Wiggins always seems to find out about the murders first. He did it last time, too." She stared at the footman out of narrowed hazel eyes and then brushed the lock of dark blonde hair that had come loose from her topknot off her cheek.

"That's not my fault." He laughed. "I just happened to be walking past the station."

"I was by the station, too," she interrupted. "The draper's shop is just around the corner and I didn't see or hear anything. It's just not fair that you get first crack at everything."

Mrs. Jeffries glanced at the cook and smiled knowingly. Mrs. Goodge nodded and then hid her grin behind Amanda's blonde curls. Both of them could remember what Phyllis had been like when she first came to them.

She didn't speak often of her past, but they knew she'd been in service since she was hardly more than a child and that most of the places where she'd worked had treated her badly. When she'd taken Betsy's place, she'd been nervous, eager to please, and hardworking. She'd been reluctant to do anything that might jeopardize her position in a place that treated her decently. When they'd explained to her that the inspector knew nothing about the way they helped on his cases, she'd been so terrified of angering him and being back on the streets that she hadn't wanted to be involved.

But that had all changed and now she was complaining about Wiggins finding out first! She'd come quite a distance since then and they were all proud of her.

"Quit your complainin'. I can't 'elp it if I'm there and you're not." He grinned at her. "And I didn't find out all that much. Only that the inspector and Constable Barnes were called to a murder in Kensington. But when I was comin' back from Luty's, I did like you said, Mrs. Jeffries"—he looked at the housekeeper—"and nipped past the inspector's station. Davey Marsh was 'angin' about in his usual spot."

Davey Marsh was one of the many street urchins that loitered in front of the railway stations, police stations, and even shops, hoping to earn a few coins by running errands, taking messages, and carrying packages. Davey knew and liked Witherspoon's household and had often done errands on their behalf.

"Did he know anything?" Betsy asked eagerly.

Wiggins grinned. "'Course 'e did, 'e's a sharp one is our Davey and 'e knew where the murder 'ouse is. 'E didn't know the exact address, but he overheard one of the constables say they 'ad to go to the Rayburn house on Bellwood Place."

"Oh my gracious," Lady Cannonberry gasped. "That's Helena Rayburn's home."

"You know her?" Mrs. Jeffries asked.

"I do. I mean I've met her on a number of occasions. She's a widow. Was she the one murdered?"

Wiggins winced. "Sorry, but Davey didn't know who'd been killed. Is this lady a particular friend of yours?"

Ruth shook her head. "Not really, in truth, she's a rather

an obnoxious snob, but even so, I wouldn't wish any harm to come to her."

"So our first task is to find out who was killed?" Mrs. Jeffries glanced at the clock and saw that it was almost five.

"Don't worry, Mrs. J." Smythe got to his feet. "Bellwood Place is close by, and we've time to get there and see if we can find out anything."

Wiggins rose as well. "Murder always draws a bit of a crowd, and if they've gone, we'll just 'ead off to the pubs. They'll be plenty of talk there."

"Mind you get home at a decent hour," Betsy said as Smythe bent down to kiss her cheek. Amanda held out her arms as Smythe straightened and came around the table. He picked her up, gave her a quick kiss and hug, and then started to hand her back to Mrs. Goodge, but Betsy was already up and around the table. "Give her to me and I'll take her upstairs for a quick walk. If she sees you leave, she'll start to cry. She's turned into a right little daddy's girl."

"You're both my girls." Smythe put Amanda in his wife's arms and then waited until she disappeared up the stairs before he and Wiggins headed for the back door.

As soon as they were gone, Mrs. Jeffries looked at Ruth. "Even though we don't know who the victim might be, what more can you tell us about Helena Rayburn?"

Ruth glanced toward the stairs. "Shouldn't we wait for Betsy?"

"I'll tell her what you tell us," Phyllis offered. "I usually walk her to the corner when she and the baby are on their own."

"I don't know all that much about the woman. She's only

an acquaintance I've met socially. She's spent most of her adult life in India."

"India," Mrs. Goodge exclaimed. "Oh, sorry, that startled me for some reason." She laughed. "Go on."

"Well, as I was saying, she spent most of her adult life in India but came back to London some years back when her husband died. He was a colonel in the army. I believe she's the president of a garden club." She nodded her head vigorously. "Yes, yes, that's right. I ran into her once at Kew Gardens when there was an exhibition of orchids. She was so engrossed in the flowers she barely acknowledged my presence, and just last week, Jean Turner, she's the correspondence secretary of our women's group and a very keen gardener, mentioned that the Mayfair Orchid and Exotic Plant Society is having their annual competition soon and that Helena Rayburn is the favorite to win. Apparently, she always wins."

CHAPTER 2

—————◆—————

"If the keys were gone, then the doors to the conservatory were both unlocked. Is that what you're saying?" Witherspoon looked at Helena Rayburn for confirmation.

"No, that's what Mrs. Stanway just told you." She glanced at the two women on the sofa. "But I will concur with her statement. The keys did go missing, but luckily the doors were both unlocked when it happened so I could get in and out."

"Which means it was possible that Mr. Filmore went inside the conservatory on his own?"

"It certainly looks that way. He didn't come into the house and announce his presence, and the staff know better than to let anyone, even Mr. Filmore, into my conservatory without my permission."

"Have you any idea why he was here?"

She shrugged. "None. I wasn't expecting him."

"He didn't come here to bring you a new plant?" He rose and edged toward the drawing room doors.

Surprised by his movement, she stared at him but said nothing except to answer his question. "Certainly not. Mr. Filmore wouldn't have just shown up on my doorstep with something I'd not ordered."

"But he did that once before, Helena." Thea smiled helpfully. "He brought you that beautiful Forest Calanthe last spring. We were all so envious, they're very difficult to obtain, but he found you a lovely specimen, remember?"

"Of course I remember," Helena snapped. "But that was the one and only time he ever arrived without an appointment and with something I hadn't specifically ordered. He only took such a liberty because we'd had a prior discussion about that particular species of orchid and I'd let him know how much I desired one."

"Then it is possible he was bringing you a plant?" Witherspoon was now at the drawing room door. "After all, you've just admitted he'd done it on a previous occasion."

"Yes, when you put it like that, I suppose so," she conceded. "But when I was in the conservatory, I didn't see any new specimens, so if that was Mr. Filmore's reason for coming here today, where is it?"

"If you'll wait just a moment, I may be able to answer that question for you." Witherspoon opened the door and stepped out.

Helena glared at Thea and then flicked her gaze to the door, which was cracked open a few inches. "For goodness' sakes, can you please keep your comments to yourself?" She kept her voice low. "I told that policeman Filmore never came here on his own."

"But that isn't true. He has."

"Yes, I know that now, but you contradicting me in front of the police makes it appear as if I was lying. For God's sake, Thea, it's bad enough that the fellow got murdered here and that in and of itself is scandal enough. If the police even hint that I may be a suspect, I'll never get the appointment to the Narcissus Committee."

"Don't be ridiculous, Helena. The police aren't going to consider you a suspect just because you had a memory lapse." Isabella interjected as she waved a hand dismissively. "Besides, even if you were a suspect, how would the Narcissus Committee find out about it?"

"They put all manner of malicious things in the newspapers," Helena argued. "And I'll not have Thea's loose tongue ruining my chances with the Royal Horticultural Society. I've worked too hard to let anything keep me out."

Thea looked hurt. "I was just trying to be helpful. I thought you'd forgotten about the calanthe."

"I did forget," Helena muttered.

"Then you shouldn't get so angry about it." Isabelle leaned toward her and started to say something else, but then straightened as Witherspoon reappeared. Behind him was a constable carrying a burlap bag. They stopped in the open doorway.

"Mrs. Rayburn, I've no wish to get dirt on your lovely carpet, so if you'd be so kind, I'd like you to come here and look at this. We'd like you to identify it."

For a moment, he thought she might refuse, but finally she stood up and stalked across the room to the constable. She looked at the bag, frowned, and then reached over and pushed the edges of the burlap down, revealing the mangled bulb and stem. "Where did you find this?"

"It was at the bottom of the stairs outside the conservatory. It had been tossed underneath a plant, a fern, I think. Do you know what it is?"

"I'm not sure," she murmured. "The plant has been so thoroughly smashed it's difficult to identify it properly. What I can see of it leads me to believe it is or was an orchid of some kind."

"Would looking at the blooms help?" the constable asked. He propped the bag on his hip, stuck his hand down the back, and pulled out the petals. "I collected them with the plant and stuffed them in the burlap for safe keeping, sir," he explained to Witherspoon. "You said it was evidence, so I retrieved as much as I could." He opened his hand, trying to keep the petals centered in his palm, but there were too many of them and two of the colorful blooms fell to the floor.

Helena's brow furrowed as she studied the plant. "I'm not sure what it is."

"It looks like a red vanda." Isabelle Martell had come up behind her and was staring fixedly at the blossoms on the constable's rather large hand.

Helena turned sharply. "You can't be sure of that. There isn't enough of the plant here to be absolutely sure as to what it might be. We'd need to see the entire specimen to know for certain it was a vanda."

Thea joined them. She slipped past the other two, bent down, and picked up the blooms that had fallen to the floor. She studied them closely as she straightened. "It is a vanda. See." She held the blooms toward her two friends. "There's a dorsal sepal here and the red spots are quite clear against the pale orange body. There's nothing else I know of that has those kind of red spots. It's a vanda." She pushed closer to the constable and stared at the smashed plant. "And look, you can see how the stem is thick here"—with her other hand she pointed to the bottom of the plant—"so it can support a lot of branches."

"Are you certain, Mrs. Stanway?" Witherspoon asked. He'd no idea why the identity of the plant might be useful, but his "inner voice," as the housekeeper called it, was telling him it was very important indeed.

"I'm fairly sure, but if you'd like the opinion of a real expert, you might contact Mr. Harry Veitch. He's the chair of the Orchid Committee for the Royal Horticultural Society."

"There's really no need to bother anyone at the Royal Horticultural Society." Helena said quickly. "I'm certain you're right, Thea. It is a red vanda. As you pointed out, the stem is thick at the bottom and the red spots on the sepal are proof enough."

Thea smiled at Witherspoon and handed him the blossoms. "The vanda generally has twenty or more separate blooms. That's why a thick stem is important. It's a beautiful orchid."

"And a rare one." Isabelle eyed Helena speculatively. "They cost a fortune."

"Is this yours? Was it in your conservatory?" Witherspoon watched Helena as he spoke. He didn't like to make assumptions about guilt or innocence until all the facts of a case were thoroughly investigated, but he found some of her statements to be very suspicious. But her expression didn't change as she shook her head.

"Absolutely not. I've never seen it before."

"You can take this into evidence now." Witherspoon eased the blooms back into the bag. "Give it to Constable Griffiths and ask him to find some way to preserve it if possible."

"Yes, sir." The constable hoisted the bag onto his chest and covered the dirt with as much of the burlap as possible. He moved carefully out the door and into the corridor.

Witherspoon turned his attention back to Helena. "Could Mr. Filmore have been bringing you this orchid because he thought you might want it?"

She shook her head. "As Isabelle, I mean Mrs. Martell, said, they've very expensive."

"They're from India," Isabelle added.

"I don't think he'd bring something that valuable to any of his clients without discussing it beforehand," Helena continued. "The one he brought me before without asking was nowhere near as valuable as the vanda."

"But it's possible? Right?"

"I suppose so, but I don't think it likely."

"Why not?" Isabelle asked. "You told me yourself that Mr. Filmore had gotten you some wonderful plants for next month's competition. Perhaps he knew you'd want this one as well."

"What competition?" Witherspoon asked.

It was Thea who answered. "It's our gardening club, the Mayfair Orchid and Exotic Plant Society. We have it every year. This year Lord and Lady Prentiss are going to be two of our judges."

"Inspector, can we please get on with this?" Helena sighed wearily and went back to the sofa. "I'm exhausted."

"I'll be as quick as possible," he said kindly. "But I do have more questions I must ask. The three of you were here for luncheon, is that correct?"

"There were four of us," Isabelle said. "Mrs. Attwater had gone home by the time we found the body."

"There was another lady present? What time did she leave? Also, I'll need her name and address."

"She's Mrs. James Attwater and she lives at number 26 Webster Crescent in Mayfair," Thea supplied.

Helena gave Thea an irritated frown. "Luncheon was early today, we sat down at twelve thirty. But she didn't leave until almost half past two. Well past the time when a luncheon guest should go, but Mrs. Attwater has a habit of ignoring social convention."

Witherspoon silently repeated Mrs. Attwater's address to himself. He did it three times so he wouldn't forget. His memory was good, but without Constable Barnes and his little brown notebook, he didn't want to risk losing important facts. "When was the last time any of you saw Mr. Filmore?"

"I saw him yesterday," Thea said. "Actually, he brought me some new *Cattleya trianae* that he'd just acquired. I've a conservatory as well. It's not as big as Mrs. Rayburn's but it's adequate for my orchids."

"Mr. Filmore acquired exotic plants for all of you ladies?"

"He was one of many sources," Helena replied.

"Really?" Thea chirped. "I've never heard of you buying from anyone else. Have you got a secret supplier you've not shared with the rest of the club?"

Helena ignored her. "Go on, please," she said to Witherspoon.

"Was Mr. Filmore a member of your gardening society?"

"Don't be absurd, Inspector. He wouldn't be allowed to be a member." Helena looked at him as if he were a half-wit. "Only ladies can join and then only with a recommendation from two members of the board. Mr. Filmore supplied some of us with various orchids and exotic plants, that's all."

The inspector nodded as if he understood and turned his attention back to Mrs. Stanway. "When you saw him, did he mention he was coming here today?"

She shook her head. "I'm afraid not."

He looked at Helena Rayburn. "And you've no idea why he was in your conservatory?"

"None, Inspector."

"Prior to today, when was the last time you had any communications with the victim?"

She thought for a moment. "Let me see, he brought me two clematis plants about ten days ago. Yes, I believe that was the last time."

"Were the keys to the conservatory missing then?"

"No, I remember because I had to go into my day room to get them and he had to wait outside. It was raining and he was a bit annoyed about how long it took Mrs. Clements to go around the house and unlock the outside door."

"Mrs. Martell, have you had any dealings with the victim?" Witherspoon asked.

"I buy some of my flowers from him. But the last time I saw him was three weeks ago."

Constable Griffiths stuck his head into the room. "Excuse

me, sir, but you wanted me to let you know when the police surgeon was finished and the body removed."

"I heard he had his throat slit from ear to ear," the barmaid muttered to the man standing next to Wiggins.

They'd had no luck in front of the murder house, because if there had ever been a crowd of gawkers standing about, they'd gone. So to avoid being spotted by one of the constables that knew both Wiggins and Smythe on sight, they'd deemed it wise to move to the nearest pub.

The Plump Partridge was a pub on a side street less than an eighth of a mile from the murder house. Wiggins had wedged himself into a narrow space at the crowded bar while Smythe surveyed the other customers sitting at the tables before ordering two pints and then making his way to the far side of the noisy, crowded room.

"Someone really got killed, then?" Wiggins asked innocently. He gave the barmaid a respectful nod that also included the tall, thin, bearded man standing beside him.

"Some sort of gardener got himself killed at the Rayburn house on Bellwood Place." She put down the glass she'd been wiping and nodded as someone behind Wiggins shouted for another pint. She was a tall, slender woman with brown hair and the kind of bone structure that meant she'd be turning male heads for years to come.

"He weren't a gardener," the man corrected. He slanted Wiggins a quick glance. "My wife said he was the fellow that owns that exotic plant and seed shop in Hammersmith. Hiram Filmore is his name."

"How does she know who got killed?" the barmaid demanded.

"'Cause today was her afternoon to help at the Adams house and that's right next door to the Rayburn house. She overheard two of the coppers natterin' about it. That's how she found out."

"Would she talk to me?" Wiggins asked.

The bearded fellow looked at him suspiciously. "Why do you want to speak to her? You interested in murder, then?"

"Who isn't? But the reason I'm askin' is because I work for a newspaper and they got wind of it. My guv sent me along to find out if it's true." This was a fiction he often used when he was gathering information, and as he had on decent clothes, he thought he could get away with it.

"Why aren't you chattin' up a constable, then?" The barmaid filled a pint with bitter and slid it across the counter to the fellow standing at Wiggins' elbow. "Ta," she said as she took his coins.

"'Cause you're a lot nicer lookin' than any of that lot." Wiggins wasn't lying. She was probably a good ten years older than he, but she was very pretty. "And the coppers won't talk to the likes of me when their guv's around."

Both the barmaid and the other patrons close enough to hear laughed. "You're a cheeky one," she said. "But you seem nice. What does your paper want to know?"

"What it always wants to know." He grinned, "Who did it."

On the other side of the room, Smythe was in deep conversation with one of the young lads who'd been sitting at the table when the stool had emptied and he'd grabbed the seat.

"Thanks for the pint." Harold Miller, who was all of eighteen, skinny as a beanpole, and trying desperately to grow a mustache, took another sip of the beer Smythe had generously provided.

"Yeah, it's right nice of ya," Johnny Chambliss, Harold's companion at the table, added. Like his friend, he, too, was growing a mustache and, from the heavy dark lines sprouting over his mouth, doing a fine job of it. "But don't you want a pint as well?"

Smythe gave a negative shake of his head. "I'm fine. Actually, I'm workin' so it's best if I keep a clear head."

"Workin'?" Harold's pale eyesbrows rose in surprise. "At what? I don't know of any job that lets you 'ang about in pubs."

"Mine does." He grinned. "I work for a private inquiry agency and I was hopin' you lads might be able to help me."

"You wantin' to know about that bloke that was murdered at the Rayburn house?" Johnny leaned forward eagerly. "I know all about that, he's a man named Filmore."

"How do you know that?" Miller demanded.

"Because I was standing two feet away from the fixed point constable, the one on the corner, when the house-maid come running up sayin' this Mr. Filmore been murdered in the greenhouse."

"You're makin' it up, you were at work today." Harold looked disbelieving. "So what was you doin' there?"

"Mr. Bagshot had sent me to the newsagent's for a tin of tobacco, and I was comin' out when the maid was tellin' the copper. I overheard everythin' she said. She said Mr.

Filmore had a pair of garden sheers stickin' out of his chest."

"You never said anythin' about this earlier." Harold eyed him suspiciously as he raised his glass for another sip.

"You never give me a chance. From the minute we met, you've done nothin' but talk about seein' Fiona on Sunday and followin' her to Our Lady of Victories for the nine o'clock mass and bein' so pleased about her bein' a Roman Catholic because your mum'd not object to her. Mind you, you've not said more than ten words to the girl, so I think worryin' about how your mum's goin' to take to her is putting the cart before the horse. You don't even know if she likes you."

"You're just hoping she likes you," he charged. "But your mother'd die before she let you marry a—"

"Excuse me," Smythe interrupted. "But can you tell me a bit more about the dead man?"

Barnes was finishing up his notes on Mrs. Clemments' statement when the door to the pantry opened and a house-maid entered. She was thin as a fence railing and carried a steaming mug of tea. Her brown hair was pulled straight back from a narrow face and tucked under her white maid's cap. "Mrs. Clemments thought you might like a cup of tea." She smiled shyly as she put the mug down in front of him.

"Thank you, miss, and thanks to your housekeeper." He took a quick sip. "Now, I know this isn't very pleasant, but I'm going to ask you a few questions."

"That's what Mrs. Clemments told me, sir, that's why

I'm here. But I've got to say, I don't know anything about that poor Mr. Filmore being murdered."

"Yes, I'm sure you don't." He opened his notebook to a blank page. "What's your name, miss?"

"Margaret Pooley, sir, but everyone calls me Peggy." She gave him a wide grin. "Mrs. Clemments said you wanted a word with all of us, and Cook is still fussing with her pastry dough so they sent me down. It's a bit exciting, isn't it, sir. I've never been in a place that had a dead body before. Well, not one that had a pair of shears stickin' out of the chest, only my great-aunt Frannie's wake. But that doesn't really count now, does it. I mean, it were a wake so there was supposed to be a body lying about the place."

Barnes eyed her speculatively. She was no more than seventeen but not in the least nervous of him. What's more, she was a chatterbox. Sometimes that worked to his advantage and she'd do more than give brief replies to his inquiries. But sometimes, the talkative ones loved the sound of their own voice so much they could barely pause long enough to hear the question let alone answer it.

"Of course, poor Mrs. Wickham is all in a state over the situation and says that dinner'll need to be put back an hour at least, and if that happens, the mistress will be screaming to high heaven because she hates anything disturbing her day. But mind you, she doesn't like to cross Mrs. Wickham. She's a good cook and there's plenty in London that would snatch her up in a second—"

Barnes interrupted the steady stream of words. "Miss Pooley, Peggy, how long have you worked here?"

Peggy didn't so much as pause for breath. "A year, sir.

I used to work for Mrs. Stanway but I come here when Mrs. Rayburn hired Mrs. Wickham to be the cook. Mrs. Rayburn pays better, you see, and Mrs. Wickham told her she'd not come unless I got a position, too. Truth to tell, sir, Cook is my mother's first cousin and she looks out for me."

"So Mrs. Wickham has only been here a year as well?" He made a mental note to interview her next.

"That's right, sir."

"And you both used to be employed by Mrs. Stanway?" he clarified.

She nodded. "Then Mrs. Rayburn offered us positions and we come here. Mrs. Stanway was bit put out when we give notice but there wasn't much she could say, was there. She couldn't afford to match the pay Mrs. Rayburn was offering."

"Did you see anyone hanging about the area earlier today?" he blurted out. Interesting as these domestic details might be, they had happened over a year ago and probably had nothing to do with the murder. "Anyone who looked suspicious."

"No, sir, but then I wasn't looking."

"I understand that Mr. Filmore supplied Mrs. Rayburn with all her plants, is that correct?"

"Not all of them, sir, only the fancy ones, the orchids and the ones for the greenhouse. They're the ones that Mrs. Rayburn likes to show off to the other ladies. The ones out in the garden proper come from Bennington's out on Wood Lane—they're a big nursery that everyone 'round here uses."

Barnes nodded. "My wife buys from them as well. Now, what can you tell me about Mr. Filmore?"

"Not much, sir. He didn't have naught to do with us when he came here. Sometimes he'd speak to Mrs. Clemment. But he never spoke to me."

"Then I suppose you wouldn't know where his place of business might be?"

"But I do, sir." She grinned proudly. "I don't know the exact address, but I know it's in Hammersmith on Ridley Road." She giggled, revealing a set of surprisingly straight, white teeth. "Last time he was here, the mistress was complaining about how long she'd been waiting for him. I overheard him telling her it was a long way between here and Ridley Road, and what's more, if she didn't like the way he did business, he'd be happy to take his specimens elsewhere."

Upstairs, Inspector Witherspoon was getting a headache, but that didn't keep him from giving his subordinate a grateful smile. "Thank you, Constable Griffiths, I'll be right out. Can you go downstairs and ask Constable Barnes to meet me in the conservatory?"

"Yes, sir," he said before shutting the door.

"What do you need to do in the conservatory?" Helena Rayburn demanded.

"We'll be searching it, ma'am," he told her.

She got up from the sofa. "I insist on being present, Inspector."

Witherspoon hesitated. Though it wasn't strictly against procedure, he didn't like the idea. "I'm afraid that wouldn't be wise, Mrs. Rayburn. There might be important clues in the area—"

"I don't care," she interrupted. "It's my property, and

as far as I can tell, you've no sort of warrant to search my property. You've no right to keep me out."

"We're not trying to keep you out, ma'am, we're trying to investigate a murder, and we have both the obligation and the right to search the premises," he argued.

"Again, I don't care a fig for your rights or obligations." She crossed her arms over her chest and fixed him with a hard stare. "I've already told you, my plants are rare and delicate. Most of them are valuable. I'll not have policeman stomping about in there and making a mess of things."

"Madam, I assure you we'll be very careful."

"How do I know you or that Constable Barnes won't try to steal a cutting for yourself?"

His jaw dropped. "Really, ma'am, I assure you, neither myself nor my men would ever do that."

Thea Stanway chuckled. "Don't be silly, Helena, your plants are no more valuable or rare than the ones Isabelle and I have. Don't make such a fuss and let the inspector do his job."

"I'm not being silly," she cried. "And I've a perfect right to make a fuss. You'd feel the same way if we were at your house and it was your conservatory that was being invaded by all and sundry."

"The inspector is hardly invading." Thea smiled sympathetically. "He's just trying to do his job."

"She's right, Helena," Isabelle added. "You'll feel better if you let them get on with it and then leave you in peace."

"I most certainly will not feel better." Helena glared first at Isabelle and then at Thea. "And despite your ridiculous assertion, Thea, my collection is far better than yours"—she looked at Isabelle again—"or yours. I'm not going to allow Mr. Filmore's unfortunate death to mar my perfect record. Come the first week in July, my orchids are still going to beat out both of you and I'll bring home the first prize."

Half a mile away, Chloe Attwater entered the drawing room of her enormous five-story home in Mayfair and grinned at her housekeeper. "As expected, I had a wonderful time. I can't say the same for my hostess or her companions, though Thea Stanway did seem to be enjoying herself some of the time."

Kareema Dhariwal gave her mistress a disapproving frown. She wore a coral-colored sari over her small, slim frame and held a vase of yellow tea roses in her hands. She had a very prominent nose, a lovely olive complexion, and black hair, which she wore pulled back in a bun at the nape of her neck. "What do you think to achieve, mistress?"

"Achieve." Chloe chuckled. "Why, everything, of course. But for the moment, I'll be content with making them as uncomfortable as possible. After I've watched all three of them squirm for a while, I'll decide what to do next."

Kareema put the vase on an end table and then looked at her employer and friend, her expression somber. "Why do you do this, mistress?"

Chloe's smile disappeared. "You know why."

"I know why you think you should do it, but the reasons are long ago and in the past. You found another life, a good life. We both did. Can't you forgive and forget?"

Chloe stared at her. "Have you forgotten? Have you forgiven?"

"No, but taking vengeance has a cost."

"I'm prepared to pay it."

"I don't think it is wise."

"It may not be wise, but it is most certainly a lot of fun."
She flopped onto the sofa, kicked off her elegant black court
shoes, and took a deep breath. "Don't fret so, Kareema, I
know what I'm doing and I'm doing it for both of us."

"People always think that way, but it is rarely true.
Every action has unforeseen consequences. You should
know that better than anyone." Her housekeeper stared
at her with a disapproving, tight-lipped expression on her
face. "This is a dangerous game you play, mistress. I do
not want to see harm come to you."

"No harm will come to either of us," Chloe declared.
"I'll see to that. I'm not the powerless little nobody I was
twenty years ago, Kareema. They're going to pay, Kareema,
they're going to pay for what they did to both of us."

Both the other ladies decided to accompany Mrs. Rayburn
and the inspector to the conservatory. As they trooped
down the long hallway, the inspector considered pointing
out that as Mrs. Rayburn was the owner of the property,
she was the only person with the legal right to witness the
search. But he didn't wish to wield his authority like a
cudgel, and furthermore, the exchanges between Helena
Rayburn and her friends were very interesting.

He was certainly no expert on female friendships, but
it did seem to him that some of the remarks tossed back
and forth between the ladies revealed more than they realized. He had the distinct impression that Mrs. Rayburn
had a far higher opinion of herself than she had of her
companions; as a matter of fact, he was certain of it. In

his experience, the kind of arrogance that Mrs. Rayburn exhibited often had unforeseen results, and he wondered if she realized her friends might not be so kindly disposed to her when he interviewed them on their own.

When they reached the door of the conservatory, Barnes went in first. Witherspoon entered next with the three women trailing at his heels. Constable Griffiths and another constable were already inside. They stood at the far door awaiting instructions.

"Are there going to be four of you tramping around in here?" Helena demanded as she marched to the center aisle and planted herself there like a battlefield general. Thea Stanway leaned against the end of the row of tall cupboards while Isabelle Martell stayed back, propping herself against the door frame.

"We'll be very careful of your plants, Mrs. Rayburn," Witherspoon assured her for what he thought must be the tenth time. He motioned for the constables to start searching the long counters on his right. Constable Griffiths headed to the table nearest the outside door while the other constable started with the one along the wall. Barnes went past Mrs. Stanway to the cupboards and opened the top cabinet on the one at the end of the row.

Witherspoon headed to his left, to the oilcloth hanging from one of the metal supports on the ceiling.

"Be careful there," Helena warned. "That covering is there to keep those plants at a constant temperature."

"Yes, ma'am." He pushed the cloth to one side. A table was shoved up against the glass wall. Plants at various stages of growth were arranged in long, neat rows along the wood. Some of them were barely pushing out of the

soil, some had green shoots arching toward the light, and
two were completely blooming. The inspector stared at one
of the blossoms, entranced by the loveliness of the deep
purple color and the delicate, unusual shape of the petals.
"Mrs. Rayburn, what kind of flower is this? It's absolutely
exquisite."

Helena rushed across the small space separating them.
"It's a *Vanda amesiana* and it's very fragile. Please put
the cloth back. The temperature needs to be as stable as
possible."

Witherspoon peered under the table and saw there was
nothing, then dropped the oilcloth back into place.

Constable Griffith squatted down and shoved his head
under the counter. Unfortunately, he was larger than the
space, and his shoulder bashed one of the leg supports,
causing some of the pots to wobble dangerously. "Oh, for
goodness' sakes," Helena cried. "Watch what you're doing.
Those are my lady slippers and they're very delicate."

"Helena, you told me you didn't have any of those."
Isabelle hurried forward and poked her friend on the arm.
"I asked you for a cutting and you claimed they'd all died."

"Nonsense, I said no such thing," she replied. "You must
have misunderstood me."

"But Isabelle was very clear." Thea joined the other
two. "I was there when she asked you."

"Then I must have misheard what she was asking. For
goodness' sakes, we've had a murder here, the police are
mucking about in my conservatory, and the two of you are
complaining about something I may or may not have said
last week." Helena started forward as the other constable
lifted a tray of seedlings so he could look underneath.

"It wasn't last week, it was two days ago." Isabelle pointed to the plants.

Helena ignored her and continued on toward the constable trying his best to cram the tray of seedlings back into their narrow space.

"Take a look at this, Inspector." Barnes held up a thick brown burlap-wrapped bundle he'd just taken off the shelf of the second cupboard. "It's very heavy." The constable put the bundle on the edge of the table in front of him and shoved a potted fern out of his way.

"Of course it's heavy." Helena turned on her heel and retraced her steps. The inspector, Isabelle, and Thea trailed after her. "Those are gardening tools, Constable," she continued. "Please be careful with them, they're very valuable."

"As is everything else in this place," Isabelle muttered.

"Don't be rude, Isabelle." Helena gave her friend a quick, disapproving frown. "It doesn't become you."

Barnes untied the two straps that held the bundle together and unrolled the fabric, revealing a row of polished gardening implements. They were tucked into long pockets sewn onto the cloth. The constable pulled out a small pruning knife and handed it to Witherspoon. "It's very fancy, sir, and the wooden handles are carved in the same pattern as the shears that stabbed Mr. Filmore."

The inspector held it up and studied it carefully. "It certainly looks like the same pattern that was on the murder weapon."

"And there's an empty space here where the shears should go." Barnes pointed to the largest pocket, which was now empty.

"Are you saying my gardening shears murdered Mr. Filmore?" Helena demanded. "That is absurd."

"Then where are yours?" Barnes asked. "Surely a set like this would contain a pair of shears?"

"Tufts, he's my gardener, has probably misplaced them. He's old and getting forgetful."

"Is that the reason you're sacking him?" Isabelle asked sweetly.

"You're one to talk," Helena shot back. "You've gone through six gardeners in the last two years, but none of them has been good enough to get your orchids so much as an honorable mention at our annual competition."

"Our annual orchid competition isn't important now." Thea put her hand on Helena's arm. "Someone has been murdered here, Helena, and the truth is he was killed with your shears. I know this is difficult for you and you're terrified of a scandal, but you must tell the truth. I saw the handle poking out of Mr. Filmore's chest. It was exactly like that one."

"Didn't you see it, Mrs. Rayburn?" Witherspoon pressed.

"Of course I didn't see it," she replied. "No decent person stares at something sticking out of a dead man's chest."

"And your eyesight isn't all that good," Thea said. "But mine is and I did take a good look at it."

"My eyesight is just fine." Helena took a deep breath and looked down at the implements spread out on the table. "This is unbearable. These aren't just tools, they're works of art—the handles were carved by a master artisan. My mother-in-law bought them in Paris fifty years ago. They are priceless."

"If they were so valuable, ma'am, why were they in an unlocked conservatory?" Barnes asked.

"I've already told you, the keys have gone missing and the only way in here was to leave the doors unlocked. Obviously, Inspector"—she turned away from the constable's hard gaze—"someone used my shears to murder that man."

Mrs. Jeffries came into the kitchen and stopped in the doorway. Mrs. Goodge was sitting at the table staring off into space. Samson, her massive, orange-colored tabby cat sat on the floor next to her chair. He'd come to the household after one of their investigations. He was bad tempered, cranky, and would swat anyone who went near his food dish. The only person he liked was Mrs. Goodge and she, for her part, adored him and spoiled him rotten. She genuinely couldn't understand why the rest of the household didn't like him. Samson made a soft mewling sound and butted his head against her shins, but for once, she ignored him.

"Are you alright, Mrs. Goodge?" Mrs. Jeffries stepped into the room.

The cook snapped out of her trance and gave the housekeeper a weak smile. "I was just woolgathering. I'm fine."

"Good, I'm glad there's nothing wrong. You had the oddest expression on your face. It was a bit worrying."

The cook waved her hand. "There's nothing amiss, I was just lost in thought."

"I do wish Ruth had known a few more facts about Helena Rayburn." Mrs. Jeffries headed for the table. "If our information is correct, the victim was murdered on her property. That could be very important."

"True. Usually people don't just wander in and get themselves killed at a stranger's house, so it's probable that Mrs. Rayburn knew the dead man."

"Ruth said that Mrs. Rayburn has spent most of her adult life in India. I know very little about that part of the world," Mrs. Jeffries admitted. "Frankly, hot, tropical climates have never appealed to me."

"Never been there, but I do know a bit about the place and I'd be cautious about believing anything you read in the press." The cook looked off in the distance again.

"Why is that?"

"The newspapers never tell you what's really going on in foreign lands. You only read what the army and the government want you to read. India might be part of the empire but it's a law unto itself. Good Englishmen get that far away and they start forgetting there are rules to be followed. I've heard some ugly stories, that's for certain."

"Whatever do you mean? What kind of stories?"

"The usual ones, wives and husbands get strange ideas when they're in hot climates, makes people feel they can do what they like regardless of who gets hurt. You know, the sort of stories that could embarrass the foreign office or the military. When something horrid happens, it gets reported, but it's always couched in terms that don't make Her Majesty's government look bad."

"Gracious, you make it sound like a den of sin." Mrs. Jeffries pulled out her chair and sat down. It wasn't like Mrs. Goodge to be so cynical but perhaps she wasn't feeling well. Her rheumatism might be acting up.

She shrugged. "Well, I'd not go that far, but as I said, I have heard stories and most of them didn't do our nation credit. The way we've treated native peoples is often downright sinful. I've never admitted such a thing before, even to myself, but our investigations over the years have changed my attitude about Queen and country. Mind you, on the other side of the coin, we've gone to these places and put in railways and roads and built hospitals, so that's all to the good. And of course, India was one of the few places where decent but poor young women could find a good husband."

"I've heard that. When I lived in Yorkshire, my neighbor's daughter went out to India as a nanny. She ended up marrying a nice young lieutenant."

"Lots of them ended up marrying well," Mrs. Goodge agreed. "Can't say that I blame them. If my choice was working in a textile mill in Leeds or Bradford and I had a chance to better myself by going to India, I'd have done it, and I hate the heat." She broke off as they heard the back door open. Fred, the household's mongrel dog, leapt up from his spot by the cooker and trotted out to the hall.

Wiggins, with a tail-wagging Fred on his heels, entered the kitchen first. Smythe followed at a more leisurely pace.

"We didn't find out a lot." Wiggins yanked his hat off as he went to the coat tree.

"But we did find out a few bits." Smythe sat down. "Not as much as I'd like, but at least we found out his name. Our victim was a man named Hiram Filmore."

"'E's a buyer and seller of rare plants and herbs." Wiggins took his spot next to the cook. "He runs a small shop in Hammersmith."

"Does he live there as well?" Mrs. Jeffries asked.

"We didn't find that out as yet," the footman admitted. He reached down and stroked Fred's head.

"Did you find out how he was murdered?" Mrs. Jeffries noticed that the cook was staring down at the tabletop, seemingly uninterested in the conversation.

"Not really. There are two different versions of how the man died," Smythe explained. "We couldn't 'ang about the murder house because there was too many constables about the place that know the two of us by sight." He jerked his head slightly to include Wiggins. "So we went 'round the corner to the pub."

"But the news had already spread," Wiggins added. "And the people I was chatting with seemed sure Filmore's throat had been slit."

"While the lot I was talking to was certain he'd been stabbed in the heart," Smythe said.

CHAPTER 3

Mrs. Jeffries was waiting at the front door when Inspector Witherspoon arrived home. "Gracious, sir, you look very tired." She took his hat and hung it on the coat tree.

"It's been a rather exhausting day, Mrs. Jeffries, and if it's not going to inconvenience the household, I'd love a glass of sherry."

Mrs. Jeffries wasn't surprised by his thoughtfulness regarding the kitchen staff. The inspector hadn't been born to wealth or servants, but had, instead, inherited his house and a large fortune from a relative. Consequently, as he'd been raised in very modest circumstances not far above those who now served him, he treated them as human beings and not instruments put on this earth to cater to his needs. He wouldn't put either the cook or the maid to any unnecessary work.

"But of course, sir. Mrs. Goodge said the steak and

kidney pie isn't quite ready as yet and the pudding needs some time to cool before it's served." She turned and led the way to the study off the drawing room.

They frequently had a glass of sherry together before he took his evening meal, most often when he had a murder. Witherspoon liked talking to her about his cases and she, for her part, encouraged that behavior. As they walked down the corridor, she kept up a steady stream of comments about mundane household matters. She wanted him relaxed when they chatted, and more to the point, the focus on the daily domestic routine would keep her from accidentally letting on that they knew about the murder.

Opening the double doors to the study, she crossed to the drinks cabinet while he settled into his favorite chair. The room was a comfortable place of bookshelves filled with books and magazines, dark wine-colored wallpaper, a desk in one corner, and a faded maroon and gold carpet that the inspector had inherited from his mother.

Mrs. Jeffries handed him a glass of his favorite sherry, Harveys Bristol Cream. "Now, sir, I've talked your ear off about the new curtains and the silly clerk at the draper's shop so it's your turn. Tell me, sir, why do you look so tired? Did they give you even more paperwork than usual?" She sat down on the settee across from him.

"No, no, Mrs. Jeffries, it's far worse than working my way through more police ledgers." He paused and took a sip of his drink. "There's been a murder."

"Oh dear, sir, in your district?" She knew that was the case, but in keeping with her supposed ignorance of the crime, she thought it a logical question. "Or were you sent out somewhere else?"

"No, it's in our district. A man named Hiram Filmore was found stabbed in the conservatory of a private home on Bellwood Place in Kensington. Poor fellow wasn't just stabbed, either. His murderer knocked him on the head and then shoved a pair of fancy gardening shears into his heart."

"Gracious, sir, that's awful." She shook her head in feigned disbelief. "What do you mean by 'fancy' gardening shears?"

"There was an elegant, beautifully carved pattern on the handles. I'm not an expert on wood types, but I think these might have been made of rosewood. They were lovely and one could tell the metal used in the prongs and blades was of an excellent quality."

"What kind of a pattern was it?"

He tapped his finger on the side of his glass. "Constable Griffiths called it a Celtic knot and he ought to know, his people are from Ireland. The shears were part of a set that was kept in the conservatory. The poor fellow was found splayed out in the most undignified manner."

"Was it his conservatory?"

"No, the property belongs to Mrs. Helena Rayburn. Unfortunately, it was a very strange situation and I'm not sure I handled it properly."

"Gracious, sir, I can't imagine you doing anything untoward," Mrs. Jeffries protested.

He laughed self-consciously. "I didn't do anything wrong, and my reasons for doing what I did, for conducting Mrs. Rayburn's interview in front of the other ladies, might turn out to have been a very good idea. The way the ladies spoke to one another leads me to believe that when I interview Mrs. Stanway and Mrs. Martell, they may be very forthcoming about Mrs. Rayburn and her relationship with the deceased."

"I'm sorry, sir, I don't follow."

"Mrs. Rayburn was having a luncheon today and two of her guests were with her when she was shown the body," he explained. He gave her a brief, but to his mind, very thorough accounting of the day's activities. When he'd finished, he stared at her expectantly. "You do understand what I'm getting at? It seems to me that by the time Mrs. Stanway and Mrs. Martell excused themselves, they were both a bit annoyed with Mrs. Rayburn."

"It certainly sounds that way," she agreed.

"But then again"—he finished his drink—"perhaps not. At one point, I thought Mrs. Stanway was very upset at some of the comments Mrs. Rayburn made, yet she seemed quite sympathetic to her friend about the murder weapon."

"What about it?" Mrs. Jeffries drained her glass as well.

"Mrs. Rayburn didn't tell us the murder weapon belonged to her. When we searched the conservatory and Constable Barnes found the set with the missing shears, I asked why she hadn't told us it belonged to her. She claimed when the body was originally discovered, she'd not looked at the weapon closely and that's why she hadn't mentioned it belonged to her." He handed her his glass. "Let's have another, shall we. It's been a dreadfully tiring day."

She took his glass and picked up her own. She was glad of the respite because her mind was whirling feverishly to take it all in. As she crossed the room, she forced herself to take a long, deep breath and clear her head. In just fifteen minutes, he'd given her an enormous amount of information. But she needed more details. She needed to know the bits and pieces that he'd not thought to mention but which might turn out to be very important.

Yet right this second, she couldn't think of a single, solitary useful question to ask him. Gracious, what on earth was wrong with her? She caught herself—it was still early days yet and there would be plenty of time to dig a bit deeper. Besides, tomorrow morning they'd have a chat with Constable Barnes and he would fill in some of the gaps.

She uncorked the sherry and poured each of them a second drink. Right now, all she had to do was see if the inspector could give her some sense of the emotional nature of the crime. Surprised, she blinked as that idea popped into her head. Now where did that come from, she asked herself as she shoved the cork back into the bottle. The emotional nature of the crime, what did that mean? Picking up their glasses, she went back to her seat. But the thought, as silly as the words had sounded, was true. Crimes did have emotions. "I don't quite understand, sir." She gave him his drink and sat down. "Do you think she was lying?"

"I don't think so. When she claimed she hadn't looked closely at the body when it was found, she seemed genuinely distressed. I don't mind admitting, Mrs. Jeffries, bodies of murder victims are usually quite frightening and I understand why she might have just taken a quick glance and looked away." He continued speaking as he sipped his drink. Talking seemed to help him get his thoughts in order, so he spoke freely, telling her more and more details as they occurred to him.

As he spoke, Mrs. Jeffries gave up trying to commit every word to memory, and instead, she simply listened. "So the keys to the conservatory are gone?" she asked when he paused to take a breath.

"Indeed, and they have been for about a week. Constable Barnes asked Mrs. Rayburn why she'd not had another set made, and she claimed she simply hadn't gotten around to it as yet."

"Hmm, well, most of us procrastinate," Mrs. Jeffries murmured. "Was the police surgeon able to estimate the time of death?"

He shook his head. "No, but we know it must have been within a specific time frame. The gardener had gone into the conservatory at ten fifteen to get a tray of plants Mrs. Rayburn wanted put outside. But the body was discovered by the housekeeper at about half two so the murder must have taken place within that time period."

"Why did the housekeeper go into the conservatory?" Mrs. Jeffries asked.

"One of the maids heard something, and Mrs. Clemment, she's the housekeeper, is the only person except for Mrs. Rayburn and the gardener who is allowed in the conservatory."

"And she found the corpse. That must have been awful for the poor woman."

"Of course it was, but she handled it well. She closed the room up and got her mistress." He sighed. "I wish she'd have sent directly for the police, but from what I saw of

Mrs. Rayburn's character, if the housekeeper had done so, she'd probably have lost her position."

"I take it Mrs. Rayburn is one of those 'take charge' sort of women?" She was interested in his assessment of the people involved. Despite his protests that he knew little of women, he was an excellent judge of character.

"Indeed she is. As a matter of fact, as I said earlier, none of the ladies appear to be shy and retiring. When we went to search the conservatory and Mrs. Rayburn insisted on accompanying us, as a gentleman I know I should have insisted the other ladies excuse themselves, but there was something compelling about listening to them, and as a policeman, I thought perhaps I might hear something useful about the murder."

"Which, of course, is why you said earlier that letting the two women come with you might end up being a good idea. That was very clever of you, sir." She finished her own drink and put her glass on the side table. "And I shouldn't feel overly concerned with their relationship to one another. Sometimes very old friends do talk to one another in a manner that seems discourteous to outsiders."

"They are old friends. They all were together out in India." He sighed heavily. "I have a feeling this isn't going to be an easy case."

"They never are, sir."

"True, but we've already gotten word from the chief superintendent that I've got to go to the Yard and give him an update within the next day or so. Honestly, Mrs. Jeffries, I don't want to waste valuable time doing that. We're already behind on this one. The constables I sent to search both the victim's flat and place of business weren't able to get inside."

"There weren't any keys in the dead man's pockets?"

He shook his head. "No. I sent some lads to see if there was a porter or landlord for one of the properties and there is. Filmore's landlady lives in the flat below him, but she's out of town until tomorrow morning."

Mrs. Jeffries thought for a moment. "That's odd, isn't it, sir? Most people carry their keys in their pockets. Do you think the killer took them?"

"It's a possibility but not as yet a fact. He might have hidden his keys somewhere in the vicinity of his flat or his business. The lads had a quick look but they found nothing. I've notified the constables on patrol to keep an eye on both properties. They're close together. We'll know more once we speak with the landlady." He put his empty glass on the table and got up. "Let's see if our supper is ready. Despite a nasty murder, it's a lovely evening, and after my meal, I'd like to see if Lady Cannonberry would care to take a stroll in the garden."

"I'd best get upstairs, we've a lot to do today, and there's a chance the inspector will be called to the Yard." Barnes put his empty mug down and got up from the table. As was his custom, when he and the inspector were on a murder together, he always came to the house first, ostensibly to get the inspector, but also to have a quick word with Mrs. Jeffries and Mrs. Goodge.

Being a smart old copper, he'd long ago realized that when they were on a murder, seemingly like magic Witherspoon would suddenly come up with a huge amount of material about the victim and the suspects. He'd watched, asked a few discreet questions, and most important, he'd listened. It wasn't long before he'd realized Mrs. Jeffries was discreetly feeding information to her employer.

He'd wondered what, if anything, he should do. After all, Witherspoon's servants were amateurs and they were interfering in a police investigation. But when it came time to act, he realized he didn't want to. Instead, he decided to help them.

So when he and the inspector had a case, he'd gotten in the habit of having a quick word with Mrs. Jeffries and Mrs. Goodge. He passed along what he knew and found out what they'd learned. Over the course of many investigations, he'd come to have a real respect for all of their abilities. They were good at getting people who would spit on a policeman's shoe before giving him the time of day to chatter like a bunch of magpies.

"Silly waste of time," Mrs. Goodge muttered. "Why can't the chief superintendent just wait for your reports?"

"I think someone is already applying pressure to Chief Barrows."

Mrs. Jeffries rose to her feet. "Why do you say that? Have you heard anything?"

"No, but generally, unless the murder involves someone very important or the press is likely to get unreasonable, the chief gives us a few days before ordering the inspector to the Yard. But this summons came yesterday, the same day as the murder."

"And that's not a good sign," the housekeeper agreed. "The press hadn't even had time to print anything."

"Which means we've got something else to worry about

as well as catching this killer," the cook muttered. "Someone's puttin' their oar in the water and we don't know who it is."

"True, but we'll find out. I've got a source or two at the Yard who owe me a favor."

"But still, it's worryin'. There's some on the Metropolitan Police that are jealous of Inspector Witherspoon's success," Mrs. Goodge muttered. "Some who'll do anything to undermine him. People are like that, you know."

Taken aback by the undercurrent in the cook's tone, Mrs. Jeffries glanced at her and saw that she had that faraway look on her face again.

But Constable Barnes didn't notice. He grinned broadly. "Stop worrying, Mrs. Goodge, this has happened before and we've weathered it. I'm off upstairs. I'll see you ladies tomorrow." He disappeared up the back stairs.

A few moments later, they heard footsteps in the upstairs hall and the front door slammed shut as the two policemen left. Less than a minute later, the back door opened and they heard a babble of voices and the clatter of feet.

"Lordy, I thought they'd never get goin'," said a female voice with a distinctly American accent.

"Madam, I did tell you we ought not to come quite so early," said a man with a very precise English accent. "It's hardly a decent hour to descend upon people."

"Fiddlesticks," she snorted. "We ain't descendin', we're coming for our morning meeting."

"And the household is always up and about," Betsy added.

"We're all ready for you," Mrs. Jeffries said to the group trouping into the kitchen.

They were led by a small, very elderly, white-haired woman wearing a blue dress as bright as the eye of a peacock feather, a matching hat with a two-foot azure veil trailing behind her, and brandishing a blue and white lace parasol. Pearl earrings hung from her ears and a matching necklace was draped around her neck. Luty Belle Crookshank loved colorful clothes, jewelry, and justice.

Behind her came Hatchet, her butler. He was dressed in an old-fashioned black frock coat of excellent cut and quality, and in his hand, he carried a shiny black top hat that had been out of style now for a good ten years. But he, like his employer, wore what he liked. Despite being many years younger than Luty, he had a full head of thick snow-white hair. He carried himself with the dignity of an English admiral but the sparkle in his blue eyes made it clear he didn't take himself or the world too seriously.

Betsy and Smythe, who was carrying their daughter, completed the group.

Amanda spotted Mrs. Goodge, shrieked with glee, and waved her chubby little arms. The cook threw down the dishtowel she'd been using to wipe the worktable and hurried over to claim her goddaughter.

"She's been a right little terror this morning." Smythe eased the toddler into Mrs. Goodge's arms, pulled back the cook's chair, and braced it against his body until the two of them were safely seated.

"Nonsense," Mrs. Goodge exclaimed as she fluffed Amanda's blonde curls, "I don't believe a word of it, she's my little sweetling."

"Your little sweetling tried to have a tantrum over putting on her clothes this morning." Betsy dropped into the chair across from them. "But we soon put a stop to that, didn't we."

Amanda giggled and pointed to Samson, who was sitting on Fred's rug by the cooker. "Kitty!" But the cat simply gave them all a disgusted look, stuck his nose in the air, and stalked out of the room. "Kitty go?"

"He doesn't like little ones," Smythe said gently. "But not to worry, my darlin', he doesn't like anyone but Mrs. Goodge."

A moment later, Ruth dashed in and took her spot. "Sorry I'm a late. I had to send off some notes to my women's group. I think some of them might know Helena Rayburn quite well."

"Excellent, Ruth, thank you. Wiggins and Phyllis will be right down." Mrs. Jeffries gestured at the empty chairs. "We'll need to get started quickly."

"Guess that means you've found out a few things," Luty muttered as she took her usual seat.

Luty Belle Crookshank had been a witness in one of their very first cases. But the elderly American was both smart and observant. She'd seen the household snooping about and asking questions, and then shortly after that case had been solved, she'd come to them with a problem of her own. Ever since, she and Hatchet had insisted on helping with the inspector's cases.

Widowed, wealthy, and childless, she'd become a huge asset to their investigations. With her homespun ways and ready wit, she charmed secrets out of the rich and powerful. She was from the American West and not in the least ashamed of having worked alongside her English husband digging silver out of the mountains of Colorado. People who wouldn't have spoken to someone like her when she was running a boardinghouse in Pueblo or taking in laundry in Denver now fell all over themselves to get an invitation to one of her parties. But Luty would much rather be helping solve a murder than going to a ball, unless, of course, she was on the hunt.

"We have," Mrs. Goodge said as Phyllis and Wiggins joined them. It took a few minutes for all of them to get settled and cups of tea to be poured.

Betsy waited till Mrs. Jeffries finished pouring everyone's tea and took her seat at the head of the table before she spoke. "Before you begin, when we were waiting outside for the inspector and Constable Barnes to leave, I told Luty and Hatchet what we knew from yesterday."

"Good, that'll save a bit of time." Mrs. Jeffries looked at them. "Have either of you heard of or know anything about Helena Rayburn or the victim, Hiram Filmore?"

"I've never heard of either of them," Luty declared. "But Hatchet here claims he knows something."

"It isn't a claim, madam, it is a fact. If it is indeed the same person, I have heard of Hiram Filmore."

"But you never met him," Luty shot back.

"No, but Mrs. Jeffries asked if we knew him or had heard of him and I, madam, have heard of him."

Amanda's smile disappeared and she made a soft sound of alarm as the two of them argued. Everyone else knew that the bickering between them was a testament to their close relationship and genuine affection for each other, but the little one was too young to understand that.

Luty was instantly contrite. "There, there, sweetie, it's alright. We're not mad at each other." She shot Hatchet a malevolent glare but kept her voice soft. "Say something nice. I don't want my baby upset."

Hatchet, who was as besotted with the tot as the rest of them, leaned across and chucked her on the chin. "I'm sorry, we didn't mean to raise our voices."

"Don't worry about it," Betsy told them. "She's alright now."

Mrs. Jeffries looked at Hatchet. "Tell us what you know of Hiram Filmore."

"He was in the army in India for years, and when he retired, he stayed on in Bombay and established a business selling rare plants and herbs."

"How do you know this?" Ruth asked curiously.

Hatchet smiled. "In my younger days I spent a lot of time in the Far East. I still keep in contact with a number of friends who are still out there. One of my friends is a plant collector who specializes in orchids. He's currently in Borneo, but a few years back he was in India working for a consortium of English aristocrats, all of whom wanted orchids and other exotic blooms for their gardens. He and I correspond regularly and he's mentioned Filmore's name on more than one occasion. Plant collectors or orchid hunters as some call them are a hard and tough breed, but even amongst them, Filmore had a bad reputation. What's more, most collectors are like my friend—they work for either a rich individual or a collective of some kind."

"Why's that?" Phyllis asked.

"Because it's expensive, and collectors need to have enough money to hire guides, buy supplies, and in many instances, employ guards to get them in and out of some very unsafe places. Even after they've found a reasonable number of specimens, they have to get them safely back to England, and according to my friend, they're lucky if they get back with even half of what they've collected. But Filmore didn't work for anyone. Which means he had enough money to finance his own expeditions."

"So that means he'd not have to share the profit with anyone else," Luty muttered.

"Can you find out more?" Mrs. Jeffries asked.

"I'll send off a telegram to Sebastian today," Hatchet said. "But it may take some time to get a reply. In his last letter, he said he was going into the jungle on an expedition."

"It can't hurt to try. Now, if no one has anything else, I'll pass along what we've learned since yesterday." For the next fifteen minutes, Mrs. Jeffries gave them a complete report on what they'd learned. Mrs. Goodge added her comments as well. When she'd finished, she sat back and looked at the faces around the table. "Are there any questions?"

"Seems like a lot of keys are missin'," Wiggins mused. "The ones to the conservatory and the ones to the victim's flat and shop. Maybe the killer took 'em."

"That's possible," Phyllis said. "But the keys to the conservatory have been missing for days and—"

Mrs. Jeffries interrupted. "No speculating, you both know what happens when we start down that road."

"It's not speculatin', it was just a thought," Wiggins protested. "But I know what you mean. Right then, I'll have a go at the Rayburn house and see if I can find a housemaid or a footman to chat with. If that doesn't work, I'll see if I can chat with one of the neighbors."

Amanda gave a tiny burp and then a huge yawn. "Let me put her down for a little nap before I go out." Betsy pushed back her chair, came around the table, and scooped the child into her arms. She disappeared in the direction of Mrs. Goodge's quarters, where a baby cot had been set up on the day the child was born.

"Guess you'll be wantin' me to have a chat with the local cab drivers," Smythe offered.

Mrs. Jeffries nodded. She knew that before Smythe bothered with the hansom drivers, he'd go to the Dirty Duck and have a word with his best source, Blimpey Groggins, a professional seller of information.

"After I send off my telegram, I've a few other sources I can speak with regarding the late Mr. Hiram Filmore," Hatchet said.

"I'm goin' to Hammersmith," Luty interjected. "There's bound to be people there who know plenty about the dead man."

"Madam, there's no need for you to go there," Hatchet insisted. "I was going there this afternoon."

"Why do you git to be the one who gits all the good jobs?"

"But Luty, it would be far more beneficial to us if you used your connections to find out about Filmore's financial situation or who his heirs might be," Mrs. Jeffries suggested.

Luty made a face. "That means I'll be talkin' to a bunch of lawyers and bankers. That's borin'. I want to go to the Hammersmith High Street and find out what's what. I'm good at gettin' people to talk. I kin find out lots."

"That's not a very safe area, madam," Hatchet protested. "You're much better suited—"

"I kin take care of myself," Luty cried. "And after what happened on our last case, all of you should remember that. You're all just trying to push me to the side and make me do the dull, namby-pamby work because you think I'm old and useless."

There was a stunned silence around the table as everyone stared at the elderly American. Luty's eyes watered and she blinked hard in an effort to hold back the tears.

No one said anything for a moment until, finally, Ruth spoke. "Luty, you do us all a disservice if you really believe what you're saying. We have the highest regard and respect for your abilities. You've proved your resourcefulness, your worth, and most importantly, your bravery many times. Gerald is alive today because of your courage and fast thinking. The reason you get sent to do the namby-pamby work, as you put it, is because you're the only one here clever enough to loosen a banker's or a barrister's tongue."

Luty glanced down at the floor. "I'm sorry. I shouldn't have said what I did. I know you don't think that way. I just wanted to do somethin' a bit more excitin' is all," she said softly. "Don't pay any attention to me. Sometimes I git a bit down in the mouth about things. I guess today is just one of those days."

"I get down in the mouth about things, too," Phyllis said. "Especially when I hear or see something that reminds me of the my first position. My mother died and I had to go to work for an awful family in Mayfair. I still avoid even walking down the street where the house is, and sometimes, if

I see someone who looks like the mistress or her son, I get a terrible feeling that makes me feel sick inside. Like I've done something wrong. So I know just what you mean, Luty. I really do."

"It wasn't a total waste of our time, sir." Barnes grabbed the handhold in the hansom as the cab swung around the corner onto Webster Crescent. "We found out from Mrs. Clemment and the housemaid that Mrs. Rayburn was gone for a period of time yesterday morning. Both of them insist that sort of behavior is out of character for her. She's never left the house before guests are expected because she oversees the kitchen and the dining room herself. The maid claims that when Mrs. Rayburn did return home, she was in a terrible mood."

The hansom pulled up to the curb and Witherspoon opened the door. "True and I find it significant that Mrs. Rayburn neglected to mention this herself when we interviewed her." He and Barnes stepped out onto the pavement and the constable turned to pay the driver. "What's even more annoying is that she knew we were coming by this morning to take her statement in fuller detail. We made that abundantly clear when we left yesterday."

"She's probably gone to speak to her solicitor," Barnes suggested. "She was really rattled when we found the rest of that gardening set, sir. Mind you, she doesn't strike me as a stupid woman, so if she was the killer, you'd think she'd have had the brains to get rid of the evidence."

"She may not have had time and we both know that even clever killers often make very stupid mistakes. But she did have a point—as the conservatory has been unlocked for days, anyone could have gotten in and taken her shears. Well, let's go in and see what Mrs. James Attwater can tell us."

The Attwater home was a five-story Georgian in light gray brick. A box hedge enclosed a small garden of blooming rosebushes in brilliant shades of red, pink, coral, and white. A walkway set with intricately patterned paving stones led to a short, broad set of stairs and a front door painted a bright scarlet.

"She's not hurtin' for money." Barnes headed up the walkway.

"So it would appear," Witherspoon agreed. "Let's just hope this lady is home and we've not wasted our time."

The lady wasn't just home, she was waiting for them.

The door opened before they'd even knocked, and Barnes found himself facing a small, black-haired woman dressed in flowing green robes that he thought were called a sari. From the depths of the house, they heard a woman shout, "Is that the police, Kareema? If it is, bring them straight into the drawing room."

"Do come in, sirs." She stepped back and held the door wide. "Mistress has been expecting you."

They stepped inside a huge foyer. A staircase curved to the upper floors, the walls were painted a pale green, and overhead, a crystal chandelier hung from the high ceilings.

"This way, please." Kareema led them down the long, white-tiled corridor and through a set of double doors. The drawing room was huge, elegant, and furnished with the lightest of touches. Walls of pale cream, upholstered furniture in a blue and green muted paisley, sheer curtains open to capture the sun, and an oak floor covered with a beige and green oriental rug.

A slender, dark-haired woman rose from the love seat. She wore a pink taffeta day dress with leg-o'-mutton sleeves, which rustled faintly as she moved. She came toward them with a welcoming smile. "Do come in, gentlemen, I've been waiting for you. I'm Chloe Attwater."

"We're sorry to intrude, Mrs. Attwater," Witherspoon said. In truth, he was rather taken aback. The woman was probably close to the same age as Helena Rayburn, but she was far lovelier. "And I promise, we'll not take up too much of your time. I'm Inspector Witherspoon and this is my colleague, Constable Barnes."

Her eyes flicked from one to the other, and the constable realized she'd caught the fact that the inspector had introduced him as a "colleague," not an inferior. She smiled broadly when she caught his expression and waved them toward two matching chairs across from where she'd been sitting. "Please don't concern yourself, Inspector, I am at your disposal today. I heard about what happened at Helena's yesterday and I knew you'd want to speak with me. Please make yourselves comfortable."

Just as they sat down, Kareema entered. She pushed a tea trolley loaded with a silver tea service, a tray of cakes, and a plate of biscuits. "Shall I serve, mistress?"

"You will have tea?" She looked from Witherspoon to Barnes.

As he was gaping at the food, Barnes was oblivious to the fact that his superior might want to decline the offer and nodded quickly.

"We don't want to trouble you, Mrs. Attwater," Witherspoon began, but she interrupted.

"Nonsense, Inspector, I've had this at the ready and it's no trouble at all." She smiled at her servant. "Can you please pour for us, Kareema," she instructed before turning to Witherspoon. "Now, while we have our tea, ask me anything you like. I'll help with this ghastly business in any way I can."

"Do you take sugar, sir?" Kareema asked the constable.

"One lump, please." Barnes took out his little brown notebook and balanced it on his knee.

"Would you like a biscuit, a cake, or both, sir?" She placed a cup of tea on the table next to him.

Barnes hesitated for a fraction of a second. "Both, please."

"Mrs. Attwater, what time did you arrive at the Rayburn house yesterday?" Witherspoon asked.

"Luncheon was at half past twelve and I arrived about fifteen minutes before we went into the dining room. It must have been twelve fifteen or thereabouts."

"Were all the other luncheon guests present when you arrived?"

"Mrs. Martell arrived soon after I did but Mrs. Stanway was already there. I'd seen her in the water closet off the cloakroom when the butler took my wrap. Our hostess was nowhere to be seen. But I wasn't surprised. Helena, Mrs. Rayburn, always loved to make an entrance. I was surprised by Isabelle arriving before Helena came downstairs. Isabelle loves to make an entrance as well." She laughed. "You should have seen those two in India—there wasn't a picnic, luncheon, dinner party, or ball where those two didn't try to come in just a few moments later than the other."

Barnes nodded his thanks as Kareema put a plate of treats next to his teacup. "You've known Mrs. Rayburn for a number of years?"

"Oh yes, we were in India together years ago," Chloe explained. "Of course, back then our status was very different. I worked as a governess while Helena, Isabelle, and Thea had come out to stay with relatives who were in the army. Isabelle had a brother and I think Helena had come to stay with a cousin—no, I tell a lie. It was Thea Stanway who had a brother. Isabelle was there with a cousin as well. But I left India years before any of them. I went to live in America and lived there for twenty years. But when my husband passed away, I got homesick and came back to London."

The constable nodded and then waited for Witherspoon to ask the next and, to him, the obvious question, but when his superior said nothing, Barnes plunged ahead on his own because, awkward as it might be, it had to be asked. "Mrs. Attwater, I hope you won't be offended but—"

"But you'd like to know why those women became friends with a mere governess," she interrupted. "The truth is, they didn't want to, but they had no choice. My mother's family was and still is related to a number of highly placed officials and army officers in India. So even though I was just the 'hired help' as they say in America, the ladies were afraid of offending me so I was always invited to social events."

"Didn't that interfere with your work?" Barnes asked.

"Not really, you see, the children had an ayah. I was

just there to give them lessons. I didn't take care of them all the time, and as I was a very good teacher, my employers were happy for me to have a social life as long as it didn't interfere with my duties."

"An ayah?" Witherspoon asked as Kareema put a cup of tea and a plate of pastries on the table next to him.

"An ayah is a nursemaid," she explained. "A native Indian woman who took care of the children when they weren't having lessons or with their parents."

"I see." Witherspoon reached for his tea. "How long have you been in London?"

"June of last year," she said. "Of course, the first thing I did was to contact my old acquaintances from India. I wasn't certain they'd even be here. After all, Helena had managed to land herself a rich English colonel so I thought she could be anywhere in the empire, and Isabelle had married a major so the same could be said of her. The only person I was relatively sure would be in London was Thea Stanway. I knew she and her husband had come back to London, though I didn't know he'd passed away. Then, of course, I found out the other two were widowed as well. It's quite sad; both Thea and Isabelle lost their husbands when they were relatively young. I had no idea, of course, until I remembered a bit of gossip I heard in San Francisco years ago. We had a mutual acquaintance who had come from Madras to the United States, and she told me that there were some very nasty rumors about the Mrs. Martell's late spouse." She paused for breath and Witherspoon opened his mouth to ask another question, but she was too quick for him. "Naturally, I'm not one to believe gossip, but some say where there's smoke, there's fire."

"Did you use a carriage to take you to the luncheon?" The constable helped himself to a delicate thin biscuit and took a bite.

"I took a hansom cab. It's simply too difficult to keep a carriage in the city though I am considering purchasing one of those lovely horseless carriages I saw displayed at the Imperial Institute."

"You saw the Horseless Carriage Exhibition?" Witherspoon asked. He'd gone and had a look himself. "What did you think of it?"

"I thought it was wonderful, but I suspect it might be a few years before they are sufficiently practical to drive about London." She gave him a rueful smile.

"I agree, but it is exciting, isn't it. Just imagine if in the future, we're all moving from one place to the next in horseless carriages."

"Indeed, they were most impressive, and impractical or not, I was tempted to buy one. I quite like new things, you see, and even better, if I had bought one, it would have made both Isabelle and Helena green with envy, and that would have made the entire enterprise worth it."

Slightly bemused by the frankness of her statements, Witherspoon was caught off guard and couldn't think what to ask next.

"Did you see anyone hanging about the Rayburn home when you got out of the hansom yesterday?" Barnes looked up from his notebook.

"Not that I recall. But I wasn't particularly observant."

"Had you ever met Mr. Hiram Filmore?" Barnes shoved another biscuit in his mouth. They were delicious.

"Yes, I met him in India. He worked in the infirmary.

I remember because he was in charge of sending the personal effects of the dead soldiers home. He used to ask me to help him write the letters to the families. Thea Stanway used to help him as well—his handwriting wasn't very good."

"Isn't that the sort of thing a commanding officer does?" Witherpsoon helped himself to a small pink frosted cake.

"The commanding officer writes the initial letter to the family, but this was the one that accompanied their personal effects." She smiled sadly. "Often, it took time to gather things up and get them posted. It was an infirmary, Inspector, and not a very well run one, I might add. The officers that were nominally in charge were sometimes simply not very good administrators. All of the ladies, the wives, the sisters, even those like myself that had come to India to work helped out as best we could. But things often got lost. Actually, right before I left, I remember there was a bit of commotion over things going missing. Several letters arrived from the families claiming some of their loved ones' possessions weren't in the boxes of personal effects. But you know the British army; they got that hushed up as soon as possible and so nothing ever came of it."

"Had you seen Mr. Filmore since you came back to London?" Barnes waited till she glanced away before he licked the crumbs off his fingers.

"Twice. Both times he was with Mrs. Rayburn. The first time was last year at the Mayfair Orchid and Exotic Plant Society annual show, and the second time was when he was going into Mrs. Rayburn's garden. That was several months ago. It looked as if he was bringing her a box of cuttings."

The inspector swallowed the last bite of the tiny cake. "While you were having luncheon, did you see or hear anything that was unusual?"

"Not really, it was a very boring luncheon. Isabelle Martell was playing coy and trying to find out how many items Helena and Thea were entering into the upcoming competition. But that was all." She frowned and put her tea on the table next to the love seat. "Come to think of it, Helena was very quiet, uncharacteristically so."

"Mistress, would you like more tea?" Kareema asked.

"No, I'm fine, but thank you."

"Do you know if Mr. Filmore had any enemies?" Barnes asked.

"I'm afraid I don't." She shrugged. "I'd only seen him the two times since coming back to London. Frankly, Constable, I never liked the man and I don't think my friends did, either."

"Did any of them ever tell you that specifically?" Witherspoon asked.

"No, it was simply an impression I received whenever his name would be mentioned, that's all. Helena used to make rude comments about his dress and his manners."

"But they used him to acquire their specimens," the inspector pointed out.

She laughed. "Helena likes to win so badly she'd use the devil himself if he could find her an orchid that would win first prize at their annual show."

"Don't you want to win?" Witherspoon asked.

"It would be nice, but I'm not obsessed with it."

"I take it you didn't get your plants from Mr. Filmore?" Barnes finished his tea and put the cup down.

"No, I buy my plants from local merchants, and I use an old friend from San Francisco for the exotic blooms and the orchids. As I said, I'm not obsessed the way the other three ladies are. I joined their club for social reasons and to renew my acquaintance with them."

"Forgive me, Mrs. Attwater, but why would you renew your acquaintance with these ladies? From what you've said, it doesn't sound as if you liked them all that much," Barnes blurted out.

She grinned. "You do get right to the heart of the matter, don't you, Constable."

"Sorry, ma'am, I didn't mean to be offensive."

"You're not, you're doing your job, and you're absolutely correct. I don't particularly have fond feelings for any of those women. My reasons were entirely pragmatic. I was new in town and old acquaintances can be very useful in establishing oneself socially. London can be a very lonely place for a woman on her own."

The inspector didn't think a woman as lovely as Mrs. Attwater would be on her own for long, but he kept his opinion to himself. "Is there anything else about yesterday that you can tell us? Anything you saw or heard that struck you as out of the ordinary or unusual?" he pressed.

"I'm afraid not. It was just an ordinary lunch."

Witherspoon couldn't understand how in a house full of people, a human being could be murdered but no one saw or heard anything. So he tried another tactic. "I'm sure this whole episode has been very upsetting for you, Mrs. Attwater. Sudden death can be very shocking, so perhaps later you'll be able to remember something about yesterday's events once you've had some time to think."

"Sudden death?" She snorted delicately. "Really, Inspector, what do you think I was trying to tell you when I said I'd heard some nasty rumors about Isabelle Martell's late husband? But she isn't the only one to know something about sudden death. Helena Rayburn is a bit of an expert on the subject as well."

CHAPTER 4

Amanda was sitting up in her pram as Betsy pushed it into the little park tucked away on a side road off the Kensington High Street. It was the closest public space to the Rayburn house on Bellwood Place, and though she didn't think she'd have much chance of finding anyone who knew anything about the murder or the victim, she had to try.

A paved oval footpath lined with elm trees bisected the small green and ended at a tall gate in the ivy-covered walls of a neighboring churchyard. A group of children ran, skipped, and chased one another between the trees and the grass. Amanda grinned and waved her hands at them, blissfully unaware that they were ignoring her. Three wooden benches sat beneath the tree limbs and provided shade against the warmth of the June sun. Two of the benches were occupied so Betsy headed for the empty one right in the center.

She angled the pram so Amanda could keep watching the children play before she sat down. She needed to think. This morning's meeting had unsettled her and she wasn't sure what she should or even could do about it.

Luty's outburst had shocked them, but from Betsy's point of view, there had been a grain of truth in her complaint. Her bravery and resourcefulness might be admired, but what all of them really wanted Luty to do was sit in some banker's or barrister's office and dig up what she could.

Betsy understood Luty's frustration. She felt the same way. Sometimes she itched to get back out onto the streets and use her smile, her wits, and her guile to pry information out of a reluctant store clerk, shopkeeper, or publican. Amanda giggled as one of the boys raced past her, and she banged her hands against the rail of her pram to get his attention, but he kept on going.

Oh, it wasn't anyone's fault, Betsy understood that, but she knew that while her overprotective husband hunkered at the table, no one wanted to upset any apple carts by asking her to do anything interesting. Since Amanda's birth, everyone had entered into a silent conspiracy to make sure she never was at risk. Which was nonsense really, because like Luty, she could jolly well take care of herself. One didn't survive the back streets of the East End without learning a few useful lessons. But there had been enough drama this morning and she'd been grateful when Phyllis had spoken up. The girl had shared some of her own painful past just so that Luty could salvage her pride about her outburst. So Betsy had held her tongue and not protested when they'd asked her to go to the murder neighborhood and see what she could learn. But that was ridiculous. She glanced around the park and made a face. Who was she supposed to chat with, the children chasing each other, one of the elderly nannies seated on the far bench, or the young couple holding hands on the other?

"How old is your daughter?"

Startled, she turned. A middle-aged red-haired woman stood there, her gaze fixed on the toddler. The lady's stare was intent, too intent. Betsy got up and put her hand on the pram's handle. "She's two."

Amanda giggled and the woman smiled, transforming her face. "Oh my gracious, she is precious, isn't she. She reminds me of my daughter." She looked at Betsy. "Mine is all grown up now, but like yours, she had those lovely curls and big blue eyes. Sorry I was staring, but my eyes aren't what they used to be and it takes them a few moments to focus properly."

Betsy relaxed. "She's our only baby and I'm afraid we spoil her a bit."

"I spoiled my Jeannette as well and she turned out just fine. Children are such a blessing, aren't they. I shouldn't be dawdling here, I ought to be home sewing my curtains, but after all the rain we've been having lately, I needed to get out of the house. It's such a lovely day."

"You live nearby then?" Betsy eased back onto the bench.

"Just up the road and around the corner." She waved her hand in an arc. "We're the third house along, the one with the tiny hedgerow in front and the spaniel at the window. He'll be ever so annoyed at me because I didn't bring him. He likes to come with me when I leave the house, but I was going to visit my friend Lucy and she has three cats. Simon, of course, can't be trusted around cats so he had to stay home. Though I did take him for an extra-long walk this morning, so he shouldn't be in too bad a temper."

Betsy kept a friendly smile on her face, but a hard, sharp disappointment cut through her. She probably wasn't going to learn a ruddy thing. "I guess we've all been a bit housebound with the rain." She reached into the pram, grabbed one of the clean nappies she always carried, and wiped the drool off Amanda's chin.

"It's no worse than it usually is for this time of year." The redhead chuckled. "We just like to do a bit of complaining. But I remember when my Jeannette was little, being stuck inside because of the rain was a right old misery. I best get moving, those curtains aren't going to hem themselves, and if I don't get them up today, everyone on Bellwood Place will get an eyeful of us having our supper." She grinned at Amanda, nodded at Betsy, and turned on her heel.

It took a moment before Betsy realized exactly what the woman had said. "Wait a moment," she called, "I'm going that way myself, I'll walk with you."

"What do you mean by 'sudden deaths'?" Barnes asked.

She shrugged. "Exactly what I said. I left India years before either of them, but before I went, Helena Rayburn, she was Helena Blackburn back then, she hadn't managed to pry a marriage proposal out of Malcolm Rayburn yet, but I digress. She accused a young man of inappropriate behavior towards her and the very next day he was found drowned."

"Are you implying she was responsible for his death?" Barnes looked skeptical.

"Of course I am, Constable; otherwise, there'd be no point in mentioning it at all."

"But if this young man was in the army," the inspector said, "surely the military conducted a proper investigation."

She laughed cynically. "He wasn't in the army, and even if he had been, I highly doubt there'd have been any sort of real investigation done on the incident. They were all too eager to have his death classified as an accident."

"What was his name?"

"Anthony Treadwell," she replied. "He was an engineer working for an Anglo-American mining company."

Barnes scribbled the name in his notebook.

"And Isabelle Martell?" Witherspoon couldn't quite believe his ears. It was usually very difficult to get women or for that matter even men of this class to speak freely. Yet Mrs. Attwater was almost hinting that her "friends" were capable of murder.

"That one was simply gossip, but I heard it years ago, presumably just after the incident occurred." She paused as Kareema put a fresh cup of tea in front of her.

"Your tea, mistress, and don't forget you've an engagement soon." The housekeeper shot a quick, disapproving glare at her mistress and then went to stand next to the tea trolley.

"Nonsense, Kareema, I've plenty of time." She flashed the constable an amused smile. "Now, as I was saying, about Mrs. Martell. Supposedly her husband died under very mysterious circumstances. He fell off a second-story balcony to his death right after they'd had a dreadful quarrel."

"And I take it, Mrs. Martell was the only one present when this accident happened?" Barnes guessed.

"Indeed." Chloe grinned. "That's what I was told. The Martells had a terrible argument, and ten minutes later, he was lying on the ground-floor terrace with a broken neck. In all fairness to Isabelle, he did have a reputation as a drunk and the balustrades on the balcony were quite low, so I suppose he could have tripped and fell."

"You learned of this from someone who was in India with Mrs. Martell?" Witherspoon asked. "Someone who then renewed her acquaintance with you in San Francisco?"

"That's right."

"And how long ago did this accident occur?"

"Ten or eleven years ago," she replied. "I don't know the exact date. But I can find out. It was right before Isabelle came back to England."

"No, no, that won't be necessary," Witherspoon said. This information, while interesting, was about as useless as a broken umbrella during a downpour. The army wouldn't be keen to release any information about the incident, and he wasn't sure it warranted further investigation. In his experience, any sudden, accidental death often led to gossip.

A housemaid stuck her head around the door. "Sorry for interrupting, ma'am, but there's a constable here for the inspector. He says you're to go to the Rayburn house and that it's urgent."

"Oh dear, and we were having such a nice chat," Chloe said as the two policemen got up and headed for the door. "You must come back if you've anything else you'd like to ask me."

"Indeed we will, ma'am," Witherspoon called over his shoulder.

"And thank you for the tea," the constable added.

"Anytime, gentlemen, I'm at your disposal. I just hope there hasn't been another murder at Helena's. It would ruin her chances to get that open position on the Narcissus Committee."

Though it had only just opened, the Dirty Duck Pub was filling up fast. Dock workers, delivery drivers, street vendors, bread sellers, and casual laborers lined up at the bar and filled the benches along the walls. The tables were full, too, save the one nearest the unlighted fireplace, which was reserved for the proprietor.

Smythe pulled out a stool, sat down, and grinned at his old friend. "Are you feelin' more settled now, Blimpey? Betsy said she had a nice chat with Nell."

Blimpey Groggins, the proud owner of the Dirty Duck, was ginger-haired, rotund, and dressed in a yellowed white shirt with a brown and cream checkered waistcoat. He laughed. "We're a bit better now, but Smythe, I've got to tell ya, the whole idea about becomin' a father at my age is dauntin'. Dauntin', I say, and though I'd never say it in front of Nell"—he leaned closer, lowering his voice as he spoke—"she's no spring chicken, either."

Smythe glanced toward the bar, making sure that Lily, the barmaid, and Eldon, Blimpey's man-of-all-work, weren't close enough to overhear. "Be careful, Blimpey. Your people like you but they love your Nell, and you'll not want that comment repeated to her. Women don't find jokes about their age funny. Beside, you're wrong, Betsy told me that lots of women Nell's age have children."

"But it's her first and even the sawbones said she

needed to be careful. But give my thanks to your lady. Ever since she and Nell had their chat, Nell's been much calmer. But you're not here to chat about my impendin' fatherhood. I heard your inspector caught that murder over on Bellwood Place."

"That's why I'm 'ere." Smythe took a sip from his pint. He wasn't surprised Blimpey was already aware of the murder; that was the man's job. He made his living buying and selling information. Groggins had a small army of paid informants that kept him current on everything of interest in the south of England. His people worked at newspapers, insurance companies, all the law and police courts, the docks, shipping lines, telegraph offices, Parliament, and there were rumors he even had sources at Buckingham Palace. His clients came from all classes and all walks of life: businessmen, thieves, bond traders, estate agents, and more than a few politicians. Anyone who needed information came to him. But he didn't give his help for free. He charged huge fees.

But that wasn't a problem for Smythe; he could afford them. Everyone thought he was a coachman, and to some extent he was, but he had made a fortune in Australia.

When he'd come back from Sydney, he'd stopped in to pay his respects to his former employer, Euphemia Witherspoon, and found her dying. Surrounded by thieving servants, with only a very young Wiggins taking care of the sick, elderly woman. Smythe had sacked the staff, sent Wiggins for a doctor, and nursed his old friend. But despite the best medical care money could buy, it was too late for the lady. Her one request to him before she died was that he stay on at the house and make sure her nephew, Gerald

Witherspoon, was settled in properly with people he could trust.

By the time Smythe felt it was safe to leave, they were already "on the hunt" with the inspector's cases and he'd fallen in love with Betsy. So he stayed and kept his secret to himself for a long time. He'd told Betsy before they married, and Mrs. Jeffries had figured it out on her own.

"You know now that we're expectin', I'm thinking my Nell and I should move on. We've plenty of lolly so we could go anywhere in the world."

Stunned, Smythe stared at him. "What are ya goin' on about? Go where? Why?"

"Come on, Smythe, you know what I'm talkin' about. We've lots of money but what's the use of havin' it if no matter where we went, we'd be treated like the bottom of the barrel. My Nell and I don't mind it. We've carved out lives for ourselves that suit us both. But what about our little one? I don't want people lookin' down their noses at him or her because of us. You know 'ow things are in this country. You can go out and buy the biggest 'ouse in London, you can put fancy clothes in your closet and hire someone to teach you to talk proper, but that won't make a difference. Your child won't be allowed in the best schools and certainly won't have any friends in the neighborhood because the toffs won't let theirs have anythin' to do with yours."

"But you'll find toffs and their ilk wherever you go." Smythe felt panic surge through him. Blimpey was his best source for investigating, and if he closed up shop and moved on, it would be a disaster.

"'Course there would be, but we could go to Australia

or America or even Canada once the little one is born. Life would be different but at least our child would get a decent start. They've got good schools all over the world, and from what I've seen and heard, people in San Francisco or Sydney don't judge a person based on the class they was born in—you get judged on what you do in this world."

"What would you do, Blimpey? Even with plenty of lolly, you'd still want to keep busy." Smythe knew exactly what his friend meant; he and Betsy had had this same conversation more than once. They, too, had considered leaving England for a less class-ridden society, but they'd both decided that, for the moment, they'd stay put. Amanda was still a toddler.

Blimpey thought for a moment. "I could do what I do 'ere, I could open a pub."

"That'd keep you occupied for about an hour a day. Be honest, Blimpey, would you really be happy not knowing everything that was goin' on in your patch of the world? One of the reasons you're so good at your work is because you're one of them people that just have to know everything."

Blimpey frowned. "I just know I want my child to have all the opportunities I never had."

"And if you'd had those opportunities, would you be doin' something different?" He leaned toward his friend, his expression earnest. "Admit it, ya like what you do. Ya like seeing some toff climbing out of a hansom and knowin' he's so close to bein' bankrupt that 'e can't even pick up the tab for his dinner or watchin' a titled lady stroll down Regent Street all the while knowin' that her husband's rollin' about in the hay with half her friends and the lover she thinks is faithful has half a dozen other women. Admit it, Blimpey, ya like that."

"I do, I like it a lot," he admitted with a laugh. "Bloomin' Ada, I don't know what I'm on about, do I. When I mentioned leaving to Nell, she wasn't keen on the idea, said this was our country, and if we didn't like the way things were, instead of runnin' off, we ought to fight to change it."

Smythe relaxed. "She's right. Promise me you'll not close up shop just yet."

"You're just worried I won't be 'ere when you need help on one of the inspector's cases."

"Bloomin' right it worries me. But as you are 'ere, let's get on with this."

Helena Rayburn glared at her gardener. "How dare you insinuate those are mine." She pointed to the bloodstained garments spread out on the pristine lawn.

"Because they are yours," he insisted. "I've been the gardener here since Colonel Rayburn was a lad and there's nothing wrong with my eyesight. I've seen you wearin' these things when you're larkin' about in your conservatory pretendin' you know something about growing plants."

Witherspoon studied the man. Tall and bald, he had brown eyes, excellent posture, and bushy eyebrows. His face was red, though whether that was from shouting at his employer or a lifetime of braving the elements, it was impossible to tell. "Mr. uh . . ."

"It's Tufts, Howard Tufts." The gardener turned to Witherspoon. "And I know what I know. I found them things rolled up and stuffed under the ivy bed. Soon as I saw 'em,

I sent for one of your lads. But she come out and started demanding that I give 'em to her."

Barnes looked at Helena Rayburn. "Is that true, Mrs. Rayburn?"

"Of course it isn't," she snapped. "He's only saying that because I've given him his notice and he's angry at me."

"You didn't give me the sack," Tufts charged. "I'm the one that give you notice and you did too try to make me give them to you. But I held my ground and wouldn't let you take them."

Barnes kept a wary eye on the gardener and Helena Rayburn while Witherspoon knelt and examined the clothes spread out on the ground. There was a full-sized apron, an oversized duster, and a pair of gardening gloves, all of which were stained with blood. "When did you find these?"

"This morning," Tufts smirked at his employer. "I went to cut the ivy back and found them. Like I said, I went and got that constable who's been on the front door and he sent for you." He jerked a thumb at Helena Rayburn. "But then she come out and told me to hand them over."

"That is utter nonsense. I did no such thing."

The inspector rose to his feet. "Mrs. Rayburn, do these belong to you?"

"I've already said they don't. How dare you take his word over mine."

Tufts snorted.

"Mrs. Rayburn, are you certain?"

She bit her lip and looked away. "I'm not going to answer any more questions. You've no right to harass me like this."

"We've every right, ma'am," the inspector said softly. "A man was murdered on your property, and according to the evidence here on the ground, whoever killed him might have been wearing these garments, which your gardener claims belong to you."

"And that's not all." Tufts waved toward the fence. "Them boards over there weren't loose last week. I was weeding along that fence, and one of the things I do when I weed is check that there's no rot on the wood."

"You're saying the boards weren't loose last week?" Barnes clarified.

"That's right, they were good and tight when I checked them."

"That proves that anyone could have gotten in here and murdered Filmore," Helena interjected eagerly. "The killer obviously loosened them to get into the garden and then to the conservatory." She lifted her hand, pointed, and turned slowly, moving in a semi-circle. "You're all trying to make it look as if I killed that man, but I didn't, and I'll not have you ruining my reputation with your nasty implication that I'm a murderer."

"Mrs. Rayburn, no one is trying to imply anything of the sort. We're simply asking questions." Witherspoon hoped she wouldn't become hysterical. He wasn't very good with that sort of thing.

"But you're asking the wrong questions." She jerked her chin at the gardener. "Why don't you find out what he was doing when Filmore was killed? He never liked him, he was always hinting that the man was up to no good."

"I never said that," Tufts cried. "I just said that it was

odd the only thing he knew about gardening was stealin'
plants from their native soils and selling them off. Why
should I want to kill the fellow?"

"Because you were jealous of him," she charged. "You
were upset that I was making you retire and I was hiring
someone Mr. Filmore recommended."

"You didn't tell us this before," Barnes said to her.

"I'm hardly in the habit of sharing my domestic details
with all and sundry. But nonetheless, it's true. If you don't
believe me, you can ask Mrs. Clemment. She was present
when I told Mr. Tufts that as of the first of July his services
will no longer be required. But after today, I do believe I
can dispense with his services immediately." She turned
her attention to Tufts and pointed to the gate. "Get off my
property now."

"Not so fast, Mrs. Rayburn," Witherspoon said. "We'd
like to ask Mr. Tufts a few questions before he leaves."

"Ask him your questions, then." She turned on her heel
and stalked toward the house.

Witherspoon waited till she was out of earshot. "Mr.
Tufts, did you have any sort of quarrel with Mr. Filmore?"

"No, I thought the man was no better than a confidence
trickster, but that was no skin off my nose." He grinned.
"He sold them women the most god-awful plants. As long
as he claimed it was a rare orchid, he could sell them anything he liked."

"You're saying he often gave them worthless plants
that he'd misrepresented?" Barnes asked.

Tufts grinned even wider. "That's right, but he was quite
a clever sod. He didn't do it all the time, and he stopped

altogether once he realized that Mrs. Rayburn and Mrs. Martell was always bringing members of the RHS around to have a look at their greenhouses. Now, them folks do know something about plants."

"RHS, oh you mean the Royal Horticultural Society," Witherspoon muttered. "Mr. Tufts, where were you on the morning of the murder?"

"I was here until about half past ten," he explained. "But it was too wet to get much done so I went home. My missus can vouch for me, and despite what Mrs. Rayburn says, I wasn't all that bothered about being let go. I was getting ready to give my notice anyway. I'm almost seventy, Inspector, and I'm tired. Besides, the late Mr. Rayburn left all of his old servants a bit of money when he passed on, so with that and my savings, the wife and I will do just fine."

"Can anyone verify your whereabouts, I mean anyone other than your wife?" Barnes asked.

"My neighbor came over and the two of us went to the Full Moon, that's the pub around the corner at about half past eleven. The barkeep will can vouch for me. I was there until two."

Witherspoon nodded. He'd send a constable to the pub just to be sure, but he was fairly certain Mr. Tufts could be crossed off the list of suspects.

"Are you absolutely sure these garments belong to Mrs. Rayburn?" Barnes nodded toward the clothes.

"Much as I enjoy riling the woman, it's the truth. They're hers. But if you don't want to take my word for it, the other servants will tell you they're hers. She had them special made by her dressmaker. Except for the gloves, she sent to France for them. Guess English gloves weren't good enough for her."

The Kensington High Street was noisy with the clatter of horses' hooves, the thump of wheels, and the shouts of drivers jockeying for position on the busy road. Shoppers and street hawkers hurried along the pavement, all of them intent on their business and, to Phyllis' mind, in a ruddy great hurry. She shifted to avoid being bumped and jostled, and stayed close to the shop fronts as she walked.

Phyllis slowed her footsteps as she approached the butcher shop on the corner. She wasn't sure she had the will or the courage to keep going. So far, she'd been to three other places but she'd learned nothing. The clerk at the greengrocer's knew of the murder but was in such a grumpy mood she couldn't get anything out of the girl, the baker had a long line of customers and barely gave her so much as a "good morning," and the woman running the newsagent's was too busy complaining about her daughter-in-law to another customer to even notice Phyllis was trying to ask a few questions. All in all, it had been a miserable morning.

But the lack of success with the local shopkeepers wasn't the only thing bothering her. Try as she might, she couldn't stop thinking about the incident with Luty. She'd spoken up hoping to make the elderly woman feel better, to let her know that everyone had moments when "they got down in the mouth" and her outburst of honesty had worked. By the time their meeting ended, Luty was back to her old self.

But Phyllis' comforting words to Luty had come with

a cost and now she was paying the price. Unwelcome memories had come flooding back; feelings of shame, worthlessness, humiliation, all those emotions she'd worked so hard to push out of her mind had taken root and sprouted with a vengeance. Try as she might, she couldn't make them go away.

All of a sudden she was a twelve-year-old girl again, grief stricken and standing in front of her old mistress, Mrs. McConnell. "Stop your sniveling, Thompson, you're not the first child to lose a parent. Now get back in the wet larder, and this time, scrub the floor properly or I'll toss you out without a reference."

Coming to a full stop, Phyllis leaned against the brick wall of an estate agent's office, lifted her shopping basket, and pretended to be searching inside it. She wanted an excuse to keep her face down and hidden from the people on the street. Tears welled up and she swallowed hard to keep them from spilling down her cheeks. The harsh voice continued, only now it was screaming in her head. "You little fool, you'll never amount to anything, I ought to put you out on the streets! I should never have let you in here, you can't do anything right. All you do is take food out of decent people's mouths."

Phyllis covered her mouth with her hand to stifle a sob just as a young lad charged around the corner and banged into her, jerking her back to the present.

"Cor blimey, miss, I didn't see ya there." His thin, narrow face was contorted in worry. "I'm so sorry, miss. I didn't mean to bang into ya. But I'm in a hurry. If I don't get back before my guv does, he'll sack me."

He was skinny, dark haired, and dressed in scruffy,

oversized clothes he'd probably inherited from an older sibling. He was so young he barely came up to her shoulder. "It's alright," she told him. "You didn't hurt me."

"Ta, miss." He bobbed his head and raced off.

She watched him disappear into the crowd of well-dressed shoppers, most of whom had no idea what it was like to worry every single minute of the day about losing your position and having nothing, not even a miserable job that kept a bit of food in your belly and a cold roof over your head. A hard, hot anger surged through her as she realized the full injustice of it all. Neither she nor that young worried-looking lad had done anything to deserve the fate they'd been given, so why should either of them be ashamed about their lives? Why did being born poor give those that had something leave to push around those that nothing? It wasn't right. Another voice entered her head and this was one she welcomed.

"You've a right to the same things the rich have," Betsy had told her. "You've a right to a warm bed, plenty of food, and being treated with respect. You're as good as anyone else. The work we do on the inspector's cases is important. We've kept the innocent from being hung and made sure the guilty, even if they're rich and powerful, pay for their crimes. So you hold your head up high no matter who you're talking to, even if it's the Queen herself."

Betsy had delivered that lecture shortly after Phyllis had worked up the courage to help them. She straightened her spine, swiped her cheeks, and took a deep breath. Betsy was right, she did deserve a good life, and by golly, she was going to have it. She was no longer going to let the past intrude on her present. Not now, not ever again.

She turned and walked the short distance to the corner, opened the door, and stepped into the butcher's shop. Stopping just inside the door, she surveyed the room. It was almost lunchtime, so the morning rush was over and the place was empty of customers. Even better, there was a young man behind the counter. She'd been surprised to find that when it came to getting information, she had better luck with males than females.

Smiling brightly, she walked up to the counter.

"May I help you, miss?" He was a short, chubby lad with thinning brown hair, deep-set blue eyes, and a lovely smile.

"I hope so," she said softly. "I'm looking for an address, and to be frank, sir, I'm desperate. If I don't deliver this letter"—she yanked a cream-colored envelope out of her shopping basket—"I'll get sacked. The awful thing is, I remember the name of the household but only because there was a murder there. When I realized I couldn't remember what the mistress said, I thought I'd try the local shops and see if any of you could help me."

"It must be the Rayburn house." He nodded his head. "They're the only ones that's had a murder around here, and you're in luck, miss, I do happen to know their address. They're one of our customers and I deliver there three times a week. It's number 16 Bellwood Place. It's not far from here, two streets up, round the corner, and then the first left."

"Gracious, you must be brilliant to remember all that."

"I'm not brilliant." He smiled shyly as a blush crept up his cheeks. "It's my job to know where our customers live, but it's not easy remembering the fastest routes to all their homes."

"I'm sure it isn't. Thank you for your help, I'm ever so indebted, sir. The mistress would have been furious with me if I didn't deliver her invitation." She leaned toward him. "She's only inviting Mrs. Rayburn to luncheon because of the murder, she pretends such things are beneath her, but she's curious about the whole thing."

"You can't blame her for that. Everyone's interested in murder as long as it's not them or one of their loved ones that's the victim."

"I know, but still, this kind of nosiness is a bit much, but the mistress won't be told. Even the master thought it was a bad idea, but she wouldn't listen to him." She broke off and giggled. "She's dying to know anything about the Rayburn household."

He glanced over his shoulder toward the door behind the counter. "Well, I can give you a few tidbits to pass along. Like I said, I deliver there thrice a week, and last week, I overheard the Rayburn cook complaining about Mrs. Stanway."

"Who is Mrs. Stanway?" Phyllis knew quite well who she was, but of course, she had to feign ignorance.

"She's one of Mrs. Rayburn's friends and one of our customers as well. That's the only reason I listened when the kitchen ladies were goin' on about her. It's no good listening to gossip about people you don't know, is it."

"What were they saying about her?"

"It wasn't just her, it was another woman, someone who'd just come here from America, but I didn't know anything about her. She doesn't give us her business."

"But they said something interesting about Mrs. Stanway?"

"Perhaps I shouldn't have said anything, it wasn't all that interesting. The cook was sayin' that Mrs. Stanway is the nosiest woman in London." He broke off and grinned again. "Mind you, it sounds like your mistress could give Mrs. Stanway a good run for her money."

Phyllis laughed.

"Mrs. Stanway's old nanny lives across the street from the Rayburn house," he continued, "and both the cook and the scullery maids were natterin' on about how Mrs. Stanway spent hours peekin' out of the upstairs curtains and watching the people on the street. Now, I like a good gander as well as the next person, but I don't spend half me life gaping out the window."

Phyllis was disappointed but forced herself to smile. This was hardly useful information. Spying on your neighbors was an old and honorable pastime in most neighborhoods, especially for bored upper-class women on duty visits to their old nurses. "Was that all they said?"

As soon as the three of them entered the Rayburn home, Barnes went downstairs to get Mrs. Clemment. He needed her to verify that the bloodied clothes belonged to Mrs. Rayburn.

Helena and the inspector continued on to the drawing room. Witherspoon took his bowler off as they went inside. "Mrs. Rayburn, may we sit down?"

She stalked to the marble fireplace and stood with her back to him. "I'm in no mood to be sociable, Inspector, so just ask your questions and then get out."

"I know this must be difficult for you," he began.

"Difficult?" She spun around to face him. "Do you

know what this is doing to me, to my reputation? It's been less than a day since that man was found dead in my conservatory, but already people are whispering behind my back and the gutter press has practically come out and accused me of murder."

"I'm sure that's not true, Mrs. Rayburn," he replied. He'd read the morning papers, and though her name had been mentioned, most of the articles consisted of the bare facts of the case.

"But now that you've found those clothes, you think I did it?"

"No, ma'am, we've not come to any conclusions about the identity of the murdered. We're simply doing our best to get to the truth. Now, if you answer a few more questions . . ."

"Why should I? Whatever I say you'll use against me." She crossed her arms over her chest and gave him a long, hard stare. "Why should I cooperate?"

"Because it's only by cooperating that we'll be able to catch the real killer," he pointed out. "It's in your interest to tell me the truth and to answer all our questions honestly. Are you absolutely sure Mr. Filmore wasn't bringing you the specimen we found in your garden, the red vanda? You've admitted he had done something like that on a previous occasion." He didn't know why that mangled plant kept bothering him, but it did, and somehow, finding out how it came to be in the Rayburn garden felt important.

"Yes, but I explained that he did it before because on that occasion he was bringing me an orchid he knew I wanted. I never mentioned a red vanda in front of him. I don't particularly like them, they're too gaudy and loud for my taste. Thea and Isabelle are vanda enthusiasts. Both of them have vanda orchids, but theirs are, of course, a more common variety."

The inspector thought about a comment his housekeeper had made. "Is it possible Mr. Filmore was bringing the red vanda to one of them? Perhaps he knew they were going to be here for luncheon?"

"That's most unlikely." She stared at him coldly. "I'm hardly in the habit of discussing my social calendar with someone like Filmore."

"He may have found out from another source." Witherspoon shifted his bowler to his other hand. "It would at least explain why he was here."

"I suppose it's possible."

He decided to change tactics. "Mrs. Rayburn, we know those garments are yours, and even without testing, I'm fairly sure the stains are blood. Why did you say they weren't yours?"

She leaned back against the fireplace. "I was scared, Inspector, wouldn't you be?"

"Of course, but as I've said before, if you are innocent, the only way we'll catch the real killer is by everyone being honest. You, however, have prevaricated on at least two occasions, the first being your denial that the murder weapon was your property and the second just now when you claimed the apron, duster, and gloves weren't yours, either."

Her hands balled into fists and she went a shade paler. "But as I've pointed out consistently, the keys to the conservatory have been missing for over a week, and anyone could have gotten in and taken those items. Obviously, that's exactly what the killer did. He used my property to commit murder and wore my gardening clothes while he did it."

"Why do you assume the killer is a 'he'?" Thea Stanway asked. She stood in the half-open doorway. "I'm sorry, the front door was ajar so I just came inside. I think your constable has disappeared," she said to Witherspoon as she advanced into the drawing room. "Really, Helena, you shouldn't assume women aren't capable of murder. All one has to do is read the newspapers to know that isn't true. Women kill all the time."

Downstairs, Constable Barnes was back in the butler's pantry with Mrs. Clemment. "You're sure the garments are hers," he asked for the third time.

"And for the third time, Constable, yes, I'm sure." She tapped her hand impatiently against the scratched tabletop. "That's hardly the sort of thing I'd make a mistake about. I've seen her wearing both the apron and the duster dozens of times."

"We just need to make sure, ma'am," he said. He'd repeated the question because he sensed that Mrs. Rayburn wasn't liked by her servants and they might be tempted to do what they could to get the lady of the house into a bit of trouble. "Can you tell me about the household's movements yesterday? I hate to put you through this again, but I need you to go over everyone in the household's movements yesterday between half ten and two o'clock."

"Specifics will be difficult, Constable, but I can tell you generally where everyone was. As you know, Mrs. Rayburn was having a luncheon, and between that and the fact that it was raining outside, no one had a spare moment. The rain makes our jobs more difficult. We've got to make certain the umbrella stands are properly polished and that the cloakroom and the water closet off the hall are clean and aired. Cook and the kitchen staff were doing the food, so all of them would have been in either the wet larder, the dry larder, or the kitchen."

"They wouldn't have gone to the dining room?"

She shook her head. "No, the upstairs and downstairs maids were helping with the linens, the crystal, and the table setting. I was overseeing everything. The tweeny was doing the fetching and carrying between the butler's pantry and the dining room, but she had everything upstairs by half eleven so I sent her to take care of the cloakroom and the water closet."

"So there were times when the staff was in and out of your sight, correct?"

"That's right, but I don't think any of the servants had a reason to murder Mr. Filmore."

"And none of the staff went outside?" he pressed.

"No."

"You seem very sure of that?"

"After you left yesterday, I asked all of them if they'd gone outside or if they'd seen anything from the windows," she replied. "None of them had, they were too busy doing their jobs."

"Were you surprised when Mrs. Rayburn went out?"

"Of course." Mrs. Clemment glanced at the closed pantry door. "As I told you when you were here this morning, it was very unlike her to leave like that. She went out about half past ten, and frankly, Constable, I was so surprised you could have knocked me over with a feather." She sniffed. "The woman doesn't trust anyone to know their jobs, but I've been a housekeeper for over twenty years and I know how to set a proper table and how to oversee serving food. But she acts like we're a bunch of heathens that don't know the difference between a soup spoon and a fish fork."

"And you've no idea why she left or where she went?"

"None and she's not the sort of person who'd appreciate her servants asking her to explain herself."

"She returned right before luncheon," he clarified. "That's what you said this morning."

"That's right, she came back right before Mrs. Attwater and Mrs. Stanway arrived, so it must have been a few moments past twelve. But she went up to her room and stayed there until all three ladies were here. Which was surprising as well. I expected her to come down and check on the dining room, but she didn't. I thought it was because of her hair but that turned out not to be the case, either."

"Her hair?"

Mrs. Clemment grinned broadly. "She doesn't like to go out in the damp because it makes her hair very curly. By the time she returned, her hair was as fuzzy around the edges as a wooly sheep so I thought she'd stayed in her room to try to fix it with that hair pomade she's so fond of, but when I went up to tell her the guests were here, it was still just as frizzy as when she'd come in . . ." She broke off and stared at him. "Oh dear, I forgot to tell that as well. I'm sorry, Constable, but this has been very upsetting, and frankly, it's made me entirely too forgetful. I ought to have told you about this yesterday."

"What was it?"

"When I went into her room, she was sitting at her dressing table and she was drinking a glass of sherry."

"I take it that was unusual behavior for her?"

"It is, she isn't much of a drinker, but wherever she'd gone and whatever she'd done had upset her and it wasn't because of her hair."

CHAPTER 5

"Good luck with the chief, sir," Constable Barnes said to Witherspoon as they walked into the headquarters of the Metropolitan Police Force.

"Thank you, Constable, but perhaps I won't need luck and the chief superintendent simply wants a progress report."

"That's an optimistic view, sir." Barnes leaned on the newel post as Witherspoon started up the stairs to the chief's office. "It's been less than forty-eight hours since we got the case, and they've already interrupted us and sent for you. Generally, the chief gives us a bit more time than that."

Witherspoon shrugged and started up the stairs. "We'll see, Constable. Hopefully, I'll be down soon."

Barnes waited until the inspector disappeared before he straightened, turned, and headed for the slightly plump policeman standing behind the counter next to the corridor.

"Still as stiff-backed and hard as when you was a lad." Mike Talbot grinned at his old friend. "How come you don't seem to get any older, Barnes, while the rest of our lot is either on desk duty or out on a pension."

Barnes laughed. "Clean livin', Mikey, and a nip of whiskey every night before bed. How have you been?"

"Right as rain." Talbot glanced up the stairs. "I found out who put the fire under the chief superintendent and you're not goin' to believe it."

Barnes' smile disappeared. Mike Talbot was one of his sources at the Yard and not given to exaggeration. "Who was it?"

"Sir Jeremy Sanders."

"Isn't he one of the top advisers to the home secretary?"

"That's right. Sanders showed up here late yesterday afternoon and asked to see Barrows."

"Are you sure he came to see him about our case?" Barnes pressed. For the life of him, he couldn't think of any connection between the murder of a plant seller and a top adviser to the home secretary.

"Yup, Barrows walked the fellow out and I was on duty when they came down the stairs. I heard every word they was sayin'. Sanders has got an even louder voice than our chief superintendent."

Upstairs, Witherspoon stared in confusion at Chief Inspector Barrows. "I'm sorry, sir, but I'm not sure I understand?"

The chief inspector was a tall, bespectacled man with a fringe of dark hair that was constantly losing ground to an ever-increasing bald spot. He took his glasses off and leaned back in his chair. "It's quite simple, Inspector, this is a very important case and we want it solved."

"You mean you want it solved quickly?" Witherspoon said. That was generally what his superiors always wanted.

"No, no, no, you misunderstand me. Take as much time as you need to catch the killer. But this case must be your top priority. You mustn't waste any of your time on anything except this investigation."

The inspector was tempted to point out that pulling him and Constable Barnes away from the Rayburn house in the middle of important interviews could be construed as a waste of time, but he wisely held his tongue. "Uh, yes, sir. We're making progress on the case."

"Of course you are." Barrows smiled broadly. "That's one of the reasons I'm glad you're on the case. You always solve them and your record has been duly noted by some very important people."

Witherspoon didn't care about important people, but he did care that he was getting credit for something that didn't just belong go him. "I don't do it alone, sir. Constable Barnes and the other men from the station do an exemplary job. I couldn't solve anything without all of their help."

Barrows got up and came around from behind his desk. "Yes, yes, yes, I'm sure that's true and it's good of you to give credit to your men." He ushered the inspector toward the door and yanked it open. "But you must use any and all means to catch this terrible murderer. We'll give you whatever assistance you require. If you need more men, let me know and I'll make sure you get them."

"There is one thing I need." Witherspoon dug his heels into the linoleum floor to avoid being pushed into the hall.

"We've sent a request to the War Department for the victim's military file."

"And you want my help to get it quickly." Barrows nodded. "Right then, I'll see what I can do. Keep me informed, Inspector. Good day." With that, he gave the inspector a gentle shove and then closed the door.

Witherspoon stood there for a long moment and stared at Barrows' closed office door. He didn't understand it, this was the first time he could recall where Barrows didn't nag him to solve the case quickly. That was most unlike the fellow. What was going on? Witherspoon shrugged; perhaps he ought not to look a gift horse in the mouth.

Wiggins hadn't planned on coming to Mayfair, but he'd had no luck at any of the other women's homes. He'd hung around the Rayburn house for a good half hour then tried both the Stanway and the Martell properties. But no housemaids, footmen, or tweenies had so much as stuck a nose out the servants' entrances. He'd not wanted to try chatting up the shopkeepers or going to the pubs because he didn't want to intrude on either Phyllis' or Smythe's territory.

But he refused to go home this early in the day so he'd try his luck here. Chloe Attwater had been a guest at the Rayburn luncheon, so there was a chance he might learn something. But now that he was here, it seemed like a waste of time. He made a face as he studied the quiet street. Save for the occasional hansom cab or carriage trundling past, Webster Crescent was as quiet as a graveyard at midnight. He'd gone to the mews that ran along the back of the Attwater home first, but that was just as empty. He'd not seen so much as a door open.

"Well, sod this for a game of tin soldiers," he muttered. "I might as well go back to the Martell or Stanway house." Wiggins turned and retraced his steps. When he got to the corner, he saw a small figure dart out of the mews and race off toward the high street.

He took off, running to catch up with the lad. "Oy," he called. "You there, can I talk to ya?"

"What do ya want?" The boy turned, put his hands on his hips, and then grinned. "Hey, Wiggins, what ya chasin' me for? I thought it was a copper after me."

"I could ask you the same thing." Wiggins was delighted to see that the fleeing figure was Kevin Nelson, a street lad who worked the area around Kensington Station and who'd also done errands and such for the Witherspoon household. "Have ya been doin' somethin' that would cause the police to chase ya? Our inspector wouldn't like that."

Kevin laughed. He was a ginger-haired lad with a narrow, pale face and a sprinkle of freckles across his nose. He wore a thin gray shirt frayed at the wrists, a pair of blue trousers with patches on the knees, and a pair of shoes so scuffed it was impossible to tell if they'd once been black or brown. "I just thought it might be coppers because there's naught but toffs 'round here, and when they see the likes of me, they usually set the constables on us. But I've got a proper reason for bein' 'ere. I've 'ad a steady job now for a month."

"Doin' what?" Wiggins asked as Kevin fell into step next to him.

"Watchin' a house in Kensington for the lady that lives down there." He turned and pointed toward Webster Crescent. "She's a right generous sort, too. Pays me a sixpence every time I come here and I come twice a day to tell her what's what. Except for yesterday, I came three times yesterday and she give me a florin, can you believe it, a whole florin."

Wiggins stopped in his tracks. "Who is this lady?"

Kevin had stopped, too. "Mrs. Attwater, she's a pretty lady, and she lives in one of the biggest houses on Webster Crescent. She meets me at the mews back of her house and pays me whether I've got anything to tell or not. Mind you, yesterday I had to go to the back door and get her 'cause she weren't expecting me. But I had news and I knew she'd want to hear it."

"You're right, Constable, that certainly explains why Chief Superintendent Barrows is being so cooperative about our case." Witherspoon nodded as the hansom cab pulled to the curb of an elegant street in Bayswater. "But now the question is why would Sir Jeremy Sanders care enough about Filmore's murder to make a special trip to Scotland Yard?"

"Constable Talbot didn't hear the why of it, sir. All he heard was Sanders nattering on to the chief superintendent about how you needed to stay on the case so the real killer would be caught." Barnes opened the door and the two policemen stepped out. He paid the driver and then turned to join the inspector, who was checking his pocket watch.

"Too bad he didn't hear anything else," Witherspoon frowned at his timepiece. "Oh dear, going to the Yard has put us behind. Let's hope Mrs. Martell cooperates and we can conduct this interview quickly. I want both of us with the lads when they search Filmore's flat and place of business."

"I told Constable Griffiths to check with the landlady about the keys and then contact us so that we could be there."

Isabelle Martell lived in a five-story red brick house with white stucco fronting on the ground floor. They climbed the broad steps and the constable banged the brass-plated knocker.

The door was opened and a tall, black-suited butler stared at them. "Yes, what do you want?" he asked.

Barnes was in no mood to tolerate snobbery from anyone, let alone a toff-nosed butler. He stepped forward aggressively. "We'd like to see Mrs. Martell."

"I'm afraid—"

"And if she doesn't wish to speak to us now," the constable interrupted, "we'll be quite happy to wait for her at the Ladbroke Road Police Station."

The butler's eyes widened, but he stepped back and held the door open. "Please come in."

As soon as they stepped inside, he led them down the thickly carpeted hall to a set of double doors. "You can wait in there," he ordered. "I'll tell the mistress you're here."

"She's not hard up for money, that's for sure," Barnes muttered as he and Witherspoon entered the opulent drawing room.

The walls were painted a pale yellow, the Louis XIV furniture was upholstered in yellow and blue stripes, and a huge crystal chandelier hung from the center of the high ceiling. Heavy damask gold curtains draped the windows, and matching portraits of a cavalier and his lady were prominently displayed over the white marble fireplace.

"My butler says you wish to speak to me." Isabelle

Martell swept into the room with her head high and a less-than-pleased expression on her face.

"Yes, ma'am, we didn't finish taking your statement yesterday," Witherspoon said.

"But I've nothing more to say about Mr. Filmore's unfortunate death. The man supplied me with plants. I barely knew him." She sat down in an armchair and folded her hands primly across her lap.

"Nonetheless, as someone who was on the premises when the murder might have occurred, we must take your statement." The inspector glanced at the constable, who, upon realizing they weren't going to be asked to sit down, had moved to stand by the fireplace. Barnes pulled out his little brown notebook and pencil, flipped it open, and propped it on the mantelpiece.

Isabelle's eyebrows rose but she turned her attention back to the inspector. "Alright, do get on with it, Inspector. I've an appointment."

"What time did you arrive for luncheon yesterday?"

"I don't know precisely, I didn't look at the clock. It was possibly fifteen or twenty past twelve."

"Were any of the other guests present when you arrived?" Barnes asked.

She looked at him sharply, as though she couldn't believe he had the temerity to speak to her. "Yes, Mrs. Attwater was present and then Mrs. Stanway arrived. No, that's not right, Mrs. Stanway was already in the house when I came inside. She was in the cloakroom fussing with one of her gloves. She hadn't closed the door all the way, which, of course is just like Thea. She's so proud of those lace gloves she's more interested in getting a speck of dirt off them than behaving properly."

"Did you see anyone hanging around the immediate vicinity when you entered the house?" Witherspoon asked.

"No, but it was raining and I wasn't looking at the neighborhood." She glanced at the gold and white French clock on the top of the armoire. "How much longer is this going to take?"

"Not much longer, ma'am," the inspector said. "You were acquainted with Mr. Filmore, correct?"

"I've already told you he supplied me with plants."

"Did you know him in India?" the constable asked softly.

Startled by the question, she drew back slightly. "Why on earth would you ask that? What does India have to do with it?"

The constable ignored her comment. "So you did know him?"

"Yes, I suppose you could say that."

"How well?"

"Not well at all." She had regained her composure. "He was in the army," she began, but Barnes, fully annoyed now because his knee hurt like the devil, interrupted.

"As was your husband," he said smoothly.

"They were in the same regiment, but my husband was a major and Mr. Filmore was an enlisted man, a sergeant, I believe. My contact with him was minimal. I saw him occasionally when I helped take care of the wounded or the sick. Hiram Filmore acted as a kind of administrator for the infirmary so I did have some contact with him."

"That's a big responsibility for an enlisted man, even a sergeant," Witherspoon murmured.

"It was India, Inspector, and there were times when officers were in short supply. From what I understood, Mr. Filmore was both competent and responsible, so he took on many of the duties one would normally expect a higher-ranking officer to have."

"When did you reestablish contact with Mr. Filmore?" Barnes looked up from his notebook to see her glaring at him. He gave her a bland smile.

"As I've already stated, I barely knew the man. I met him again at Mrs. Rayburn's house about five years ago. Helena introduced him to our gardening club, and when I saw the specimens he had available, I gave him my business."

"Have you ever been to Mr. Filmore's place of business?" Barnes asked.

"No, he always brought specimens here for my approval."

"But surely, as someone who is interested in flowers, you'd have gone there to see the whole range of plants available to you," Witherspoon suggested.

"I'm not in the least interested in flowers." She smiled at Witherspoon. "I only joined the society because my friends were members and because it adds to my social status here in London. Winning a prize at our annual garden show would add greatly to my status and that's why I used Mr. Filmore's services. I thought he could help me get the first prize at this year's competition."

Witherspoon nodded as if he understood, but in truth, he didn't understand it at all. Why anyone would join a society they had no interest in was a mystery to him. "When did you leave India?"

Again, she looked startled by the question. "Why does that matter?"

"We're trying to make certain we understand the relationships between the victim and those of you who were at the luncheon," he replied. He wasn't absolutely sure why he'd asked the question, it had simply popped out of his mouth, but thanks to Mrs. Jeffries, he'd learned to trust his "inner voice."

"For the tenth time, I had no relationship with Mr. Filmore. Even in his professional capacity, he usually dealt with my gardener, not me. But if you must know, I left India in 1887."

"Nine years ago." Barnes wrote in his notebook. "Was that when your husband died?"

"Yes."

Barnes gave her another bland smile. "We understand his death was an accident. That he fell from a second-story balcony? Is that true?"

Everyone was back at Upper Edmonton Gardens in good time for their afternoon meeting. Upon entering, Luty Belle had snatched Amanda and now cuddled the little one on her lap while Phyllis had immediately shed her hat and helped Mrs. Goodge pour the tea and pass around the cups.

A seed cake held pride of place in the center of the table and next to it was a loaf of brown bread, a pot of butter, and a dish of peach preserves.

"Who would like to start?" Mrs. Jeffries helped herself to a second lump of sugar.

"I've not found out anything." The cook sank into her

chair. "But tomorrow I've several sources coming in and I'm hoping to hear something useful."

"I had a bit of luck today." Wiggins nodded his thanks as Phyllis pushed the bread plate in his direction. "Remember that ginger-haired lad who 'angs about Kensington Station lookin' to run errands and such, we've used him a time or two." He waited till several of them had nodded. "Well, I run into him today in Mayfair."

"What were you doin' there?" Mrs. Goodge demanded. "The Rayburn and the Stanway homes are in Kensington and Isabelle Martell lives in Bayswater."

"But you're forgettin' that Mrs. Attwater lives in Mayfair."

"But she wasn't even there when they found the body." Mrs. Goodge picked up the knife and began slicing the seed cake.

"But she might 'ave been there when Filmore was murdered. Besides, I'd been to the other places and 'adn't seen 'ide nor 'air of anyone who'd talk to me. But I struck gold at the Attwater place."

"Tell us what you found out," Mrs. Jeffries said.

Wiggins grinned. "It turns out that a month ago, Mrs. Attwater asked young Kevin to keep a watch on the Rayburn home. 'E reported to 'er twice a day and she paid him a sixpence each time."

"What was she wanting him to find out?" Betsy asked as Mrs. Goodge pushed a slice of cake in front of her.

"Anything," Wiggins replied. "Mainly, she wanted Kevin to keep her informed about who came and went, but yesterday, when Kevin found out about the murder, he raced over there and told 'er about it. She give him a florin for 'is trouble." He gave Mrs. Goodge a quick smile when she shoved his cake plate next to his tea mug.

"Why on earth would Chloe Attwater want to know about who came and went at the Rayburn home?" Hatchet muttered.

Betsy frowned as she swallowed her bite of cake, glanced at the cook, and then gently pushed her plate aside.

Wiggins stuffed a huge bite in his mouth, chewed, and then made a face. "That's the question, isn't it," he croaked as he tried to choke it down.

"I might be able to answer that," Ruth ventured. "I heard some interesting information at my women's group today. It was our quarterly luncheon and everyone is generally a bit more relaxed and talkative . . ." She broke off and smiled self-consciously. "But you're not concerned with any of that, so I'll just repeat what I heard." She paused for breath. "To begin with, I heard a bit about Helena Rayburn as well as the other ladies who were at her home yesterday. All four of them were in India at the same time, though according to my source, Chloe Attwater or Chloe Camden as she was known then was considerably lower down on the social scale than the other three."

"Yes, she went there as a governess." Mrs. Jeffries noticed that both Betsy and Smythe had trouble choking down their cake. "The others had gone to stay with relatives who were military officers. But in a foreign country, the gulf between a governess and the others might not have been so deep."

"No, I think it was even deeper, and when I tell you the rest, you might agree with me. I found out that Mrs. Attwater left India years before the others did. She and one of the servants in the household where she had worked left India in the company of an American man. At the time, there was gossip that she was . . ." She broke off and took a deep breath. "Expecting a child. Do forgive me for being so blunt, but in our investigations, it's important to repeat exactly what I've heard."

Phyllis giggled, Wiggins chuckled, Luty snorted, and the rest of them laughed.

Ruth laughed as well. "Alright, I do understand that we've all learned that prevaricating and using euphemisms is pointless and stupid when a murder is the subject, but I'm not used to being so blunt."

"Is the child here in London?" Hatchet took a bite of the cake. His eyes widened as he chewed, but he gamely swallowed it down.

"No, and as far as my source knew, Mrs. Attwater never has had a child. But that's not all I heard. I also found out that the first thing Chloe Attwater did when she arrived back in London was to buy her way into the Mayfair Orchid and Exotic Plant Society. My source was certain that Helena Rayburn wasn't going to approve Chloe Attwater's application for membership. She thinks Mrs. Attwater knew it as well and that's why she used her influence with Lady Prentiss, whose husband is a member of the Royal Horticultural Society, to force Mrs. Rayburn to let her into the Mayfair group. Helena Rayburn wanted Lord and Lady Prentiss to agree to be judges at the Mayfair Orchid and Exotic Plant Society annual flower competition and certainly wouldn't risk offending them by refusing their friend's membership application."

"So you think that Chloe Attwater deliberately set out

to reestablish contact with her old friends from India?"
Mrs. Jeffries noticed that everyone who'd eaten a bite of
the seed cake had either pushed their plate aside, choked
it down, or in the case of Phyllis had tried discreetly to
spit it out.

Ruth nodded. "I do and now that I've heard what Wiggins learned from Kevin, I'm sure I'm right. Mrs. Attwater
is one of the richest women in England, yet instead of trying
to buy her way into an organization that would enhance her
social status, she buys her way into a local gardening club."

"And if your source is right"—Betsy looked at
Ruth—"and they weren't really friends in India, why did
she bother with them at all? She's rich and the rich never
have trouble finding friends."

"That's an interesting question." Ruth took a bite of cake.

"Excellent, Ruth, anything else?" Mrs. Jeffries waited
till Ruth gave a negative shake of her head, and noticed
her stop chewing the cake she'd just popped in her mouth.
"Who's next?"

"I found out something," Betsy said. "I had a chat with
a woman who happens to live near the Rayburn house.
She's got a good view of the entrance to the mews from
her sitting room window, and yesterday morning, she saw
Helena Rayburn heading into it. She wasn't certain about
the time, but she thinks it might have been a quarter past
eleven."

"The mews, isn't that the way the inspector and Constable Barnes think the killer got into the conservatory?"
Mrs. Goodge exclaimed.

Betsy nodded. "That's right, but what I don't understand
is if Helena Rayburn is the killer, why would she go in

through some loose boards in her own back garden? Why not just slip into the conservatory and do the deed?"

"That's easy, she wanted to be away from the 'ouse to establish her alibi," Wiggins suggested. "You know, pretend she was out larkin' about, goin' to the shops or something like that, but instead she slips in the back way, coshes the poor bloke on the 'ead, and then stabs 'im in the heart."

"That makes more sense than trying to avoid all the servants," Phyllis agreed. "Especially if they were setting up for a luncheon, they'd be all over the place and she probably couldn't have gotten away from them."

Mrs. Jeffries glanced at the cook. Mrs. Goodge was looking at the faces around the table, her gaze going from Ruth, who was struggling to choke down the cake, to Betsy, who'd pushed her plate aside, and then to Hatchet, who was pouring tea down his throat. Something was obviously wrong with the seed cake. Mrs. Jeffries knew she had better interrupt, both for the sake of the cook's vanity and the investigation. "Listen, everyone, we mustn't speculate. Just because Mrs. Rayburn was seen in the mews doesn't mean she's the killer. We've gone down this path before, and all of you know what happens when we do that—we fix on a suspect and we don't examine the evidence properly."

"But she was seen in the mews," Betsy argued. "Why would she go there right before she was hosting a luncheon?"

Hatchet put his cup down. "There could be lots of reasons. We could equally ask why was Mrs. Attwater paying a lad to keep an eye on the Rayburn house? That's even more suspicious. But as Mrs. Jeffries has said, we mustn't let ourselves speculate, not until we've more facts."

Smythe looked at Hatchet. "Did that source you had ever mention in his letters how long ago it was that Filmore left the army?"

"Not that I can remember," Hatchet said, "but I've a feeling that might be important so I'll try to find out."

Amanda yawned and Betsy got up, scooped the child into her arms, and then headed toward the cook's quarters.

"I heard something today that might be useful." Relieved of the child, Luty shifted to a more comfortable position. "Seems that Mrs. Rayburn ain't as rich as she pretends. Accordin' to my sources"—she flashed Hatchet a quick grin as she used the plural—"the only money she has is her husband's pension and a small annual income from his investments and they're doin' a bit poorly these days."

"But she has enough to keep up appearances," Mrs. Jeffries clarified.

"So far, but those plants she was buyin' from Filmore, they didn't come cheap. Rare orchids, the kind he sold, come with a high price tag. Now, I know we ain't supposed to be speculatin', but it seems to me that she might have gotten into a bit of a fix financially and he give her the orchids on credit. Then he wanted her to pay the piper. That'd be a good motive for murder, especially if she didn't have it."

"True, but we don't know that there weren't others with additional and even stronger motives for murdering Filmore," Mrs. Jeffries pointed out. "So let's not get ahead of ourselves. Does anyone else have anything?"

"I learned something," Phyllis said. She told them about her chat with the local butcher's clerk. "I know it's not much, but as Mrs. Jeffries always says, all the little bits and pieces help."

"And now we know that Thea Stanway likes to stick her nose where it don't belong." Wiggins laughed. "That should come in right handy. Maybe tomorrow I'll get lucky and one of 'er servants will stick their nose out of 'er back door."

"Good luck to ya, then." Smythe put down his cup. "I tried the hansom drivers at the local stands, and none of them, not a one, could recall takin' any of those ladies to that luncheon. None of them had transported Filmore, either. But I've some more sources workin' on the problem. The killer, whoever 'e or she might be, 'ad to get to there somehow."

Constable Griffiths had caught up with the inspector and Constable Barnes outside the Martell house. He'd informed them that Filmore's landlady was still out of town, and according to the neighbor who'd received a telegram from her, she wouldn't be home until tomorrow. So they'd decided to interview Thea Stanway before going back to the station.

The Stanway home was a three-story red brick row house with a small paved forecourt surrounded by a black wrought iron fence. A row of potted ferns stood like sentries along the walkway leading to the white-painted front door.

"Not quite as posh as the others," Barnes murmured. The brass lamps flanking the entrance were dull and corroded in spots, paint was chipping off the window trim, and there were chunks missing off the edges of the concrete steps. He had lifted his hand toward the corroded metal knocker to knock again when the door opened.

"You're the police." The housemaid stepped back and

waved them inside. "Mrs. Stanway said you might be here today. Please come inside."

They stepped into the entryway. A red and green rug went from the entrance and ran all the way up the staircase. Paintings of brilliantly colored flowers hung on the cream-colored walls, and two tables covered with emerald green silk cloth stood opposite each other in the small space. A large black lacquer box inlaid with mother of pearl stood on one and a tall gold and white Chinese vase stood on the other.

The housemaid led them past the staircase and down the hall to the drawing room. Tables covered with fringed runners, glass-fronted cabinets filled with china knickknacks, bookcases, a wicker rocker, two settees upholstered in dark green and gold damask, and three matching armchairs crowded the room. The walls were so covered with paintings of pastoral scenes, portraits, and seascapes that it was difficult to see the pattern in the pale pink wallpaper.

Thea Stanway rose from one of the settees. "I've been expecting you, gentlemen. Please come in and sit down." She waved at the two armchairs that were catercorner to her.

"Thank you, Mrs. Stanway." Witherspoon eased into one of the armchairs but Barnes took out his pencil and notebook before sitting down.

Witherspoon relaxed a bit as he sat; the cushion wasn't one of those wretched slippery ones. "Mrs. Stanway, I know Mr. Filmore's death must have been a shock to you, but it's necessary that we ask you some questions."

"Of course. Would you or the constable care for tea?"

"No, we're both fine. Now, can you tell me what time you arrived at the Rayburn home?"

"I'm not sure of the exact time. I think it was almost half past twelve. But I was in the neighborhood at half past eleven. My old nanny has a flat in a house just across the street from Mrs. Rayburn, and I often go to visit her, especially when I've a social engagement at the Rayburn home."

"Did you see anyone hanging about the Rayburn home when you arrived either to see your nanny or when you went to the luncheon?"

"I didn't, but it was wet out so I was more concerned with keeping myself dry than looking around the neighborhood," she replied.

"Did you take a hansom cab that morning?" Barnes asked.

"I walked, Constable. I like walking. I got in the habit when I was in India."

"But you said it was wet out?" he pressed.

She smiled. "I've a very good umbrella, Constable, and this time of year, it wasn't cold. Cabs are ridiculously expensive and I quite like exercise and fresh air."

Witherspoon thought back to his interviews with Mrs. Attwater and Mrs. Martell. "When you arrived at the Rayburn home, were all the other ladies already present?"

"No, I was the first, then Mrs. Attwater came, and after her, Mrs. Martell. The one person who wasn't present was Mrs. Rayburn. She didn't join us until right before the housekeeper announced that luncheon was served. I was surprised about that, too. Helena isn't one to ignore proper etiquette and not be present to greet her guests."

"Did she say why she'd been delayed?" Barnes stopped writing and looked at her. He wondered if she had any idea that Helena Rayburn had gone out.

"She did not, nor did she apologize, which I thought most odd. As I said, Mrs. Rayburn is very strict about proper etiquette, and considering the way she went on and on about Mrs. Attwater's behavior, you'd think she could have at least had the decency to apologize to us. But then we're all like that, aren't we. Finding fault in others while excusing our own actions."

"Was there anything unusual about Mrs. Rayburn's appearance when she joined you and the other ladies?" The constable wondered if Mrs. Stanway had noticed the frizzy hair.

Thea smiled. "I shouldn't mention it, Constable, but as you've asked, I supposed I ought to tell the truth. Her hair was frizzy; it was as if she'd been outside in the damp. Oh dear, that sounds unkind, doesn't it, but you did ask."

"What did Mrs. Rayburn say about Mrs. Attwater?" Witherspoon asked.

"Only that she'd stayed far too long after the meal was over and that she ought to have known better. Of course, both Isabelle and I were there longer than Mrs. Attwater, but Helena excused us on the grounds we were old friends."

"Wasn't Mrs. Attwater an old friend as well?" Witherspoon asked. "Weren't you all in India together at the same place?"

"We were. But Mrs. Attwater left years earlier than we did." She thought for a moment. "I quite like Chloe Attwater. I did when we were in India as well. But I don't think Helena, Mrs. Rayburn, liked her very much, and I know that even back then, she never considered Mrs. Attwater a friend." She shrugged. "Back in those days, Helena felt it was unseemly to have more than just a passing acquaintance with a governess. But times change and she, along with the rest of us, must change with them."

"How long were you a customer of Mr. Filmore's?" Barnes asked.

"I'm not sure, let me see. We started the club right after we all got back to England, but he didn't start supplying plants till, oh, five years ago or so . . . Yes, that's right, Helena brought him to one of our meetings and had him show his plants."

"She arranged for him to meet everyone in your gardening club?" Witherspoon clarified. "Is that correct?"

"That's right. If it hadn't been for her, he'd have probably gone out of business," she replied. "At least that's what Isabelle, Mrs. Martell, told me."

"Do you know if Mr. Filmore had any enemies?"

"Well, he must have, mustn't he. Someone killed him."

"I feel such a fool." Mrs. Goodge shook her head in disbelief as she grabbed the plate and glared at the remaining slab of seed cake.

The kitchen at Upper Edmonton Gardens was empty save for the two women and Samson, who was staring at his empty food dish.

"Don't be ridiculous." Mrs. Jeffries stacked the empty teacups on a tray and headed for the sink. "You made a simple mistake, something we all do from time to time."

"Simple mistake! I put salt instead of sugar in the cake. No wonder no one could eat the ruddy thing. Oh dear Lord, everyone must think me a complete and utter idiot." Mrs. Goodge began gathering plates and dumping the uneaten slices back on the cake plate. Then she stopped and sat down. She said nothing. Samson, annoyed that the food dish was still empty, butted her shins with his head and gave a pitiful meow.

Mrs. Jeffries put the tray on the counter by the sink and picked up the bowl filled with meat scraps. She crossed the room, eased him to one side, and used her arm to block his paws so couldn't swipe her hand before dumping the food into his dish. He shoved his fat head in and noisily gobbled down the food. She put the empty bowl next to his dish for him to lick and went back to the table.

Saying nothing, she stood for a moment and studied the cook.

Mrs. Goodge was staring off into space, her expression morose. Finally, Mrs. Jeffries said, "Are you going to tell me what's wrong?"

"Nothing's wrong."

"Please don't say that. You've been distracted ever since the inspector's gotten this murder. There's something about it which is bothering you."

"Maybe I'm just going senile," Mrs. Goodge muttered. "Maybe it's time for me to quit. I've got a bit saved now. I could move into one of them places by the seaside that cater to old women without families. Old women like me."

Mrs. Jeffries wasn't sure if she should let the cook ramble on, wallowing in self-pity, or whether she ought to stop it before the woman talked herself into a major case of melancholy. "You're not going senile and it certainly isn't time to quit. Furthermore, we may not be related by blood, but your contention that you have no family is insulting to me and would be heartbreaking to the others. We are family. So stop this nonsense right now and tell me what's wrong. Something has caused you to fall into this state of mind, now what is it?"

"India." She looked down at her hands.

"India? What on earth does that mean? Why should India upset you so much?"

"It's not the country that upsets me. It was when we found out that the ladies in this case were all military widows from the Raj. It made me remember something I've tried hard to forget." Her eyes filled with tears.

Mrs. Jeffries went to the pine sideboard, opened the cabinet on the lower right, grabbed two cut glass aperitif glasses, and put them on the table. The cook didn't seem to notice. Then Mrs. Jeffries ducked back to the cabinet and yanked out the bottle of excellent brandy she kept on hand for either quiet celebrations or emergencies.

To her way of thinking, Mrs. Goodge's current state of mind was most definitely an emergency.

She poured the brandy into the glasses, slid one across the table to the cook, and then sat down.

Mrs. Goodge blinked. "Oh dear, what's this, then? If I have this, I might ruin our supper."

"Don't worry about it, I'll supervise you. Now, tell me why the thought of army posts in India upsets you so much."

Mrs. Goodge picked up her glass and poured the brandy down her throat like a sailor. She sighed and then sat back. "Because I'm responsible for a decent young woman's death in that country. Oh Lord, I hate thinking about it, but the moment I found out our suspects were all connected to the army and India, I couldn't stop myself from thinking of Janet Lawler. She died out there and it was my fault."

She pushed her empty glass toward the housekeeper.

"May I have another? It helps, and at my age, it doesn't really matter if I become a drunk, does it."

Mrs. Jeffries laughed and poured another shot. She slid it across the table, "I hardly think that's likely. Now, tell me why you think you're responsible for this girl's death."

"Because I am, Hepzibah. If I'd behaved differently, she wouldn't have died." Mrs. Goodge nodded her thanks and picked up the glass. "It was years ago and I worked for a family in Kent. The cook left to go to London and she recommended me to take her place. She said I'd worked hard and I deserved it. So I got the position and I was so proud. It was a prominent family and they entertained a lot, so there was a large kitchen staff." She took a sip of brandy. "Janet Lawler was one of the scullery maids. She was a silly girl, always talking and laughing and a bit lazy. I was eager to prove that I was in charge, that my word was law in the kitchen. That's the way I'd always been treated, and back in those days, that was simply the way it was. Mind you, if I was young and in a kitchen now, I'd not put up with such ridiculous nonsense, we should have demanded better treatment, all of us, but we didn't. Back then, we were always being told we ought to be grateful just to have a position and a roof over our heads. It never occurred to anyone that we had rights. But none of that matters now, what's done is done. Anyway, the long and short of it is that Janet got on my bad side very quickly. Behavior that hadn't bothered me when I was the under-cook could no longer be tolerated now that I was in charge." She closed her eyes as the memories flooded back. "I gave Janet several warnings, but it didn't do much good—she was still always larking about and laughing. The worst happened while we were getting ready for a huge dinner party, and the silly child dropped an expensive platter with a prime rib of beef on it—that was really my fault, not hers, I should have called one of the footmen to carry it up to the dining room. We were able to salvage the food but the lady of the house was furious that her plate had been broken. Instead of speaking up for the girl, I let her take all the blame and she was sacked the next day and not given a reference."

"And back in those days, without a reference, a decent job was impossible," Mrs. Jeffries said softly.

"That's right. After that, the only position she could get was with a family going to India for the husband to join a regiment. Janet didn't want to go, but she was desperate for a job. A few days after arriving in India, I found out she'd come down with one of those fevers they have there and died."

"How did you find out?" Mrs. Jeffries took a sip of her brandy.

"Her cousin worked in the kitchen and she told me. That's how Janet had gotten the position there in the first place." Mrs. Goodge tossed back the rest of her drink. "That poor child was only sixteen years old and she died of a fever in India. In a foreign land amongst strangers and it was my fault. If I'd stood up for her, if I'd taken responsibility for giving that slip of a girl that heavy platter of food, she wouldn't have dropped it and broken it. She'd have not gotten sacked and she'd still be alive."

CHAPTER 6

—◆—

"How was your day, Inspector?" Mrs. Jeffries asked as she hung up his bowler hat.

"Very tiring, Mrs. Jeffries, I shall enjoy our glass of sherry this evening." He hurried down the hall and she followed a bit more slowly, giving herself a few moments to think. She was very concerned about Mrs. Goodge but she had no idea what, if anything, she could do about her friend's misery. The only thing she could think of was lending both a sympathetic ear and reassuring her she wasn't responsible for the girl's death. But now she had to concentrate on everything the inspector said. There was no doubt that he was going to speak about the case, and she simply couldn't afford to be distracted.

When she reached the study, she went to the liquor cabinet in the corner, pulled out two glasses, a bottle of Harveys, and poured them both a drink.

"Something smells wonderful, Mrs. Jeffries." He inhaled deeply. "And I do hope that whatever it is, there is plenty. I am very hungry. It feels as if Constable Barnes and I were all over London today, and yet, I'm not sure we actually learned anything of use to the case."

"Nonsense, sir." She handed him his glass. "That's just your mind muddling you up a bit so your 'inner voice' is free to work on the case without interference. That's precisely what you do in every case and thus far, sir, you've had a rather good success rate."

"You do make me feel better, Mrs. Jeffries, and I do hope you're right and my 'inner voice' will actually help us solve this one. It's quite frustrating, though—we still can't get into the victim's home or place of business. So we don't know much about the man except for what we've learned from the ladies at Mrs. Rayburn's luncheon."

"His landlady still hasn't returned?"

"No, she sent a telegram to her neighbor saying she'd be back tomorrow. But as I said, we had a busy day nonetheless. It didn't start off well at all. We went to the Rayburn home to have another word with Mrs. Rayburn, but she'd gone out. So we went to Mayfair and interviewed Mrs. Attwater."

"Isn't she the luncheon guest who wasn't there when the body was discovered?" Mrs. Jeffries asked. She knew perfectly well who Chloe Attwater was but she had to keep up a pretense of ignorance.

"Indeed, and she was a most interesting witness. Not only was she waiting for us with a full tea trolley at the ready, but she was positively eager to answer any and all our questions."

"That's certainly unusual," Mrs. Jeffries commented.

As far as she was concerned, that kind of cooperation was also rather suspicious. The rich rarely liked speaking to the police, but perhaps she was being overly cynical. She pushed her doubts to the back of her mind and listened to his account.

"I'm not certain, but I do think that some of the comments Mrs. Attwater made were deliberately fashioned so that I'd think that both Helena Rayburn and Isabelle Martell were capable of murder."

"From what you've said, sir, Mrs. Attwater wanted to make it very clear that both women were familiar with, uh, what was it?"

"'Sudden death,'" he repeated.

"So she implied that Isabelle Martell might have pushed her husband off a balcony when he was drunk and that, before she married, Helena Rayburn's accusations of inappropriate behavior led to a young man being drowned. Is that right?"

"That's right. The only person she didn't accuse was Thea Stanway." He took another sip of sherry. "But then perhaps she didn't have time to include Mrs. Stanway as we were interrupted and called back to the Rayburn house." He told her about the gardener finding the bloody clothes in the ivy bed. "At first, Mrs. Rayburn did exactly what she did when we found the gardening tools that matched the murder weapon—she denied the clothes belonged to her."

Mrs. Jeffries listened closely, trying to take it all in as he reported the events surrounding the discovery of the garments and the ensuing fracas between Helena Rayburn and her gardener.

"Of course, I knew it was pointless for the two of them

to simply stand there accusing one another of everything from murder to jealousy, so when she went into the house, I had a quick word with Mr. Tufts, who despite what Mrs. Rayburn said, had no reason to want the victim dead." He took another quick sip. "While I was interviewing Mrs. Rayburn, Constable Barnes showed the bloodstained clothing to Mrs. Clemment, and she confirmed they belonged to Mrs. Rayburn," he continued. "Earlier that day, the housekeeper had also told us that Mrs. Rayburn had gone out sometime before the luncheon and only returned a few moments before the meal was served."

"Where had she gone?"

"I haven't asked her that as yet." He shrugged. "The truth is, we got called away to the Yard before I could finish my interview so I'll ask her tomorrow."

When he paused to take a breath, she said, "I can understand why she's frightened. It doesn't look good for her, does it?"

"No, but I don't know that I think she's guilty. She had no reason we know of to murder Hiram Filmore. But we'll find out more when we do finally get to search his flat and shop. We might find evidence that there's a whole host of people who wanted the fellow dead. Mrs. Rayburn is lucky in one sense—Mrs. Stanway seems to be coming by frequently to make sure she's all right. But she does seem to be one of those friends that mean well but end up being cold comfort." He told her about Thea Stanway's assertion that women were just as capable of murder as men.

"A Job's comforter," Mrs. Jeffries murmured, though she thought it most likely that Thea Stanway was simply a nosy sort who used friendship as an excuse to see what was going on at any particular moment. "I suppose Chief Superintendent Barrows was pressuring you to make an arrest."

"No, quite the contrary," he replied.

Surprised, she stared at him. "Really sir?"

"Really. I was quite stunned when I got there." He repeated everything Barrows had said and then added the information Constable Barnes had learned. "What's odd, of course, is that we know of no connection between Sir Jeremy Sanders and Hiram Filmore or anyone else on this case."

"I'm sure something will turn up, sir. It always does." She concentrated hard as she tried to keep the facts in some semblance of reasonable order. But then she gave up and just listened.

"After that, we interviewed Isabelle Martell," he said. "She was very uncooperative; the only thing she could recall about the time she arrived at the Rayburn home was that Mrs. Stanway was in the cloakroom fussing with her gloves." He downed the last of his sherry. "But we'll learn more tomorrow. I'm sure of it."

The next morning, Mrs. Jeffries came downstairs and found Mrs. Goodge was up and had made tea. "Gracious, you don't look like you've slept at all," Mrs. Jeffries exclaimed as she entered the kitchen.

The cook sat at the table staring off into the distance. A cup of tea was in front of her and Samson was on Fred's rug by the cooker, glaring at both of them.

"I'm fine. Don't mind me, Mrs. Jeffries, it's just the miseries of old age." She got up and went to the worktable, limping as if her rheumatism was bothering her. She pulled out her big baking bowl. "I'd better do a batch of scones, just in case one of my sources show up."

"Didn't you send out notes? That's what you normally do." Mrs. Jeffries sat down in her chair, reached for the teapot, and poured herself a cup. Once again, she had no idea how to react to her friend's obvious melancholy. She'd hoped a good night's sleep might have helped the cook put her past into perspective, but from her red-rimmed eyes and the sharp lines etched around her mouth, it hadn't.

"I sent some off, but you never know who is going to respond and who isn't." She turned when they heard a knock at the back door just as Samson gave out a piteous cry for his breakfast.

"I'll get the door." Mrs. Jeffries got up. "You feed your cat."

The housekeeper had to shove her worries about Mrs. Goodge to the back of her mind as their morning routine unfolded. Constable Barnes gave them more details on yesterday's activities, and they, in turn, told him what the household had learned.

"What will you and the inspector be doing today?" Mrs. Jeffries asked as they completed their short meeting.

"Hopefully, Filmore's landlady is back and we can get into the flat." He downed the last of his tea and stood up. "If we're lucky, there'll be keys there for his shop as well. Otherwise, we'll have to break into it. We can't go another day without learning more about our victim. The postmortem report ought to be ready today, and if the chief superintendent is good as his word, we might even see Filmore's military file sometime in the next day or two."

* * *

Half an hour later, Constable Barnes and the inspector were politely introducing themselves to Mrs. Olive Rhodes, Hiram Filmore's landlady.

"I'm so sorry I wasn't here," she exclaimed as she led them up the stairs to the second floor. "But I was given a lovely return ticket to Bournemouth and I simply had to go. My sister lives there and we've not seen each other for ages. Mind you, I thought Millie had sent me the ticket and just forgotten to include a note, she does that sort of thing all the time, you see, but when I arrived, she'd no idea what I was talking about. So now I've no idea who to thank, though, of course, it was probably Mr. Filmore who did it. He's given me gifts before, but generally he says something when he does. I was so sorry to hear he'd been killed—he was a good tenant, paid his rent on time, and generally was a nice gentleman."

By this time they'd reached the first-floor landing. "What kind of gifts did Mr. Filmore give you?" Barnes took a deep breath.

"Oh, lovely little things. He knew how fond I was of music so he often got me tickets to a recital or concert." Her eyes filled with tears. "He was a nice man, a rather lonely man, and he was very kind to me. He'd even pay for a hansom cab home for those times he'd given me a ticket." She blinked hard to beat back the tears, unlocked the door, and then stepped back. "Go on in, sir," she said to Witherspoon. "I'll be downstairs in the parlor."

They waited till she'd gone halfway down before opening the door and stepping into the flat. Filmore's home consisted of a large sitting room with a brown and green herringbone three-piece suite, a small wooden desk on the far wall, and a set of bookcases. Just off the sitting room an open door led to the bedroom, which consisted of a bed neatly made up with a cream-colored spread, a trunk shoved under the window, a wardrobe, and a chest of drawers with a mirror on the wall above it.

"I'll take the bedroom." Barnes headed in that direction while the inspector began a search of the sitting room. First, he checked beneath the seat and back cushions of the furniture but found nothing but some crumbs, a button, and a sixpence. Then he went through the bookcase, the shelves of which were filled with books and periodicals about plants, flowers, gardening techniques, herbs, and spices.

Witherspoon was methodical, fanning the pages of each and every item and checking the back of the bookcase and even underneath it. But he found nothing. Lastly, he went to the desk. The top was bare save for an inkpot with two matching pens on a marble stand and a stack of envelopes. He sat down in the chair and pulled open the top left drawer and began to rummage through the contents. There was nothing but a stack of blank invoices, a packet of white notepaper, a bottle of black ink, and a stack of small brown envelopes. The drawer on the right contained much the same. He worked his way down through the others but found nothing except file boxes containing bills of ladings; invoices; shipping lists; customer lists; old ledgers filled with names, dates, and amounts in both pounds and dollars; and blank customs forms. He was almost at the bottom of the last drawer when he found the box. It was a lovely object—black lacquer, inlaid with mother-of-pearl in an exotic pattern.

Witherspoon pulled it out from beneath a packet of insurance forms and put it on the top of the desk. "Constable, I've found something," he called. Barnes, who had almost completed his search and was now going through the shoes in the wardrobe, dropped the slipper he'd been holding and raced into the sitting room.

"This was in the bottom desk drawer." The inspector waited till the constable was close enough to see before he lifted the lid. Inside was a set of three keys, an unsealed envelope, and a letter. He pulled the envelope out, opened it, and then separated the edges with his fingers so he could see inside properly. "Gracious, look at that, Constable. It's a five-pound note."

"Looks like there's a lot of them." Barnes jerked his chin toward the cash in the envelope. "That wad is as thick as a fat man's thumb."

Witherspoon pulled the notes out and fanned them. "And they're five- and ten-pound notes. There must be several hundred pounds here." He tucked the cash in the envelope. "I think we'd best take this into evidence, though I'm not sure it's evidence of anything except the man ran a business." He put the envelope back in the box and picked up the letter. Opening it, he frowned as he began to read. "It's addressed to 'My darling Nigel,' and it appears to be a love letter of some sort." He felt his cheeks start to flame as he continued reading. "A very passionate love letter," he mumbled. "And it's signed, 'Your loving Helena.'"

"Filmore's Christian name was Hiram," Barnes said dryly. "So I doubt the letter is to him. Do you think 'Helena' could be Helena Rayburn?"

"It's possible," Witherspoon said. "But as I recall, her late husband's name was Malcolm, not Nigel."

Barnes pointed to the writing at the top. "It's dated October third, 1882. I wonder if Mrs. Rayburn was married to Mr. Rayburn by then?"

"I'm sure she was," the inspector replied. "She mentioned she went to India in 1871 with a cousin. She'd have been married within a few years or she'd have come home. At least that's the impression I got when I spoke to Lady Cannonberry about the women who went out there. But we'll confirm the dates of Mrs. Rayburn's marriage and the date her husband died."

"You're thinking Filmore might have been blackmailing her?" Barnes asked. "That she might have had an illicit relationship with this Nigel person and he managed to get hold of this evidence?"

"That's possible." Witherspoon frowned. "But if that were the case, why kill him now? She's widowed, so her late husband certainly isn't going to complain about her behavior."

"There might be other reasons she'd not want that kind of news spread all over London," Barnes pointed out. "According to the other ladies, she's wanting to get on some committee at the Royal Horticultural Society, and a scandal might put an end to it."

"I'd like to say that no one would kill for such a trivial reason, but it's not true—people kill for the most ridiculous reasons all the time." He put the letter in the box and picked up the set of keys. "If we're very lucky, these might be the spare keys to the shop."

"And if we're not lucky, sir, we'll simply have to break into the place. We've got to keep searching, sir. If Filmore was a blackmailer, she might not have been his only victim."

The morning meeting was over and the others had gone out "on the hunt." Mrs. Jeffries had dashed upstairs to do the inspector's bedroom and then hurriedly dusted the drawing room and his study. Phyllis had cleared up the breakfast things from the dining room before leaving for the shops in Bayswater and Mayfair.

Mrs. Jeffries put the feather duster and her workbox in the cupboard under the staircase and hurried down to the kitchen. She was going to have it out with the cook once and for all.

When she came down the stairs, Mrs. Goodge was pulling her scones out of the oven. Mrs. Jeffries steeled herself for a confrontation and moved toward the table. There was a sharp knock on the front door. "I'll get it." She turned and retraced her steps. She hurried down the hall to the front door and flung it open.

A young man dressed in a rather tatty-looking, old-fashioned green footman's livery, complete with white leggings beneath his tight, knee-length trousers, gave her a toothy grin. "Are you Mrs. Jeffries?" he asked. When she nodded, he handed her an envelope. "This is for you, ma'am."

"Who is it from?" she asked. The only thing written on the outside of the envelope was her name.

"Someone at St. Thomas' Hospital, ma'am. My mistress was just there, and as we live close by, one of the doctors asked her if we could get this to you."

She dug in her apron for a sixpence and handed it to him. "For your trouble, young man."

"Thanks, ma'am." He took the coin, nodded politely, and leapt down the stairs and onto the back rail of a huge, black carriage.

Mrs. Jeffries tore open the envelope, yanked out the note, and eagerly read it.

Dear Mrs. Jeffries,

If it is at all possible, I would like you to come and see me as quickly as you can. It is about the inspector's latest case. Unfortunately, I'm on duty and cannot come to you.

Best regards,
Bosworth

Dr. Bosworth must have something important to tell her; he wasn't the sort of person to waste either of their time. Stripping off her apron as she walked, she hurried back to the kitchen. Mrs. Goodge's melancholy would just have to wait.

"Mrs. Goodge." She rushed to the coat tree. "I've got to go out. Dr. Bosworth has sent me a note. He wants to speak to me about the case."

The cook, who was brushing melted butter on the top of the scones, paused. "Did he do the postmortem?"

"That should have been done by Dr. Procash. But Dr. Bosworth must know something important. I should be back before our afternoon meeting."

"Right, then, I've got a source coming by in a few moments. Is there anything you need me to do while you're out?" When everyone was on the hunt, both the cook and the housekeeper took over as many of the household chores as possible.

"No, we should be alright." She put on her bonnet and grabbed her purse and gloves off the top of the pine sideboard. "I'll be back as quick as I can, but it's already past eleven and Dr. Bosworth might not be available right away, so if I'm not back by the time the others get here this afternoon, start the meeting without me."

"Of course," she agreed as the housekeeper disappeared down the corridor to the back door.

Mrs. Goodge put down her pastry brush and set about making a fresh pot of tea. No matter how miserable she felt, if one of her sources did show up, she was determined to be ready. Her past sins were no excuse for her to neglect her present duty.

Someone did come, and less than ten minutes later, Miss Eliza Baker was sitting in the kitchen. She took a delicate nibble from the edge of her scone and then put the pastry back on her plate. She was a tall woman in her seventies with gray hair, blue eyes, wire-rimmed spectacles, and a nose that was made for looking down on people.

"I was surprised to get your note." She stared at Mrs. Goodge curiously. "We haven't been in contact for years. Actually, I thought you were dead."

"As you can see, I'm alive and well." Mrs. Goodge tried to smile. She'd known within two minutes of letting the woman in the house that inviting her had been a mistake. She'd never liked Eliza, and from the way her guest was behaving, the feeling was apparently mutual.

"And still in service." Eliza's cocked her head. "That's surprising. You're far older than I am and I retired years ago. Why on earth are you still working?"

Mrs. Goodge eyed her speculatively. She wasn't going to get anything useful out of the woman so she might as well say what she wanted. "I like working, it makes me feel useful. More importantly, it gives me the opportunity to be with people who genuinely care about me. Our generation had it hard—we weren't allowed to have a family and still keep our positions."

Eliza gave her a pitying smile. "Really, you think your current situation is 'family'?"

"I don't 'think' it, I know it is," Mrs. Goodge retorted. "I've a beautiful goddaughter, friends that are like sisters, and young people in the household who think of me as a grandparent. What's more, my employer has told me that I'll have a home here for the rest of my life. Not that I would need it as I've plenty saved and could take care of myself if I had to."

She laughed. "How quaint. You work for a policeman, don't you?" She looked around the well-furnished kitchen.

"Quite a successful one as well. Not only that, but he has plenty of money, and having not been raised in the upper class, he treats his servants like human beings. I understand that since you've retired, you're living with your nephew and his wife in Shepherds Bush. How many children do they have?"

Eliza's smile disappeared. "Three and my nephew is an estate agent. He's very successful. They've put him in charge of the West Kensington office."

"How good of you to help out. I'm sure it takes a great strain off the mother."

"Why did you invite me here?" Eliza got up and put her hands on her hips. "You never liked me and I most certainly never liked you."

"You went to India with Major Kirkwood and his family and I wanted to ask you some questions." There was no reason not to tell the truth; Eliza Baker wouldn't be darkening her door again. "So sit yourself down and finish your tea. I happen to know you'll do anything to have a few hours away from your nephew's home."

"Who told you that?" But she sat back down.

"Does that matter? I know what your life must be like, and oddly enough, even though we weren't friends, I do have some sympathy for you and all the other women of our generation who got thrown on the scrap heap."

"I wasn't thrown on a scrap heap," she cried, but her eyes were pooling with tears.

"Get off your high horse, Eliza. You were sacked just like I was when they got someone younger and cheaper to cook their meals. You spent half your life at the Kirkwood home and they sent you packing without so much as a by-your-leave."

"You were sacked?" Eliza picked up the scone, took a bite, and swallowed. "Really? But you were, still are, a wonderful cook."

"I was told I was too old and shown the door. But luckily, I landed here. I'm sorry you had to go to your nephew's home. I'm sure it isn't pleasant."

"It's not that bad." She shoved the rest of the scone in

her mouth, chewed hungrily, and swallowed. "Eleanor, that's my nephew's wife, is a decent sort and I do what I can to help, but it's hard and I always get the feeling I'm not doing enough."

"I'll wager you do plenty," Mrs. Goodge said softly.

"I'm only there because Paul, he's my nephew, feels he ought to do his Christian duty, not because they really want me." Eliza's lip trembled and she looked down at her hands.

"What about the children?"

Eliza lifted her chin and brushed at her eyes. "They're really quite lovely. Edna and Jane, they're the twin girls, they're very sweet. When the weather's good, I take them to the park, and Enoch, he's their oldest, he's a smart lad. We read together every afternoon when he gets home from school."

"It doesn't sound as if the children think you're there because of Christian charity. I'll bet they love you being there."

Eliza smiled shyly. "I like to think so. I want to feel that I'm not just a burden, but genuinely helping." She sighed. "I'm sorry, I know I was rude when I first arrived, but honestly, I've always been so intimidated by you that I didn't know what to think when I got your note. How did you find me anyway?"

"Ida Leacock." Mrs. Goodge grinned. "She knows everything that goes on in this city."

"Oh my gracious, I haven't seen her in years." Eliza laughed. "She obviously hasn't changed one whit. Even when we were all in service together, she always knew every little thing that went on."

"She was and still is a good source of gossip," Mrs.

Goodge said. "And she knows where so many of us ended up."

"Really, did she ever say what happened to Martha Smathers?"

"She got married and went to Canada," the cook replied. For the next ten minutes, the two women spoke of the past, of their old colleagues and friends, who had emigrated, who had married, and who had died.

"I'm glad that Ida has done well for herself," Eliza said. "Mind you, her being such a gossip was probably a help to her in business and now she owns three newsagents shops."

"Gossip is only bad if it's mean or malicious." Mrs. Goodge pushed the plate of scones closer to her companion and nodded for her to help herself. "Speaking of gossip, when you were in India, did you ever hear anything about Helena Blackburn, she became Helena Rayburn, or Isabelle Martell, I don't know what her maiden name might have been." She made a mental note to try and find out. She had other sources coming in the next few days, and she didn't want to miss learning something useful because she didn't know the Martell woman's maiden name. "I believe they were in Madras at the same time you and the Kirkwoods were in India."

Eliza shook her head as she popped another scone on her plate. "Oh dear, I'm afraid I can't help you there. Major Kirkwood was stationed in Bombay and that was miles away."

"How about Chloe Attwater or Thea Stanway?"

"Thea Stanway?" Eliza repeated. "I didn't know she'd been in India."

"You know her?"

"I know of her," Eliza corrected. "She's a dreadful busybody. My nephew Paul had a client he was trying to find a suitable flat to purchase. A nice elderly woman named Mrs. Gilchrist. Thea Stanway butted her nose in, and no matter what flat Paul found, Mrs. Stanway found fault with it. The one the poor woman ended up buying was dreadfully overpriced and had been owned by a policeman's widow. It was the most unsuitable of the lot— it was cold, damp, and on the top floor of a four-story building."

"Mrs. Jeffries, I'm so sorry to have kept you waiting, I got called into the ward." Dr. Bosworth, red-haired and with a long, bony face and deep-set hazel eyes, took her arm and led her down the hall toward his office.

"I've only been here a few minutes," she fibbed. In truth, she'd been sitting in the lower-ground-floor corridor near the good doctor's office for over a half hour. But it was one of the few quiet spots at St. Thomas' Hospital, so she hadn't minded. It gave her a chance to think.

"I'm glad you sent a porter to let me know you were here," he said as he ushered her into his small office. "I was walking the corridors upstairs looking for you."

"I've been here before and I know where your office is," she said.

The small room hadn't changed much since she was last there. Behind his desk were two tiny windows that provided very little light; a tall cabinet filled with jars, boxes, bandages, and medical equipment flanked one side of the door; and a bookcase filled with medical books, stacks of periodicals, and topped with what she thought might be a human jawbone was on the other side. Bosworth swept a stack of files off the straight-backed chair in front of the desk and nodded for her to sit.

"But's it has been a good while since you've needed my opinion on one of the inspector's cases," he complained with a tight smile.

Dr. Bosworth was one of the household's "special friends." He'd helped them on numerous other cases. He'd spent a number of years in San Francisco working and studying with an American doctor. His time there had convinced him that one could tell a great deal about a crime by studying the size and shape of both gunshot and stab wounds. "I was beginning to think you'd found someone else to assist you and no longer needed me."

"That's not true," she replied. "You know how much we value your help."

"Do you?" He sat back in his chair and steepled his fingers together as he stared at her.

It took her a moment before she realized he was dead serious. "Dr. Bosworth, the only reason I haven't been banging on your office door asking for your help on the inspector's last few cases is because the manner of the victim's death hasn't required it. You're an expert in gunshots and stab wounds and these murders required nothing more than a general postmortem." She wasn't sure what to say. Finally, she simply told him the truth. "Dr. Bosworth, you know you've been invaluable to our investigations. Luckily, the inspector's recent investigations didn't require your level of expertise. Now let's be honest here, you're a very busy man and I don't want to come calling upon your very unusual set of skills unless it's necessary.

I don't want to wear out my welcome and get to the point where you'll hide when you see me coming."

He finally gave her a genuine smile. "Well, in that case, I won't take offense because I've not been involved. But I was beginning to get a bit put out about the matter. I am busy these days. But I do so like helping and I'll always make time to give you any assistance you need."

"Thank you, Doctor, we're very grateful. Why don't you come to dinner soon? The others would love to see you." She knew that Luty Belle would be happy to host them all for a summer supper.

"That would be lovely. Just let me know the time and the place and I'll be there. We'd better get down to business, I've more patients to see this afternoon." He flipped open a file on his desk and took out several sheets of paper. "This is the postmortem report on one Hiram Filmore. Dr. Procash sent me a copy. In layman's terms, the cause of death is a deep, deep cut to the heart muscle. Dr. Procash called me in to take a look at the wound and that's why I've called you here."

"I take it there was something odd about it," she guessed.

His homely faced creased in a frown. "Yes, there was, but it's the sort of thing I couldn't swear to in court. It looked as if the tip of the shears, which is very rounded, was not only shoved through the heart at the precise point where it would do the most damage, slicing through the aorta to the pulmonary, but once the killer shoved it inside, it appears as if the end of the weapon was used to . . . well, gouge the wound. That's the only way I can describe it."

"When you use the term 'gouge,' do you mean the murderer twisted the tip once it was inside the poor man's heart?"

He nodded. "That's what we both think, but again, it's

the sort of situation which doesn't make any sense. The wound in and of itself would have caused death in a matter of minutes."

"So gouging the wound wouldn't have speeded things up a bit?" She swallowed uneasily at the idea of someone doing such a thing.

"No, the first strike would have killed him quickly. It was a very precise wound, almost surgical. At least that's both our opinions. But that's not the only thing that was odd about the body. We both examined the head wound and came to the conclusion he was indeed unconscious when death occurred. Filmore was struck twice, not once. From the size of the impressions on both head wounds, either of them would have rendered the fellow unconscious."

"So why strike him twice if the first one did the job?" she asked.

Bosworth shrugged. "I don't know, perhaps the killer was enraged about something and just kept hitting the victim. You know I'm the police surgeon for K District and I've done a number of postmortems. Unfortunately, even with the best of intentions, some criminals die because they've been involved in altercations with the police."

"What are you getting at, Doctor?"

He leaned toward her. "From the size and shape of Hiram Filmore's head wounds, my guess is that they were made with a police truncheon or something shaped very much like one."

"A police truncheon? Gracious, are you certain?"

"One can never be absolutely sure, but I took very careful measurements and that's my best estimate. I don't know if that is important, but I wanted you to know."

"Would there have been a lot of blood?" she asked.

"Yes, the heart would have kept pumping for several minutes after the initial strike." He put the paper back on his desk and leaned forward on his elbows. "So I leave you to it to make some sort of sense of this. I know I can't make heads nor tails of it."

Octavia Wells laughed merrily and poured a glass of wine. "Now don't look at me like that, Ruth. It's past three so a nice claret is perfectly acceptable and I'm going to pour you one as well. I'll have my driver see that you get home safely. But I've not seen you in ages and I want to celebrate the occasion. Besides, this is an utterly delightful vintage." She poured the wine and handed Ruth her glass.

"Really, I shouldn't, but well, you're right, we've not seen each other for a long time." She took a sip and then grinned at her friend. "You're right, this is delightful."

Octavia was a short, plump, middle-aged redhead with sparkling brown eyes, a perfectly unlined complexion, and a sunny disposition. She was rich, flamboyant, and a staunch supporter of women's rights.

"I know I've not been in London since before Christmas"—Octavia flopped down on the chair across from Ruth—"but I simply adore traveling. What have you been up to? Are you still seeing that charming police inspector, the one who has solved so many cases?"

"I am." Ruth put her claret on the side table. "As a matter of fact, that's one of the reasons I'm here." She knew it would be foolish to try and hide her true intentions from Octavia. The woman might appear to be a flighty socialite with nothing in her head but ball gowns and parties, but nothing could be farther from the truth. She was smart, organized, and the chief fund-raiser for the London Women's Suffrage Society. "I was hoping you would know something about the people involved in his current case."

"You mean the one where the orchid hunter was stabbed in Helena Rayburn's conservatory?"

"Orchid hunter? So you have heard of him?"

"Indeed I have. He procured some orchids for Dolly Trainer, and he charged her so much money she complained about him for days afterward. But you're more interested in Helena, aren't you?"

"Well, yes."

"Helena Rayburn is a dreadful snob," Octavia interrupted. "The gossip I've heard is that when she came back from India after her husband died, she ran her sister-in-law out of the Rayburn home by browbeating the poor thing until she went off to live with some distant cousin in Newcastle. She and Isabelle Martell may be good friends, but they're highly competitive with one another." She laughed. "Helena generally wins the top prize at that gardening club they're both involved in, and of course, Isabelle responds by buying even better specimens than Helena. The word for this year's competition is that Isabelle is going to win the blue."

"But I heard that Isabelle isn't particularly interested?" Ruth picked up her wine and took another sip. "That she only participated in the Mayfair Orchid and Exotic Plant Society for social reasons and to be with her friends."

Octavia snorted delicately. "Isabelle likes to give that impression, but I happen to know she sent all the way to France to find one of the rarest specimens she could get her hands on." She chuckled. "She likes winning, especially against Helena Rayburn. As I just said, those two might appear to be friends, but they certainly don't trust one another. I've heard that Isabelle has paid a commercial nursery to house her plants until the contest. She doesn't want Helena sneaking into her conservatory and seeing what she has. What's more, Isabelle isn't just a snob, she's also a social climber; once when she'd had too much champagne, she confided to Dulcie Makepeace that she wasn't going to stop till she'd reached the highest levels of English society."

"That's amazing, how do you know all this?" Ruth was truly impressed by Octavia's intimate understanding of society, yet she couldn't see that a petty competition between two women could be a motive for murder. On the other hand, her involvement in the inspector's cases had taught her that it was certainly possible.

Octavia raised an eyebrow. "Knowledge is power and I make it my business to know these things. Navigating the English social structure is an intricate and complex endeavor, and understanding it properly has been very helpful to our cause."

"I didn't mean to imply you were a gossip," Ruth said quickly, afraid she'd offended her friend.

"But I am a gossip," Octavia countered with a grin. "And a very good one. That's how I'm able to procure funding for our cause. My analysis of the current social scene enables me to know who will be sympathetic to women's rights and open their purses when our funds run low and who to go to for help when one of our members gets arrested."

Ruth raised her hand in mock surrender. "Forgive me, I didn't realize what a valuable commodity gossip is."

"And it's fun, too, don't forget that." Octavia took a quick drink. "Now, what else do you need to know?"

"What about Chloe Attwater and Thea Stanway?" She took another sip and promised herself she'd not drink it all. But goodness, it was the best wine she'd ever drunk.

"Chloe Attwater is a mystery," Octavia said. "There were rumors that she was engaged out in India and then the fellow died so she married an American. But I don't know much about that. All I do know is that when she returned to London, she had enough money to buy her way into any social circle in England."

"I've heard that." Ruth knocked back the last of the wine and held out her glass to her friend.

Octavia took it, finished her own wine, and then got up. "What was odd was that Mrs. Attwater didn't buy her way into anything except Helena and Isabelle's gardening club." She poured them both another glass of claret. "What's more, Mrs. Attwater is still a very lovely woman, but she's gone out of her way to avoid entanglements with any eligible men. Lord Derring was supposedly smitten with her, but she made it clear she wasn't interested."

"I don't understand why Mrs. Attwater wanted to reacquaint herself with the women she'd known back then," Ruth mused. "From what I've heard, when they were all in India, they weren't particularly good friends even then. So why buy her way into their circle now?"

"I don't know, but I'm sure she has her reasons," Octavia said. "Dolly Trainer says she's supportive of women's suffrage and has even given money to our group, but that's the extent of her involvement. Oh and Dolly also mentioned she heard that Mrs. Attwater's housekeeper left India with her when she went to the United States."

"What about Thea Stanway?" Ruth took another sip and promised herself it would be her last.

"I've heard a little about her. When the three women were in India, Helena and Isabelle married fairly high-ranking officers—one a colonel and the other a major, I can't remember who married which—but Thea ended up with a young lieutenant. The gossip was that though she might have married the lowest rank, she outdid the other two because her husband was quite the catch. He was supposedly very handsome and quite a brilliant young man. There was other gossip, too." Her brows drew together as she tried to remember. "I think there was talk that handsome Lieutenant Stanway was straying from his marriage vows with another officer's wife and the only reason blood wasn't shed about it was because he came down with a dreadful illness and left the army. Lucky for him that Thea Stanway had spent so much time in the infirmary. She kept him alive and got him safely home. But he never fully regained his health, and despite her expert nursing, he died."

"I've heard that all the officers' ladies volunteered in the infirmary and they were a great help." Ruth finished her wine and put the glass down.

"A great help," Octavia scoffed. "Is that what you've heard? I doubt it's true. The army medics and the trained nurses did the real work and still do in most postings. The women just played about reading to the soldiers and writing letters for them. The only one of that group that did any real work was Thea Stanway. Her brother was a doctor, and supposedly, she knew as much as he did."

CHAPTER 7

The day had clouded over by the time the inspector, Barnes, and Constable Griffiths arrived outside the dingy brown brick building that housed Hiram Filmore's business. The establishment was at the end of a busy street beside a secondhand furniture shop and across from a workingman's café and a bustling warehouse. The only indication that the place was a business was a small sign on the front door that read, H. FILMORE, SUPPLIER OF EXOTIC PLANTS, SEEDS, AND HERBS.

"Let's hope these keys work." Barnes put the first one into the lock and heaved a sigh of relief when he heard a faint click. He turned the handle and shoved the door open.

"Good," Witherspoon said as they crossed the threshold. "Now we'll just have to find out what the second key opens," he said.

The day had clouded over and blinds covered all the windows, but inside, there was a surprising amount of light. A

brightly polished, round oak claw-foot table and three matching chairs stood next to one of the front windows and beside
it stood what looked like an apothecary cabinet, but when
Witherspoon moved closer to it, he saw the names of flowers
written in fancy script on the small, square drawers. Along
the far wall, rows of long, flat drawers were built into the wall
and went as high as a tall man's waist. A long counter ran
along the opposite side of the room and ended at a metal set
of bars that stretched the breadth of the property and ran from
the ceiling to the floor. There was a gate in the center of it.

Barnes pointed at the contraption. "Ye gods, he's got a
ruddy wrought iron fence in the middle of his shop. Good
Lord, look at that. No wonder it's so bloomin' bright in here.
Half of the roof's been taken off and covered with glass."

They all moved to the gate and peered through the bars.
Plants in various stages of growth were displayed in neat
rows. Some were mere trays of seedlings, some sprouts
leading to the back three rows, which were blooming flowers in reds, pinks, purple, white, yellow, and golds.

"He'd not just got light in here"—Constable Griffiths
pointed through the bars to his right—"there's heat radia-
tors and empty misting pans as well."

"Guess he wanted the place to be a bit like the jungles."
Barnes looked at Witherspoon and then held up the key ring
they'd taken from Filmore's flat. "Should I give the lock on
the gate a try, sir? At least then we'd know what two of the
keys opened?" The inspector nodded and Barnes shoved the
second key into the lock. It clicked and he pushed it open.

"I know a bit about plants, sir," Griffiths offered. "And
I'll do my best to make sure none of them are damaged
if you'd like me to search in here."

"Thank you, Constable." Witherspoon nodded.

"Would you like me to start over there?" Barnes pointed to the counter. "There's probably shelves under there."

"Yes, and I'll start with the drawers along the wall," Witherspoon said.

Witherspoon started at the corner nearest the street. He squatted down and pulled out the bottom drawer. Surprisingly, it was empty. He went to the next one up, yanked it open, and saw that it was filled with burlap bags of various sizes, tiny clay pots stacked neatly in rows, and a tray of flat wooden sticks. The rest of the drawers in the row contained the same, so he moved farther down the wall, started again at the bottom drawer, and yanked it open. This one was filled with seed catalogs. He groaned inwardly, pulled the top one out, and saw that it was from America. He fanned the pages, found nothing, and took out the next one. All of the drawers in the row were filled with seed catalogs; there were dozens of foreign ones in languages he didn't recognize, half a dozen in French—which he did recognize—three from Canada, and one from Australia. He went through each and every one. By the time he'd finished every drawer in the row, his fingers hurt and his knees were killing him. He stood up. "Any luck, Constable Barnes?"

"Not yet, sir." Barnes held up a stack of paper. "He's got written care instructions for every ruddy plant in the world." He slapped them onto the counter and then reached underneath and pulled out a file box. "And this is filled with maps. I think they're from when he was out in the wild, sir, in India and even further east. He's marked where he found some of his specimens."

"I've found something, sir," Constable Griffiths shouted. He charged through the gate carrying a black metal box the size of a carpetbag and raced to the counter. Barnes pushed the file box out of the way to make room for it as Griffiths put it down. Witherspoon joined them.

"It's very heavy, sir. It was shoved back against the wall behind a bin of fertilizer."

"You mean manure?" Barnes pulled a face as he caught a whiff of the box.

"Yes, sir," Griffiths said with a quick grin. "And as you can see, it stinks to high heaven."

"But it's a clever place to hide something," Witherspoon muttered. "No one except a policemen would voluntarily go near a manure bin. Let's get it open."

Barnes pulled the key ring out of his pocket, found the smallest of the three keys, and inserted it into the lock. "Ah, it seems to have done the trick, sir." Inside was a packet of letters tied together with a blue ribbon and a cream-colored piece of stationery folded neatly in half. Witherspoon reached for the piece of paper, opened it, and read.

Mr. Filmore,

I have urgent business with you. Please come to my conservatory on June 15th at 11:00 A.M. Kindly bring me another specimen of a red vanda. The one you recently sold me has died.

Helena Rayburn

"June fifteenth is the day of the murder." Barnes looked at Witherspoon. "And she did instruct him to bring her a red vanda."

"If the note is really from her," Witherspoon pointed out. "It could easily be from someone else."

"That's easy enough to check, sir. We can obtain a sample of her handwriting and compare it with the note," Griffiths added helpfully. A split second later, his eyes widened and a flush crept up his cheeks. "Of course, you already know to do that, I am sorry. I didn't mean to speak out of turn, sir."

"It's quite all right, Constable," Witherspoon said kindly. "And you're correct, a handwriting sample should do the trick." He put the note back in the box, pulled out the stack of letters, and set them on the counter. "Let's see what's in here." The ribbon was loose enough for him to pull the top one out. He slid out the letter, opened it, and read it. Then he handed it to Constable Barnes before turning to Griffiths. "I want you to take charge of the Rayburn house. Get over there now and tell the constable at the front to guard the back of the property and make sure no one leaves. You take the front door. We'll send you some extra men as soon as we get back to the station."

"Yes, sir." Griffiths nodded. "What should we do if Mrs. Rayburn attempts to leave the city, sir?"

"Stop her and contact me immediately," he ordered.

The others were seated around the kitchen table by the time Mrs. Jeffries arrived for their afternoon meeting. "I'm so sorry I'm late, but the traffic was dreadful and I foolishly took a hansom cab instead of the train." She shed her bonnet and gloves as she rushed to the coat tree.

"Take a minute to catch your breath, we've all just sat down." The cook put a plate of shortbread biscuits next to the big, brown teapot.

As soon as the housekeeper took her seat, Betsy said, "May I go first? Amanda has been fussy all afternoon and I don't know how long she'll stay asleep." Much to the annoyance of Luty Belle, the little one was in her cot in Mrs. Goodge's room.

"But you can't leave, you need to hear what we've learned today," Phyllis protested as she poured a cup of tea and passed it to Mrs. Jeffries.

"Smythe can catch me up. I spoke to a housemaid from the Stanway home. I caught her when she slipped out to meet her young man." Betsy grinned. "She doesn't think much of her mistress and says that underneath that smile Mrs. Stanway shows the world, she's a right mean-spirited cow and that she'll do anything to get back at someone she thinks has wronged her, even if it takes her years."

"How does she know such a thing?" Mrs. Goodge demanded.

"Because right after Susan, that's the maid's name, was hired, she overheard Mrs. Stanway tell Mrs. Martell that the two servants that had just left her to go work for Mrs. Rayburn better plan on staying at the Rayburn house until the day they died, because they'd never get a reference from her."

"Surely it's normal to be a bit annoyed when a trusted

friend steals your cook and a housemaid." Ruth looked at Mrs. Jeffries. "It was a cook and a maid, wasn't it?"

"That's what Constable Barnes said." Mrs. Jeffries took a piece of shortbread off the plate. "But you'd think she'd be more angry at her friend rather than her old staff. The constable also said Helena Rayburn offered higher wages that Mrs. Stanway couldn't match. Surely, Mrs. Stanway could understand why her servants moved on."

"She doesn't care why," Betsy shook her head. "She still feels hard done by and she's still angry with the two of them," Betsy insisted. "And it's been over a year. Yesterday, a letter came for the maid and Susan said she saw Mrs. Stanway put it in her pocket. Susan thought she was going to take it to the Rayburn house and pass it along, but later that day, when the cook went to the wet larder to get the meat for dinner, Susan saw Mrs. Stanway lift the plate on the cooker and shove the letter into the fire. Susan said it scared her a bit. I think that's the only reason she talked to me today. She needed to tell someone."

"She's probably worried over what Mrs. Stanway might do if she leaves," Phyllis said.

"Probably." Betsy cocked her head in the direction of Mrs. Goodge's room. "Let me finish this quickly, I think I hear Amanda thrashing about in her cot. Susan also says that the woman is such a terrible penny-pincher. She claims Mrs. Stanway sneaks into the kitchen and borrows her cloak if the weather's bad."

"Why would that make her a penny-pincher?" Wiggins asked.

"Ma . . . ma . . ." Amanda's shrill cry was loud enough that they all heard it.

Betsy got up. "Susan says Mrs. Stanway does it so she won't wear out her own things. Mind you, she admitted she'd never actually caught her in the act. But recently, when the mistress was out, Susan would snatch the opportunity to sneak out and have a word with her young man, but twice now, her cloak wasn't on the peg by the back door. The first time it happened, she just assumed she'd left it upstairs, but then it happened again, and later, she found it hanging where it was supposed to be. She said it was very damp."

"That household sounds right miserable," Phyllis declared.

"Luckily for the servants, Susan said that Mrs. Stanway is gone for hours and hours most days so they don't have to put up with too much from her." Betsy hurried off toward the cook's room just as Amanda's cries turned into bellows.

"If she's as miserly as the maid claims, where does she go?" Mrs. Jeffries mused. "She wouldn't be out shopping."

"I know," Wiggins said. "I didn't have much luck today, but I was able to have a quick chat with a Ronnie White, he's a street lad who does odd jobs for some of the households on Bellwood Place, and he says that Mrs. Stanway comes to visit her old nanny quite a bit. Last time she come, she brought a nice bottle of Laphroaig. Ronnie saw it sticking out of her shopping basket. Seems the nanny is from Islay and likes a good nip now and then."

"Thea Stanway can't be that cheap if she's buying Laphroaig." Hatchet put down his mug. "It's a rather expensive liquor. If no one else objects, I'll tell you what I found out today. I learned a few more details about Major Edward Martell's death."

"We all know he was a drunk and his death was supposedly an accident," Luty reminded him. "So what did you find out?"

He grinned at her. "A number of things, madam. To begin with, there was a lot of gossip when it happened—"

"We know that, too," Luty interrupted. "Tell us something we don't know."

"I would if you'd give me a chance," he retorted. "My source, who was in India at the time this happened, said that the inquiry into Major Martell's death was done hurriedly. However, lest you think it was because the army was trying to cover up a murder, it wasn't. They were trying to spare the Martell family further embarrassment."

Luty looked skeptical. "Why should they care about that?"

"Because Martell's older brother worked as an undersecretary to someone of importance at the War Department. The family had already suffered substantial embarrassment over the man's drinking, and when that was added to the gossip Martell's marriage to Isabelle had caused, there was substantial pressure applied to put the matter to rest as quietly as possible."

"What kind of gossip was there about the marriage?" Luty demanded.

"The usual sort. Isabelle claimed that Martell had seduced her with a promise of marriage. But he reneged on the promise supposedly because his family objected. Isabelle claimed she was now"—he paused and cleared his throat—"in the family way. Martell's commander was a staunch member of the Church of Scotland and ordered

Martell to do the right thing. Not long after the marriage, Martell began drinking."

"What happened to the baby?" Betsy asked. She held a very cranky-looking toddler in her arms. Amanda stared at them for a moment, then promptly stuck her thumb in her mouth and burrowed her head in her mother's neck.

"My source didn't know." Hatchet shrugged. "All he knew was the Martells never had a child."

"Just because the army claimed it was an accident, that don't mean that Isabelle didn't shove him off that balcony," Luty insisted.

"But there's more evidence she didn't than that she did," Hatchet shot back. "At the inquest, the servants testified they had to break the balcony door open. He'd locked it before he fell."

"Could he have been committing suicide?" Mrs. Jeffries asked.

"Probably not." Hatchet shook his head. "His manservant testified Martell always locked the door. It was his habit to go out there every night after dinner and drink himself into a stupor."

"Well, dang, that lets Isabelle off the hook," Luty muttered.

"So it would seem," Mrs. Jeffries said. "And even if there were evidence that Martell's death was suspicious, it doesn't seem to have anything to do with Hiram Filmore's murder."

"Isabelle Martell is a social climber," Ruth blurted out. She gave Hatchet an embarrassed smile. "Oh dear, sorry, I know it's not my turn. Please, go ahead and finish up."

"No apology is necessary, I was quite through," he replied.

"Go on, Ruth," Mrs. Jeffries urged.

"As I said, my source told me that Isabelle Martell is a social climber, and I'm not talking about an ordinary person who hopes to improve their lot in life by moving up a bit." She told them what she'd heard from her friend Octavia Wells. "I think what I'm trying to say is that if you're as concerned about social status as Mrs. Martell, you wouldn't take kindly to someone dredging up old gossip about your husband's death. But now that I've said it, it sounds rather silly as a motive for murder. But that's not all I heard from my source." She told them what she'd learned about Thea Stanway and Chloe Attwater.

"Now that is right interestin'," Smythe said. "It was Mrs. Attwater who hinted to the inspector that Isabelle Martell pushed her husband off that balcony and made sure she told him that Mrs. Rayburn was involved in a man's drownin'. Blast a Spaniard, I think your source is right. Mrs. Attwater's got 'er own reasons for wantin' to be friends with the other three ladies."

"And I don't think it's because of what she told the inspector," Phyllis interrupted. "She told him she'd gone to them because she didn't know anyone in London, but that can't be right. Rich people are accepted everywhere they go."

"That's true enough." Smythe knew that relationships among women tended to be more complex than the ones he shared with his mates. He looked at Ruth. "And your source 'as no idea what those reasons could be?"

"I'm afraid not," Ruth admitted. "Not only that, but

Octavia, she's my source, says that Mrs. Attwater's house-keeper is an Indian woman and that Mrs. Attwater took her with her when she went to America."

"We knew that someone had accompanied Mrs. Attwater to America," Mrs. Jeffries said. "But we didn't know who it was until now."

Betsy walked back and forth in front of the staircase, gently bouncing her cranky daughter on her hip to keep Amanda quiet so she could listen further. "I don't know, but I do think it odd." She raised her voice a bit to make sure they could hear her. "Chloe Attwater went to India as a governess, not a member of the military or the upper class. I can see why she went to America—her fiancé died and she was probably sick and tired of taking care of some-one else's children. So if an opportunity came her way, she'd take it. But why would the other lady go? I've heard that Indian women are very close to their families. So why would this lady leave hers and go to a foreign country?"

"Indian women are close to their families." Hatchet helped himself to another cup of tea. "And you're right, Mrs. Attwater is wealthy now, but she was just a govern-ess back then. She wouldn't have had the money to hire a servant to accompany her to San Francisco. I do think the situation is worth looking into."

"What's worth looking into?" Mrs. Goodge demanded. "Maybe the woman went because she was poor and needed a position. That's generally why people leave their loved ones and move about. They've got no choice unless they want to starve to death." Her voice was harsh and high, loud enough that Betsy gave a worried glance toward her husband as Amanda started to whimper. Smythe got up and scooped the baby out of his wife's arms and nestled her against his chest.

"Unfortunately, that's very true," Hatchet said quickly.

Mrs. Goodge closed her eyes as she realized that everyone was staring at her. "I'm sorry, I didn't mean to snap at all of you. I didn't sleep well last night and I'm tired." She bit her lip and looked toward the staircase, where Smythe was cuddling Amanda and crooning softly in her ear. "Is my darling alright? I didn't mean to scare her."

"It'll take more than a raised voice to scare our baby." Luty reached over and patted Mrs. Goodge's arm. "You don't look like you feel very good."

Mrs. Jeffries felt awful. She wished she'd minded her own business and not encouraged Mrs. Goodge to confide in her. The cook was still in a very dark place. Talking about her past hadn't helped her find peace, but instead, now that she'd brought the incident into the light, she seemed even more guilt ridden and miserable than before. "Why don't you go lie down," she suggested. "Phyllis and I can manage dinner tonight."

"I'm fine," Mrs. Goodge insisted. She took a breath and forced a weak smile. "Besides, I've got a bit to report and I want to do my part." She told them what she'd learned from Eliza Baker. "Thea Stanway isn't just nosy, she's a busybody, too." She took a deep, steadying breath as she completed her recital.

"But she had a handsome husband that she must have loved very much," Phyllis pointed out. "Maybe if he'd lived, she might have been a better person."

"We'll never know, will we," Mrs. Goodge replied. "That's it for me. I know it's not much, but it's something."

"We never know what will or won't be important," Mrs. Jeffries said. "Now, if no one else has anything to add." She looked at Phyllis, Luty, and Smythe, waited a moment, and when none of them spoke up, she repeated what Dr. Bosworth had told her. When she was finished, she glanced at the faces around the table and concluded the others looked just as confused as she felt.

"Here's the tea, sir," Barnes sat down opposite the inspector and pushed a mug across the desk. "We're in luck, they just made a fresh pot. I've sent two more constables to the Rayburn home. Do you think she'll make a run for it, sir?"

"I think it's very possible, Constable." Witherspoon picked up his mug and took a sip. They were in the duty office of the Ladbroke Road Police Station, and he was hoping to give his aching knees and feet a rest.

"You think she's guilty, then?"

Witherspoon pointed at the stack of letters on the desk. "You read the first one, what do you think?"

"I think if the rest of them are like the one we saw, she's got a powerful motive for murder."

"Let's see what the rest of them have to say." He slid the ribbon off, divided the stack evenly, and handed half the stack to Barnes. "You go through this lot and I'll do the—" He broke off as the door opened and Constable Roberts poked his head inside.

"Excuse me, sir, but the victim's military service record has arrived from the War Office." He held up a large brown envelope.

"Bring it in, Constable." Witherspoon took the file, nodded his thanks, and moved the pile of letters to the side of the desk. Opening the file, he frowned, "Goodness, there's only three pages here." He shoved his spectacles farther up his nose and began reading. "Filmore entered the army in September of 1871 out of the Chatham Depot. He entered the Forty-fourth East Essex as a private, and after six months there, his regiment went to Madras."

"He joined in 1871, sir?" Barnes asked. "That's after the War Office reduced the enlistment period to twelve years."

Impressed, the inspector looked at him. "You have some interesting facts at your fingertips, Constable."

"I only know that because I've a cousin who joined the army in October of that year and he only went in because there had been reforms. It was either join the army or go down to the mines and the lad couldn't stand enclosed places."

Witherspoon went back to the file. "There's a few dark spots on his record, but nothing too awful, just the usual occasional fighting and drunkenness." He handed the first page to Barnes and continued reading. "He was wounded in 1876 but stayed on and ended up as a sergeant. His last posting was in the infirmary. He left the army in October of 1882." He frowned. "But there's a note here saying he stayed on in India as a private businessman working as a procurer of exotic plants and herbs."

He flipped to the last page. "Ah, here's something interesting." He squinted to read the tiny handwriting on the paper. "It's a note from the district administrator in Madras to the commanding officer of the Forty-fourth. It says that Mr. Filmore discharged his duty as a witness in the drowning death of Mr. Anthony Treadwell, and that according to Mr. Filmore's testimony, the death was accidental and not the result of a deliberate action on the part of the regimental officers." He moved the paper closer to the light on his desk. "In addition, it says the statement of Jairaj Dhariwal will not be taken as evidence on this incident as the native man has disappeared and is no longer available to be questioned."

"That doesn't sound good, sir." Barnes raised his eyebrows. "He disappeared after giving a statement but before he could be put under oath?"

"Yes, that's rather suspicious," the inspector agreed. "Once they've given a statement, most witnesses only 'disappear' because someone either buys them off or silences them permanently."

Barnes pointed to the file. "Is there anything else, sir? Anything that might tell us more details about the drowning?"

Witherspoon examined each sheet of paper, both front and back, before shaking his head. "No, nothing, just the cryptic message which I just read. Perhaps the War Office might have some additional details in the regimental files."

"We can ask, sir, but I'd not count on it." Barnes smiled cynically. "From the little hints in that note, it sounds like it was the kind of incident the military likes to keep quiet."

"But Sir Jeremy Sanders is a very influential man," Witherspoon pointed out. "And that might have some bearing on the matter."

"Sir Jeremy is with the Home Office, sir, not the War Department," Barnes reminded him. "And he might have influence, but I doubt that he can force the military to hand over information they want buried unless we can clearly show that the information is related to our case." The constable normally wouldn't argue the point so doggedly. But occasionally, he felt it his duty to keep his inspector from making unnecessary enemies in the government.

"And we can't prove that, can we." Witherspoon sighed. "We've no idea whether or not this incident has any bearing whatsoever on Filmore's murder."

"But you think it does, sir?"

"I do, but a policeman's intuition isn't enough, is it. The principal in the incident wasn't in the army—he is referred to as 'Mr.' Anthony Treadwell."

"If he wasn't in the army, what was the fellow doing in India?" Barnes put the pages back in the file folder.

"He might have been there on business," Witherspoon speculated. He wasn't sure what to make of this new turn of events, and this, coupled with everything else they'd learned today, was both enlightening and confusing.

"Should we get started on the letters, then?" Barnes tapped the top of his stack.

Witherspoon nodded in agreement. "We should be able to make some headway before it's time to go."

"Are you sure you don't want to go lie down?" Mrs. Jeffries put the last saucer in the drying rack. "Phyllis and I can easily manage the inspector's supper. You've done all the work and even we can't muck up your wonderful lamb stew."

Mrs. Goodge put the lid back on the top of the black cast-iron pot and gave her friend a grateful smile. "It's kind of you to offer, Hepzibah, but if I sleep now, I'll be awake all night. Now stop worrying about me, I'll be right as rain in a day or two."

Through the window over the sink, Mrs. Jeffries saw a hansom pull up outside and the inspector step out. "I'd best get upstairs, he's home."

"Dinner will be served in half an hour. That should give him time to give you a complete report." Mrs. Goodge opened the oven door and carefully took out an apple tart.

Mrs. Jeffries nodded in acknowledgment as she raced to the back stairs, took them at a dead run, and then barely beat the inspector to the front hall.

"You're home, sir." She reached for his bowler. "Mrs. Goodge says dinner will be ready in half an hour."

"Excellent. That will give us time for a lovely sip of sherry." He headed to his study, and a few moments later, she was pouring both of them a drink.

"You seem decidedly more cheerful this evening." She handed him his glass and took her usual spot.

"I am. We made real progress today." He took a quick drink.

"Of course you did, sir. You always do. Now, don't keep me in suspense. You look as pleased as Samson does when he steals a nice chunk of meat off Mrs. Goodge's plate. Tell me what's got you smiling this evening?"

He grinned proudly. "I think we're going to solve this case very, very soon."

"Does that mean you have a suspect?"

"Yes."

Taken aback by the certainty in his tone, she tried to think of what to ask next. "You have proof that one of your suspects is guilty?"

"Let me amend my original statement. We don't have

absolute proof as yet, but yes, we now have a very strong suspect for Filmore's murder. It's Helena Rayburn."

"Helena Rayburn?" Mrs. Jeffries repeated. "Why would she kill him?"

"Blackmail," he said.

"Filmore was blackmailing her?"

"We think it is very possible." He put his glass on the side table and leaned back against the cushions. "From the beginning, her behavior has been suspicious. She claims she didn't look at the murder weapon and so she couldn't identify it as her property; she lied about the bloodstained duster, apron, and gloves; and she was out of the house at the time of the murder."

"Which means she had both the weapon and the opportunity," Mrs. Jeffries concluded. Even as the words left her mouth, she had one of those strange feelings that often hit her when they were on a case. She couldn't put her finger on it, but the inkling of an idea was trying to take root in her mind and she was suddenly certain that the inspector shouldn't stop looking into this case.

"That's right, but what was confusing was the motive. Why would an upper-class woman suddenly take it into her head to commit murder? We think we found our answer this afternoon when we were searching Filmore's shop." He picked up his glass again and glanced at the clock.

"It appears you've had a very successful day, sir." She pretended to pout. "But aren't you being just a bit mean?"

"Mean?" He stared at her in some surprise.

"You're telling me the conclusion without giving me the narrative. It's a bit like rushing to the back of one of

Mr. Conan Doyle's stories to see how it ends. You know how I love hearing about all the details of the investigation, sir. You're so very talented in, well, painting the picture of how your methods work."

His eyes widened as he stared at her, and for a split second, she thought she'd laid it on a bit too thick.

But then he laughed self-consciously. "Mrs. Jeffries, you flatter me. But if you want me to, uh, paint a picture for you with the details, I shall certainly oblige. Let me start at the beginning."

"Thank you, sir,"

He began by telling her about the meeting with Filmore's landlady before moving on to what they found in his flat.

"How much money was there altogether?" she asked, when he paused to take another sip of sherry.

"Over two hundred pounds, which we took into evidence. I expect once we can ascertain who the man's heirs might be, the money will eventually become part of his estate."

"Was there anything in the flat that indicated he had a solicitor?" She took a sip from her own glass.

"No, not in the flat or in his shop. Constable Barnes asked Mrs. Rhodes if she knew if he had a legal representative, but she had no idea." He continued with his narrative, going into great detail, describing the shop and then rather dramatically raising his voice when he described the letter he'd read.

"It was the stack of letters that led you to believe Mrs. Rayburn is the killer?" she pressed.

"Of course. She signed them 'Your loving Helena,' and in one letter, there was a reference to a 'Malcolm.'"

"And that's Mrs. Rayburn's late husband's Christian name," she murmured. "But was there anything that made you think Filmore had used the letters to blackmail her? The only other thing you said you found in the box was a letter from her to Filmore asking for another red vanda."

"She has claimed all along that she had no idea why Filmore was in her conservatory, but the evidence suggests otherwise." He drained his drink and put the glass down. "If the handwriting in the note is hers, it'll prove she's been lying all along."

Mrs. Jeffries nodded, though she wondered if comparing the handwriting was the best way to prove the woman a murderer. Handwriting could be faked. Phyllis, oddly enough, had a rare talent as a forger.

"But it wasn't just what we found at his flat and his business premises which might be useful to us; we also had a look at Filmore's service record." He told her what they'd found in Filmore's file and how both he and the constable found the "disappearance" of a witness in the drowning of Anthony Treadwell very suspicious. "We suspect, but we can't be sure, of course, that in some way Helena Rayburn is connected to this matter as well."

"Are you going to ask her directly?"

"From what we've seen of Mrs. Rayburn, I doubt she'd tell the truth, and unfortunately, Constable Barnes and I both realize that getting the facts about an incident that happened years ago in India might be impossible. Nonetheless, we're going to try."

"I'm sure you'll find a way, sir," Mrs. Jeffries murmured. Her mind was working furiously. Like the inspector and Barnes, she, too, was always suspicious when witnesses to a death were no longer available. "But if Filmore was a blackmailer, perhaps Mrs. Rayburn wasn't his only victim."

"We're looking into that possibility as well," he agreed. "But the only evidence we have thus far is the love letters Helena Rayburn wrote to a man named Nigel."

"She never used his surname?"

"No, but from the content of the letters, we can infer they were all written while both of them were in India."

"Which is where Mr. Filmore spent the last years of his enlistment."

"That's correct." Witherspoon finished his sherry. "And though we don't know that he had any knowledge of what she was up to back then, we know he now had possession of some very damaging letters."

"But if she wrote them in India, isn't there a chance they were written before she married her late husband?" Mrs. Jeffries pointed out. "In which case, they couldn't be used to really blackmail Mrs. Rayburn."

"But they could," he protested. "From the contents of the letters, we're positive he was married. She mentions his 'spouse' several times in the correspondence."

"From what we know of Helena Rayburn, she'd do anything to avoid a scandal, especially now."

"Why now?" He gave her a puzzled look.

For a moment, she panicked. "Didn't you tell me yesterday that she was trying to get onto the Narcissus Committee at the Royal Horticultural Society?" She was bluffing but hoped that he'd told her so many things he'd not realize this may or may not have been one of them.

"Oh, yes, I did, I'd forgotten. I suppose that this is the

sort of scandalous tidbit that might turn some members of the Royal Horticultural Society against her appointment. She'd not want that."

"Is it possible that Filmore wasn't a blackmailer, that he was running a legitimate business?" Mrs. Jeffries didn't think it likely, but she didn't want the inspector acting precipitously by arresting Helena Rayburn. They needed more facts.

"Well, I suppose it's possible." He looked doubtful. "His landlady spoke highly of his character. She thinks he was the one who gave her the return ticket to Bournemouth."

"What?"

"Mrs. Rhodes says the ticket was shoved through her mail slot. It was in a plain brown envelope with her name and address hand printed on it. She assumed her sister had sent it. But when she met her sister, she hadn't. She then said the next likely person to have done it was Mr. Filmore, that he'd often given her small gifts in the past and that she'd mentioned to him only the previous week how much she missed seeing her family."

"But aside from an envelope full of money, you didn't find any other indication that Filmore was a blackmailer?" Mrs. Jeffries asked. "I mean, you didn't come across any ledgers or anything like that?"

"Just ordinary business ledgers."

Mrs. Jeffries sipped her drink as her mind raced. There was too much information, too many facts to absorb all at once. "Well, sir, I think you've done an excellent job today, and what's more, I have every faith in your ability to find out all the facts in this case, including the incident in India."

He laughed uneasily. "You give me too much credit, Mrs. Jeffries. Besides, the War Office isn't going to be forthcoming about an old scandal in the military."

"Of course they aren't, sir." She reached for his now-empty glass, got up, and poured them both a second drink. "But you'll not let that stop you." She smiled confidently as she handed him his glass. "You'll do precisely what you always do, and what's more, sir, you know it'll work."

"And what's that?"

"Gossip, sir. You'll pay attention to housemaids, cooks, boot boys, and street lads, and you'll find out everything. You always do. Why, you've already learned so very much that I'm sure once you have another chat with the Attwater, Martell, and Stanway households, you'll find out everything you need to know."

The clock was striking ten when Mrs. Jeffries came downstairs to lock up the house. After dinner the inspector had "popped over" to have a quick drink with Lady Cannonberry, something he'd taken to doing three or four times a week. She was glad she'd held her tongue and not badgered poor Ruth into trying to get even more information out of the inspector when they had a case. The two of them deserved their private time alone. But he was home and safely abed now, as was the rest of the household.

As she came down the back stairs into the hall, she glanced toward Mrs. Goodge's quarters and sent up a silent prayer that the poor woman was sleeping properly. Reaching the back door, she stepped outside and quietly closed it behind her.

Stepping to the edge of the terrace, she took a deep

breath, inhaling the scents of jasmine and honeysuckle. The summer night was warm and inviting. She stepped to the edge of the small terrace and stared into the communal garden. From down the oval pathway, she could hear the clink of glasses and the cheerful voices of dinner guests who'd spilled out onto the first-floor balcony of the Amberson house, two doors down. Many of their neighbors were still up and the light spilling from their open windows gave enough illumination for her to see as she moved farther into the communal garden.

Crossing the gravel pathway, she stepped onto the grass and went toward the huge trees in the center. As she walked, she went over everything she could remember about the case.

Was Filmore a blackmailer? Appearances could be deceiving, and though there was some evidence he wasn't just an ordinary businessman, was there enough to conclude he'd been killed because he blackmailed people? If so, was Helena Rayburn his only victim?

When she reached the middle of the garden, she stopped beneath the spreading branches of oaks and let her mind wander. One question kept nagging at her. What was it that had precipitated Filmore's murder? They'd all been in India together; now they were all here. But from what they'd learned, Helena Rayburn, Isabelle Martell, and Thea Stanway, or the warring widows as she liked to think of them, had been back in London for close to ten years. Filmore wasn't a recent arrival, either; he'd been here long enough to establish a profitable business and make connections with his former acquaintances from India.

So why now? There had to be a catalyst, a compelling

reason to make someone decide he needed to be killed right now. Could it have been the arrival of Chloe Attwater? But she'd been back in London for over a year, so again, why now?

But was that even the right question? Perhaps there were other ways of looking at the situation. Why had Mrs. Attwater, who apparently had more money than the Bank of England, deliberately set out to befriend women who'd snubbed her in India? Did she want to rub their noses in her wealth? But if she'd wanted to do that, she could easily have gone into a higher circle and lorded it over them. Both Isabelle Martell and, to some extent, Helena Rayburn were social climbers and would have chafed at seeing a woman they snubbed moving easily among the rich and powerful. But Chloe Attwater hadn't done that. Instead she'd bought her way into their club. Why?

A shout of laughter cut through the night and she realized her feet were damp as the dew permeated her thin shoes. She started toward the house.

Perhaps the murder had nothing to do with India. Perhaps it was something else altogether. But what? Neither the police nor the household had come across anyone else who wanted Hiram Filmore dead. But perhaps they weren't looking in the right places.

CHAPTER 8

⟡

The scent of vanilla and sugar filled the kitchen of Upper Edmonton Gardens as Mrs. Jeffries, accompanied by a very cranky Samson, carried the last of the inspector's breakfast dishes down the back stairs. Their morning meeting was over and everyone was out on the hunt.

The cook put a baking tray of freshly made biscuits on top of the cooker and turned to the housekeeper. "I've got three sources coming by today so I thought I'd best do a bit more baking."

Samson, who obviously felt he'd been shortchanged on his breakfast, made a pitiful meow and trotted over to his empty food dish.

"Oh, my poor baby, I've got some nice sausage and egg leftovers for you." Mrs. Goodge shuffled to the sink, where a plate of scraps was at the ready.

Mrs. Jeffries put the teapot and two cups in the sink and

then went to the pine sideboard. Opening the top drawer, she pulled out the household ledger and tried to decide whether or not to risk a confrontation. At both breakfast and their morning meeting, the cook's red and watery eyes, pale complexion, and slumped shoulders made it clear she'd not slept well. Mrs. Jeffries took the ledger and slapped it onto the table. She opened it and flicked to the current page and then decided to speak her mind. It might be uncomfortable for both of them, but it was time for Mrs. Goodge to come to terms with the past. If this kept up, Mrs. Jeffries beloved friend was going to end up sick or dead.

Mrs. Goodge bent down and dumped the food in Samson's bowl. He shoved his head in while the last morsel was still in the air. A bit of egg bounced off his ear and rolled onto the floor.

Mrs. Jeffries opened her mouth, but before she could speak, Mrs. Goodge turned to her and said, "I didn't sleep a wink last night and that was good."

"Good?"

"It made me think, and once I started thinking, I came to a decision." She straightened, brushed her hands against the towel draped over the sink edge, and came to the table. "This case has been hard on me because it reminded me so much of Janet Lawler, and as I told you, once I had her in my mind, I felt so bad, so guilty."

"Yes, I know, but of course, we all have incidents in our past that make us feel that way." Mrs. Jeffries wasn't sure if she ought to keep talking or just shut up and listen.

She opted for the second option as Mrs. Goodge pulled out her chair and sat down. "The mere mention of India was enough to make me feel like I'd committed murder," she said. "But last night, I realized something important. Janet's death wasn't my fault."

Surprised, Mrs. Jeffries stared at her. "Of course it wasn't your doing. People make their own choices and most of those choices have nothing to do with anyone else."

Mrs. Goodge took off her spectacles, laid them down, rubbed her eyes, and then gave Mrs. Jeffries a bleary smile. "I know you've been worried about me, Hepzibah, and I appreciate it. As you've said, we're family, and I never thought to have any sort of family."

"Of course we're family." Tears pooled in Mrs. Jeffries' eyes but she fought them back to save them both embarrassment.

"Despite looking a bit like a walking corpse this morning," Mrs. Goodge continued, "I'm feeling better than I have since we got this case. I'm not responsible for Janet Lawler's death. No one is. Taking a human life is God's decision, not mine, and I'm ashamed I was arrogant enough to think otherwise. The Lord for whatever his reasons decided it was her time to die. She didn't get the sack because of that one incident, which, I will admit, might have been my fault. She got the sack because of a number of other incidents, most of which happened well before I was put in charge of the kitchen. The previous cook tried to get her sacked half a dozen times, but the mistress, being a bit on the softhearted side, wouldn't do it until the incident with the platter."

"I'm so glad you've come to this conclusion," Mrs. Jeffries exclaimed. "I hoped you wouldn't go on like you've been doing. I've been very concerned. At our age, Mrs. Goodge, our mental and emotional states can easily have an effect on our general health." When Dr. Bosworth was escorting her out of St. Thomas' yesterday, she had heard him use those very words. They'd happened upon a young medical man berating an elderly woman because she'd forgotten to take her medicine as prescribed. The young doctor had been so harsh, the elderly woman had started wailing, and Dr. Bosworth had lost his temper and lectured the fellow in front of half a dozen staff and visitors.

"I suppose I just needed to face the situation," Mrs. Goodge said. "And last night I did. About half past two I realized I couldn't have gotten her sacked—I wasn't that powerful nor had I any influence on the mistress."

"I'm so relieved, Mrs. Goodge," Mrs. Jeffries admitted. "We need you on this case. I've a feeling that the beginnings of this murder started a long time ago in India."

"And you're hoping my old sources might know something?" She yawned and got to her feet. "Let's hope so. I've got three of them coming in today. I'd best make another cup of tea. I don't want to be falling asleep just when they've got something interesting to say."

"Cor blimey, this isn't my day." Wiggins ducked into the mews as he heard Constable Barnes' voice coming out of the hansom that had pulled up a few feet away from where he stood. He flattened himself along the edge of the fence and prayed that the constables the inspector had watching the house didn't spot him.

He breathed a sigh of relief as the inspector's voice faded as he and the constable moved closer to the Rayburn home. Wiggins stood there for a moment, wondering what to do next. He supposed he ought to go to one of the other ladies' neighborhoods and try his luck there; they all had servants and surely someone would stick their nose out the back door.

Wiggins went to the end of the mews and glanced down the street. Except for the constable at the front door, there was no one else about who might know him, so if he crossed the street, he could get past without being noticed. He stepped off the pavement just as a housemaid carrying a shopping basket appeared from the side of the Rayburn home. She turned toward the Kensington High Street. Wiggins was after her like a shot.

He followed her to the corner and waited till she crossed the road before he caught up with her. "Excuse me, miss." He doffed his cap. "But I'm a bit lost. My name is Albert Jones and my mistress has sent me all the way across town to a draper's shop in this area, but I've forgotten the street it's supposed to be on."

She stopped, shifted her shopping basket to her other arm, and studied him suspiciously. Her hair was brown with just a touch of gray at the temples, her eyes blue and deep set beneath heavy brows, and her features ordinary.

He gave her a timid smile as she looked him over. She must have decided to help him because she nodded curtly. "There are two of them close by." She pointed straight ahead. "Mecham's is on the Kensington High Street or there's Martins and Sons on the Cromwell Road."

Wiggins hesitated. If he guessed wrong, she'd go in one direction and he'd be forced to go in another. "Mecham's, that sounds like it," he muttered, trying his best to sound as confused as possible in case she was going toward the other street.

"It's not far." She gave him another appraising glance. "I'm going that way, you can come with me." She started walking again.

"Ta, miss, it's ever so good of you to help me. I get confused in this part of London." He fell into step with her. She was a few years older than he was, and from her reaction, he didn't think she'd get chatty because he flirted with her. "Mind you, I generally don't get sent here but I volunteered to come because I read about that murder."

She snorted. "Like murder, do ya?"

"'Course not," he protested. "No decent person would like murder, but I'll admit to being interested in the subject. After I've saved up enough money to buy my sister a ticket home from Canada, I'm leaving my job and joining the police force. That's the reason I got lost—I came here hoping to get a chance to speak to a constable from the murder house."

"You want to be a police constable." She snorted again. "I don't know why, seems to me most of them spend their time standing about and waiting for something to happen. Did you find the murder house?" She gave him a quick glance.

"I did but the constable standing on the door stoop looked ever so fierce, you know, like he wasn't the chatty type." Wiggins made sure he pronounced his words properly. There was something about this one that made him think she wasn't sympathetic to lazy speech. "I hung out a bit, you know, hoping I could find another one to talk to, but then it got late and I knew my mistress would be angry if I was late getting back. There's three big rugs that need pounding and I'm the only one in the household strong enough to carry them out to the garden."

"So you didn't see which house I came out of." She eyed him speculatively.

"No, I got lost but then I found myself back on Bellwood Place, and from there, I knew I could find my way home. Why? Are you from the murder house?"

"I am, and let me tell you, it's not been a pleasant place since that fellow was found in our conservatory," she replied. "My mistress, who isn't the easiest person to work for to begin with, has made the household even more miserable."

They'd reached another corner and the shops were less than a quarter of a mile away. Wiggins knew he didn't have much time left. "But surely she'd leave someone like you alone, someone smart and reliable. Least that's the way you seem to me." In his experience, flattery almost always worked.

"You'd think so," she agreed with a quick nod of her head. "But her nibs has been a right madam ever since the police came, and just before I left, they were back again. I thought she was going to go mad when Mrs. Clemments came down to the kitchen and told her they were waiting in the drawing room. She started shouting at Mrs. Clemments."

"Is Mrs. Clemments your housekeeper?" he interrupted, though he already knew the answer. Still, it was important to play the part properly.

"That's right, and from the way Mrs. Rayburn was carrying on, you'd have thought it was poor Mrs. Clemments' fault the police had come back. Mind you, she stood up for herself and told the mistress if she didn't want to speak to the police, she could tell them that herself." She came to a halt and turned to look at him. "My name is Amy, Amy Broadhurst, sorry, I should have introduced myself when you told me you was Mr. Albert Jones. But if you don't mind my saying, I'm a bit upset. Hearing the mistress screaming like a common fishwife is enough to send you running for the hills."

"I understand, Miss Broadhurst." He smiled sympathetically. He genuinely felt sorry for her but he was mindful of the role he was playing. "I know how you feel. My mistress has a sharp tongue and a loud voice, too, which is one of the reasons I'm joining the police force."

"Lucky you, you've got a way out." She gave him a sideways glance. "Wish I did, but I'm stuck good and proper. What's worse is that now my conscience is nagging me. I'm not sure what to do about it."

"Worried, what about?" He could see the draper's shop ahead and was desperate to keep her talking.

She stopped, turned, and stared at him intently. "If you're really goin' to be a policeman, maybe you can help me."

Wiggins knew a mistake now would be fatal. He whipped off his flat cap and bobbed his head respectfully. "I'd be pleased to help you in any way I can, miss."

"I just want you to listen and give me your opinion, that's all." She took a breath. "If you're going to be a copper, maybe what I tell you will make you a better one, maybe it'll make you more understandin' when you're talking to people who've had a horrible shock."

"Like finding out murder's been done in your household."

"That's right. The truth is, the police interviewed me and asked me what was what that morning."

"You mean the morning of the murder." He took her arm and gently tugged her to the far side of the pavement, out of the way of the heavy foot traffic.

She bobbed her head. "I was so rattled by what had happened, that I forgot something that might be important, and now with the mistress being in such a state and the police showing back up today, I'm all at sixes and sevens and I don't know what to do."

"I'm a good listener," he assured her. Cor blimey, was she going to say something or not?

"Maybe once I tell it, it'll be easier to speak to that Constable Barnes. Peggy, she's the other housemaid, she spoke to him longer than I did and she thinks he's a decent sort. I wouldn't want him to think I'd lied or was tryin' to protect her nibs."

"I'm sure he'd not think anything of the kind," he encouraged her.

"You see, the constable asked me if I'd seen anything unusual that day, and I told him the truth, that it was a day like any other. We were busy getting ready for a luncheon the mistress was having for her friends. But what I forgot to mention was that I did see something odd."

"What was it?" Was he going to have to drag every single word out of the woman?

"Mrs. Clemments sent me upstairs with the teapot from the silver service, and just as I was passing the front hall, a letter come through the post box. Mrs. Rayburn had just come down the front stairs so she snatched up the letter. I took the pot into the dining room and immediately went back down to the kitchen. But when I passed Mrs. Rayburn, she was reading the note, and now that I think about it, she looked absolutely furious. Right after that, she went out."

Helena Rayburn stared at them through narrowed, angry eyes. "Inspector Witherspoon, your appearance here is outrageous, outrageous I tell you! It was bad enough that you've got policemen surrounding my house and humiliating me in front of my neighbors, but now you're here again. What on earth do you want me to say? I didn't kill that man and I've no idea who did. I don't know why you've focused your attention on me, but it's got to stop. You're not right to badger me like this, not right at all."

"Ma'am—" he tried to interrupt but she kept on talking.

"This harassment must stop," she cried. "I won't let you ruin me. I won't."

"Mrs. Rayburn, I assure you, we're only doing our duty," the inspector said softly.

She glared at them for a moment and then spun around so hard the glass fire screen rattled as her skirt brushed against it. She stood with her back to them and her arms folded across her chest. Once again, she hadn't asked them to sit down. "Ask your wretched questions and then get out."

"Mrs. Rayburn, we've some new evidence we'd like you to explain,"

"New evidence?" She turned to face them. "What are you talking about? There can't be any evidence. I had nothing to do with that man's murder. I've told you, someone got into my conservatory and killed him. It's nothing to do with me."

Witherspoon set the briefcase down, opened it, and

pulled out the note they'd found in the metal box. "We have a note here that appears to have been written by you to Mr. Filmore. In it, you asked him to come to your conservatory on the morning of the murder and bring you another red vanda orchid. Yours had died."

She glanced at the cream-colored paper he held and then shrugged. "I don't know what you're talking about. I wrote no such thing and I certainly didn't tell him to bring me another orchid."

"Please take a look at it." He started across the short space that separated them but she held up her hand.

"There's no need, Inspector. I didn't write it."

"Your signature is on it."

"That doesn't mean I wrote it. I can assure you, even if it has my signature, it's a forgery. I've told you since this wretched incident happened that someone is trying to put the blame for Filmore's death at my door, but I won't have. Do you hear, I won't have it."

"If that's the case, ma'am, we'd like a sample of your handwriting so we can compare it with this."

"Why should I cooperate with you? No matter what I say or do, you find a way of twisting my words and actions."

"That's not so, ma'am. We're only trying to get at the truth." Witherspoon put the note back in the briefcase and pulled out the stack of letters.

"You might want to sit down," Barnes advised. He was propped against the edge of a tall, overstuffed chair with his little brown notebook resting on the top.

She ignored him and kept her gaze on the inspector.

Witherspoon whipped off the ribbon and took out the top one. "I'd like you to read this and then tell me if you can shed any light on the identity of the writer and the recipient."

"Why on earth would I know who wrote it?" But she moved close enough for her to see what he held. "Whatever this nonsense might be, it's nothing to do with me."

He slipped the stationery out of the envelope, unfolded it, and handed it to her in such a way that the writing was clearly visible. She glanced at it with a look of derision, but after a few moments, the expression on her face changed to stunned horror.

"Do you recognize the handwriting?"

She made no move to take it from him but stood frozen in place, staring at it.

"Mrs. Rayburn," he prompted. "I asked you if you recognized this handwriting?"

"No." Her voice shook. "I've never seen it before."

It was obvious from her reaction that she was lying. "Would you take it and read it aloud, please," he instructed.

"I'm not in the habit of reading other people's correspondence." She held her hands out in front of her and started to back away, moving toward the open doors. Constable Barnes put his notebook down and stepped out from behind the chair.

"Then I shall read it," Witherspoon said.

My darling Nigel,

Prudence dictates that I should remain home tomorrow afternoon tending to my household, but I cannot bear to stay away from you, my darling, when fate has so

obligingly lent a helping hand. Filmore has told me that
she has agreed to help in the infirmary, and as you
already know, he's been sent to Bangalore. Please, my
beloved, let us meet at our usual place—

"Please stop," Helen yelled as she stumbled and
grabbed an armchair for support. "You've no right to
subject me to this. It's undignified. It's unworthy of a
police officer to read such words to a gentlewoman. Those
letters are private and personal."

"You're admitting you wrote them?" Barnes asked.

"I'm admitting no such thing." She took a deep breath
and regained her composure. "The content makes it obvious it was a communication of an intimate nature. Now,
if that's all you've come to show me, I'd like you to leave."

Witherspoon had had enough; he knew she was the
author of the letter. "Mrs. Rayburn, we know you're the
one who wrote this letter and the others. You don't seem
to understand this situation—"

She interrupted. "I understand it perfectly. You're trying to embarrass me by coming here and asking all these
ridiculous questions. I've no idea why Filmore was murdered here, but I had nothing to do with his death and
those things"—she pointed at the letters—"are simply
another police trick to annoy and bully me. As I said,
Inspector, I'm not without influence, and unless you leave
this instant, you shall force me to not only send for my
solicitor, but to use my substantial standing in this city
to make certain you and the Metropolitan Police Department permanently part company."

Witherspoon said nothing for a moment. "Mrs. Rayburn, Constable Barnes and I will wait here while you send whatever messages you like to your influential friends, and as soon as you've done that, you should send for your solicitor and have him meet us at the Ladbroke Road Police Station."

Disbelief, panic, and finally fear flashed across her face. "Are you going to arrest me?"

"I've no wish to do so at this time, but a man was murdered and it is our task to find his killer." He didn't like the way she'd threatened him, but on the other hand, he was certain her bravado was motivated by fear. "While it is true that some of the evidence is pointing in your direction, Mrs. Rayburn, it doesn't necessarily follow that you murdered Mr. Filmore."

Her face crumpled and she sank onto the chair. "I didn't do it, but every time you come here, it gets worse."

"I'm sure it feels that way to you." He smiled sympathetically. "But you must trust that we're not fools and we will get at the truth. If you're innocent, you've nothing to fear. Now, once again, I must ask you. Are you the author of these letters?"

"What makes you think I wrote them?" she charged. The color had come back into her cheeks. "Lots of people write letters. Why do you think they're mine?"

"Because they're all signed, 'Your loving Helena,'" Barnes said dryly. "And they were written in India, in Madras, at the precise time you were there."

"But there were other women named Helena, I wasn't the only one," she argued.

"Oh, but you were," Thea Stanway's cheerful voice said.

All of them turned to see her standing in the doorway. "I'm sorry." She smiled brightly and advanced into the room. "I knocked but no one came. I was afraid something was wrong so I let myself in. Do forgive me, Helena."

Barnes smiled at the new arrival. "Are you certain that Mrs. Rayburn was the only woman named Helena at the army station in Madras?"

"Why are you bringing her into this?" Helena leapt up. "Mrs. Stanway is mistaken. There was another woman with the same name, Helena Ferguson."

"But she never used that name," Thea insisted. "She was always Marie Ferguson. I ought to know, we were good friends. She hated her first name and went by her middle name. No one ever called her Helena, and other than the two of you, there was no one else there with that name."

"Are you certain?" Witherspoon asked her curiously.

"The army station at Fort George Madras wasn't that big, and I knew just about everyone, especially the women and officers. Now, what's this all about? Why is Helena so upset over a name?"

"That's none of your concern. As a matter of fact, Thea, I want you to leave," Helena said quickly. "The police haven't finished interviewing me and your presence here is making the situation more confusing."

"But I came to make sure you were all right. You've had such an awful time since that man was murdered here." Thea looked hurt. "Now you want me to leave?"

Helena gave her a tight smile. "I think that would be best. I want to get this interview over and done with."

Barnes smiled at Thea. "Not so fast, Mrs. Rayburn. By her own admission, Mrs. Stanway knew everyone at the

army station. Perhaps she can help us. Perhaps Mrs. Stanway will know who 'Nigel' might have been?"

"There's no need for that." Helena rushed toward her
friend and took her elbow. "I think Thea ought to go so
we can finish with this."

"Helena, what are you doing?" Thea jerked her arm
down and dug in her heels. "If the police ask for my help,
I'll certainly try to give it to them."

Witherspoon wasn't sure he agreed with his constable,
but he trusted Barnes' judgment so he handed the letter
to Thea. "If you could take a look at this please, we'd be
ever so grateful. I hope it won't embarrass you. It appears
to be a letter written between two people who have an,
er, intimate relationship."

"Thea, I don't think you ought to read that," Helena
warned. "It will embarrass you."

"Don't be silly," Thea assured her friend as she began
to read. "Intimacy doesn't frighten me. I was married."

As she read, Thea's smile faded and her brows drew
together. By the time she reached the end, she'd gone a
deathly pale and her hands were shaking.

Concerned she might faint, Witherspoon stepped
closer and prepared to catch her if the worst happened . . . "Mrs. Stanway, are you alright?"

But she ignored him and lifted her gaze to Helena.
"No wonder you didn't want me to read this."

"Thea, it's not what you think," Helena began.

But Thea cut her off. "Not what I think? Are you mad?
Do you suppose I'm an idiot?" She shook the paper under
Helena's nose. "It's obvious who wrote this letter and who
received it."

"It would be helpful if you would tell us, Mrs. Stanway." Witherspoon shifted uneasily and wondered if he ought to step between the two ladies. But he decided not to move and see what might happen. He had a feeling this confrontation would be important.

"How dare you pretend to be my friend." Thea kept her eyes on Helena. "All these years, I've known he had someone, and it was you all the time." She crumpled the paper in her hand.

"Er, uh, Mrs. Stanway, I'll just take the letter. It's evidence, you see."

Witherspoon tugged the page gently, prying it out of her fist. She didn't seem to notice.

Thea poked her finger in the center of Helena's chest. "Dear God, the two of you must have thought me a fool. It was true, then, all that gossip you told me was just stupid, malicious women talking. I trusted you, Helena." She shook her head and her gaze latched on to the stack on the table. "How many letters were there? How long did it go on?"

"Thea, listen, it was a long time ago and we were weak and stupid . . ."

"Weak and stupid," she cried. "Is that your excuse? You were my friend, my best friend, and you betrayed me. There's the proof of it." She lunged at the stack of letters.

Witherspoon grabbed at them, but she was faster and snatched them up, clasping them to her breast. She backed away, shaking her head as her eyes filled with tears. "You have no right to these now; they should never have been written. You have no right to any part of him," she wailed.

Barnes edged toward her and dived for the letters, but

she nimbly leapt out of the way and scurried toward the opposite corner.

"Mrs. Stanway, please, that's evidence." Witherspoon rushed after her, but she dodged toward the fireplace and wedged herself between the hearth and the glass fire screen, which contained half a dozen stuffed birds sitting on wooden branches.

Thea shook the letters toward them. "Evidence, are you insane? This isn't evidence. That man was my life, Inspector. Nigel was my husband, my beloved husband, and she tried to steal him. I took care of him when he was sick. I came back to England with him when he had to leave the army and took care of him again." She yanked the letter out of the top envelope, flicked it open, and scanned the contents.

"But do you know for sure those letters were written to your husband?" Witherspoon tried to distract her as Barnes once again edged in her direction.

"Thea, you must listen to me," Helena pleaded. "That wretched Filmore probably forged those."

Thea ignored them both as she scanned the contents. "This isn't forged. I know your handwriting and this letter was to my husband." She shook it toward Helena. "Dear God, Isabelle and the other women are right about you. You take anything you want, even if it belongs to someone else. You're a monster, an absolute monster."

"Thea, you can't mean that," Helena pleaded. "You don't understand."

"I understand everything, you miserable, murdering cow. All those years ago, you pretended to be my friend so you could have my husband. But Filmore found out, didn't he. He wanted to make you pay for your sins. Is that why you killed him? So you could save your reputation, so you could get that spot on the Narcissus Committee?" She kicked the fire screen over. It shattered, and birds, branches, and glass hit the floor with an earsplitting crash. She raced for the corridor, throwing the letters toward the inspector as she ran. "I'll never forgive you, never, and I'll see to it that you hang." She ran out the door and slammed it shut behind her.

Smythe took a sip of his pint as Blimpey sat down opposite him. "Sorry I'm late, but Nell had to see the doctor today and I wanted to go with her."

"Is everything alright?"

"It's fine. As a matter of fact, the doctor says she's fit as a fiddle and the only thing that might make either of us ill is the fact that we're worryin' ourselves to death." He sighed. "But both of us really want this baby 'cause we never thought we'd 'ave one."

"It's goin' to be fine, Blimpey," Smythe assured him. "Nell's a strong, healthy woman, and these days, 'avin' a baby isn't as risky as it used to be." He'd no idea if that was true or not, but he wanted to give his friend reassurance and comfort.

"Ta, Smythe, I've got me fingers crossed." He grinned as Lily, the barmaid, brought a pint over and put it down in front of him. He nodded his thanks, took a quick sip, and sighed in satisfaction. "Now, on to business. I've got a lot of information to pass along so listen carefully. First of all, Hiram Filmore wasn't just a businessman. The rumors I heard was that he was suspected of being a thief as well."

"A thief?"

"That's right. When he was in charge of the infirmary, there was a bit of a scandal, and what's more, it was a right ugly scandal at that, the kind the army hates."

"That could mean just about anything."

"No, this one involves the personal effects of dead soldiers. Apparently, the last year or so that Filmore was at the infirmary in Madras, there were a number of letters written to the War Office claiming that effects of the dead men hadn't been sent home."

"What kind of personal effects are ya talkin' about?"

"Rings, tie pins, small objects the soldiers had picked up in India and written home about but which never come back to England. The War Office ignored the first few letters, but when it become a flood, they sent off a nice little note to the commanding officer demanding he do an investigation. Just about then, Filmore left the army and opened his orchid-hunting business, which, by the way, if you're not sponsored by someone with more money than the Bank of England, takes a fair bit of lolly."

"So you're thinkin' that Filmore pinched the bits and pieces to get the capital to start his own business?" Smythe took another sip.

"That's what it looked like at first, but then, another source of mine said Filmore couldn't have been the thief."

"And this second source is trustworthy?"

Blimpey merely raised an eyebrow.

"Sorry, stupid thing to say, go on."

"My informant claimed Filmore wasn't even in Madras when some of the thefts took place. Most of the stuff taken was little things that had some value but not enough for the military to waste money havin' a full inquiry even if a family or two from back home raised a bit of a fuss. But the last couple of objects were valuable; one was a small pinkie ring with a black diamond, and the other was an antique lacquer box inlaid with mother of pearl. But when they were both nicked, Filmore wasn't even workin' at the infirmary. When the ring was taken, he was on leave, and when the box was snatched, he'd gone to one of the outlying towns, a place called Minjur, to give evidence in an inquiry about the disappearance of a local man. Both times, he wouldn't 'ave had a chance to take the goods."

"But if he wasn't a thief, where did he get the lolly to start his business?" Smythe muttered.

"I'm workin' on findin' that out. But that's not all I've got for ya. I found out a bit more about your garden club ladies. Firstly, Isabelle Martell was suspected of murdering her husband by shoving him off a balcony when he was in 'is cups, so to speak."

"I've already 'eard that." Smythe took a sip of beer. "The army was satisfied it was an accident, and supposedly, they rushed the inquiry into 'is death to avoid embarrassin' the family."

"If ya know so much, what ya payin' me for?" Blimpey demanded. "So I suppose ya also know his older brother worked in the War Department."

He nodded.

"Well, there is somethin' ya don't know and I don't know what it 'as to do with Filmore's death, but I'll tell ya anyway. The army was right glad to get rid of Martell. Mind ya, I don't think they murdered the bloke. Martell bought his commission in 1869."

"So what's that got to do with it? 'E was still an English officer."

"Yes, but he went in two years before the Cardwell reforms because he was the second son of a prominent family. It was expected he'd become an officer."

Smythe stared at him blankly.

"Come on, Smythe, surely you've 'eard it. It's 'ow the upper crust makes sure their sons get a leg up in this world without the family havin' to divvy up the goodies. The first son gets the title or inheritance, the second son goes into the military, and the third son goes into the church."

"What about the fourth son?"

"He usually gets sod all. But back to Martell. Even 'is friends claim 'e wasn't the sharpest fellow and it turns out the army agreed with 'em. Martell was just competent enough to 'ang on as an officer, but once the other reforms were put into place and 'e 'ad to compete with men who were genuinely competent, 'e didn't do so well. The army made sure to put him in positions where 'e'd not do too much damage. But even that proved too much, and over the years, 'e'd become less and less able to do even the simplest jobs, especially as he'd developed such a fondness for the bottle. The rumor my source 'eard was that the brass was a bit relieved when he left this world. And truth be told, his brother wasn't all that choked up about it, either."

Smythe nodded thoughtfully. "Just 'ow wealthy was the Martell family? Did he 'ave anything to leave his wife other than his army pension?"

"You mean why did his missus bother marryin' 'im in the first place? You've got to remember, these days, you don't just inherit from the father's side of the blanket. The Martells are prominent but not as rich as they used to be, but he did inherit two good-sized farms from his mother's family." Blimpey grinned. "I was savin' that bit. Major Martell inherited his property right before his accident, and once 'e was dead and out of the way, his missus come back to England, sold them both, and made a good bit of lolly from it."

"That's not all I found out," Blimpey said briskly. "Seems that for a good two weeks before he was murdered, there was a woman keepin' a close eye on Filmore. She was 'angin' about his neighborhood. Sometimes she'd sit in the café across the road from his shop and keep watch, but what really caused her to get found out was when she'd hide in a narrow passageway opposite the shop and watch the man. Guess she thought no one was payin' any attention to her, but she was dead wrong about that. Lots of people noticed her."

"You found out more than the police"—Smythe took a sip of his beer—"but then again, you've got better informants."

"I pay mine more." Blimpey grinned. "But like I told ya, orchid huntin' is an expensive and competitive business, and this mystery woman wasn't the only one keepin' an eye on Filmore."

"Who else was doin' it?"

"Filmore's competitors. Lord Pennington's syndicate paid a street lad to keep watch on him. They wanted to know if he closed up shop and took off for some hot, tropical country to hunt for more orchids. He was good at what he did, good at findin' the rare ones that bring the high prices, and the Pennington syndicate wanted to be at the ready to follow 'im if they had to."

"And this street lad works for you as well?"

"'E does now."

"Mrs. Rayburn, you really should have a cup of tea," Witherspoon urged. He flicked a quick glance toward the open doorway. Constable Barnes nodded in acknowledgment and quietly slipped out into the corridor to find the housekeeper.

"All of us could do with something hot to drink." The inspector thought a good swig of sherry might be even better, but he didn't wish to overstep his bounds. "Mrs. Rayburn, please, are you alright?" At this point, he was more concerned for her health than arresting her for murder.

She'd gone so pale the flesh around her mouth was slightly green, and despite being tightly clasped together on her lap, her hands shook. She stared over the inspector's shoulder, her gaze unfocused.

She'd allowed herself to be led into the small sitting room next to the drawing room so Barnes could rescue the letters and the maids could clear up the broken glass and mangled birds. But she'd not said one word since Thea Stanway's accusations. "Mrs. Rayburn," he began again.

Suddenly, she shook her head. "No, no, I'm not, I'm not like she said. I'm not a monster, I'm not."

"Mrs. Stanway was understandably very upset," he said. "People often say things they don't mean when they've had a shock."

"She said I killed him? She said she'd see me hang, but

I didn't. I didn't kill Filmore. I was afraid he was going to blackmail me, but I didn't even see him that day."

"You mean the day of the murder, Monday?"

She nodded. "He sent me a letter, but he wasn't there when I arrived. No one was there because it had started to rain."

"What time exactly was this?" he interrupted softly. The door opened and Barnes stepped inside.

"I don't know the exact time, but it was past half ten. I know that because I heard the clock strike the half hour when I came into the hall. I was so busy that morning, guests were coming for luncheon, and I was annoyed when the letter came through the mail slot. I almost didn't get it. But I didn't want it sitting in the letter bin when I had guests coming."

"What did it say?" Witherspoon asked.

"Terrible things, disgusting things."

Witherspoon didn't want to press her too hard, but he wanted to keep getting information. "Where did you go after you finished reading it?"

"To St. Michael's. Filmore told me to meet him in the churchyard. So I slipped out and went down the mews. I didn't want to risk anyone seeing me on the street, and there's a footpath at the end of the mews that takes you into the rear of the churchyard," she murmured. "But he wasn't there, and I waited for a while, but he never came. Then I got angry. How dare he threaten me, how dare he?"

"What did he threaten you with?" Barnes asked.

"What do you think? His letter said for me to meet him at eleven if I didn't want the whole world to know about Nigel Stanway." She laughed harshly.

"Do you still have the it, the one he sent you?"

"Do you think I'm a fool, Inspector? I burnt it as soon as I knew he was dead. Oh dear God, this is a nightmare. How can this be happening to me, to me?" She shook her head in disbelief. "This isn't right, it simply isn't right."

"If you're innocent of Filmore's murder, we'll prove it by finding the real killer." The inspector patted her hand sympathetically.

She blinked and jerked her fingers away. "Don't you understand, if Thea trots around London telling everyone about those letters, it could ruin me. Absolutely ruin me! You must stop her."

Witherspoon stared at her incredulously. Surely the woman understood she had much bigger problems than being ruined socially. "And how do you suggest we do that, ma'am?"

"I don't know and I don't care. But you've got to do it," she demanded. "If the Royal Horticultural Society finds out that I had an illicit relationship, they'll give the spot on the Narcissus Committee to Isabelle and not me. I'm not having that, Inspector, I simply am not having it."

CHAPTER 9

———

"I'm so sorry I wasn't here when you first came by." Sir Nathan Ramshaw gave Luty an apologetic smile as he rose to greet her. "But unfortunately, I was at a meeting at the Board of Governors for the bank."

Luty waved her hand dismissively. "Don't apologize, Nathan, it was my fault for stopping by yesterday without sending you word or waiting for an invitation."

She glanced around the opulent drawing room with amazement. For a man who'd started life as a poor boy from the East End, Nathan had done himself proud. Her own home was nicely turned out, if she did say so, but he'd managed to outdo just about everyone except the Queen.

The fireplace was paved in a rare bluish marble and set behind a low fire guard of highly polished brass, the walls were covered with gold leaf patterned paper, and gold and blue velvet striped curtains topped with a trio of valences draped the windows and were tied back by thick gold braided cords. Portraits of cavaliers and ladies were interspersed with exquisite landscapes of the English countryside, and the traditional English furniture was upholstered in a bold hunter green that blended perfectly with the gold and green French Aubusson carpet.

"Don't be silly, Luty, you always have an invitation here." He moved toward her with his arms outstretched. Luty forced herself to smile and stay still as she accepted his embrace. She felt foolish for even entertaining the idea, but the truth was, she'd known him for many years, and to her way of seeing things, he'd always been too free with his hands. She'd always made sure that when they were together, there were lots of people around, but she didn't have that option now—she needed him.

Sir Nathan Ramshaw had started life as a chemist in Whitechapel and then had seen there was money to be made catering to the English in India. By the time he'd come back to England, he had owned a whole network of chemist shops, general merchandise stores, and half a dozen ships that traded goods all over the world. Luty and her late husband had originally met him in Los Angeles years ago.

Sir Nathan ushered her to the settee and then plopped his skinny frame next to her. He was on the short side with a long, bony face and a fringe of thinning white hair circling his bald spot. He didn't let go of her hand and he was so close, she could see the broken veins on his cheeks. "You will stay for tea?"

"Only if it's not a bother." She gently extricated her fingers and eased away an inch or two.

"Don't be ridiculous, you know you're never a bother. Tea will be served in a moment. I ordered it as soon as the butler said you were here. I don't get many visitors these days, Luty, so it's always a treat to see you."

Luty studied him for a moment and felt a rush of shame. The poor fellow was tickled to death to have company. He was just a lonely old man. His wife and his two sons were dead, and despite his money, he probably had lots of empty hours to fill. Suddenly, she realized how lucky she was and how her involvement with the household at Upper Edmonton Gardens had given meaning and purpose to her life. Gerald Witherspoon's staff had given her a beloved godchild as well as a circle of friends that would be there until she took her last breath. Nathan only had money. So she gave him a big smile, reached over, and patted his hand. "I'm pleased to be here, Nathan, but I warn ya, I've come for two reasons."

"And what would that be?"

"One, I want to invite ya to dinner a week from Saturday, and two, I'm here to pick your brain about your time in Madras. I need your help."

"My help, of course, Luty." He stopped as the butler rolled in a tea trolley loaded with a silver service and numerous trays of cakes and biscuits.

"Shall I pour, sir?" the butler asked.

"Yes, please. Luty, would you like cake or biscuits or both?"

"Both, please."

They waited until they'd been served before resuming their conversation. "Now, what is it you need to know?" Sir Nathan asked.

"You were in Madras in the 1880s, right?" She wanted to make sure she hadn't made a mistake.

"I was."

"Did you have anything to do with the people at the army station at Fort George?" She nibbled on a piece of shortbread.

"Of course, they were customers. I opened my first pharmacy in Madras."

"Did ya ever hear any of the gossip that was goin' on?"

He eased back against the cushions and thought for a moment. "I did. But do you mind if I ask what this is about?"

Luty decided to tell him the truth. If he spoke out of turn and told anyone what she was up to, she could counter it by saying he was getting senile. "Murder. I'm helping a friend of mine on a case. He's a police inspector."

He stared at her for such a long time, she thought she'd miscalculated. But then he grinned. "Gracious, that is so exciting. What do you need to know?"

Luty thought back to the meetings in the inspector's kitchen and came up with what she thought was the best question. "Did you ever hear of someone named Hiram Filmore?"

"Oh yes, there were some very unsavory comments about that person." Nathan took a quick sip of tea. "He would say anything for the right price."

Luty tried to keep her excitement in check, but she had a feeling she'd hit the mother lode. "Say anything? What do ya mean?"

"Exactly what I said. The fellow testified in two different inquiries, and both times, his testimony ensured that no one was prosecuted, even though two people died." He broke off and looked away. "I was directly involved in one of them. I'll never forget it, either. It was awful. Absolutely awful."

"Tell me about it," Luty said.

He drew a quick breath and gave her a half smile. "I'm afraid, too, my conduct doesn't speak well of my character or my courage."

"Nathan, there isn't a man or woman alive who gets to be our age that doesn't have a thing or two in their past we'd like to forget ever happened. But take my word for it, this is right important, and I wouldn't be askin' if it weren't important."

"Alright, I've wanted to get this out into the open for a long time. When I was in Madras, a young native woman came to my pharmacy and begged me to help her. It was late at night, you see, and I'd stayed after closing time to mix some prescriptions to send off on the early train to Bangalore. The light was on and I heard someone knocking. When I answered the door, there was this young native woman. She said the local doctor wouldn't come with her and that her brother was dying."

"You know how to doctor people?"

"I'm not a physician, but back in those days I had some skill in medicine and I'd helped one or two of the local people, which is why she came to my shop. So I went with her, but even if I'd been a fully qualified surgeon, I couldn't have helped that poor man. He'd been beaten within an inch of his life." Nathan closed his eyes. "He was lying on a straw mat in one of their huts and he was covered in blood. His nose and most of his ribs were broken. I'm sure he had massive internal injuries and he had a deep head wound. But there was nothing in my pharmacy bag that could save the poor fellow. A lovely young English girl was there. She was nursing him, trying her best to save his life, but it was too late."

"What had happened to him?" But Luty suspected she knew.

"He'd been on his way to an inquest in Minjur, to give evidence in the drowning death of a young Anglo-American man, but he'd been set upon by thugs and beaten." Nathan smiled sadly and cocked his head to one side. "A few moments after I got there, the young man died. Well, as you can imagine, I didn't hang about the place and I left. But I couldn't get it out of my mind. Both the English girl and the native woman were upset. They were certain the young man's injuries hadn't been caused by thugs but were the result of a plot to stop him testifying."

"Testifying to what?" Luty asked.

"Something someone important wanted hushed up." Nathan gave her a knowing look. "This man was a witness in the death of a young American man. It was supposedly an accident."

"And you think this native man was going to testify that the death wasn't an accident."

"I'm certain it wasn't an accident, but I had no way of ever proving it, not without losing my business or possibly my life." He gave her a sad smile. "I know you must think me a coward. Back in the old days, your Leonard would have stood up for what was right without worrying about the cost to him, but I was scared, Luty, really scared, so I said and did nothing. I bitterly regret that I didn't pursue the matter."

Luty reached over and patted his hand. "We all have regrets, Nathan. Leonard was a good man and a good husband, but he wasn't any better a human being than you. During our marriage, we did things to survive that we're not proud of, and that's one of the reasons I like to help the police when I can. It's a way of makin' up for some of our sins. Tell me the details about this situation."

"Will this help your murder investigation?"

"Yes."

"Good, then perhaps there will be delayed justice for both those young men. The young native man was named Jairaj Dariwal, and he was going to testify against an English officer named Malcolm Rayburn when he was attacked. Malcolm and his friends, some fellow officers, had hazed the American fellow, a man named Anthony Treadwell—they'd held him under water unaware that he had a medical condition and he drowned. Young Jairaj witnessed this and was going to testify at the inquest for Treadwell's death. Rayburn and his cronies claimed they were just larking about with Treadwell, trying to teach him a lesson because he'd been overly forward to one of their young women."

"What young woman?"

Nathan shook his head. "Her name was Helena Blackburn, I believe she later married Malcolm Rayburn. The English girl in the hut, the one who was trying to help, had been engaged to Treadwell."

"What happened to her and the native lady?" Luty asked. But she had a feeling she already knew.

Nathan smiled. "They had a bit of a happy ending. But before I tell you that, there was another twist to the tale.

Anthony Treadwell's half brother came to investigate the whole affair and he was a rich and influential American. He used his resources to reopen the inquiry. That's where Filmore pops up again. He testified that he was on the riverbank during the incident and that there was no malice on the part of the English officers. The ruling came back accidental death."

"And the happy ending?"

"The English lady married the American man, who took her and Jairaj's sister to America." He leaned close to Luty. "But I've heard they're back in London and I'd love to meet them. Do you know either of them?"

"No, but I know people who do." Luty wanted to keep him chatting. She'd noticed he was much like her and many other older people—the more you talked about something, the more details they remembered.

They spent another half hour together, and by the time Luty stepped into her carriage for the ride to Upper Edmonton Garden, she had an earful. She chuckled as she settled back in her seat. Hatchet was going to be fit to be tied.

"She'll not be happy to see us, sir," Barnes murmured as they waited in the Martell drawing room.

"Nonetheless, we must interview her again." Witherspoon frowned at the closed double doors. They'd been waiting for the lady of the house a good ten minutes now. "She might be one of the few people in London who can confirm Mrs. Stanway's accusations against Mrs. Rayburn."

"If she knows about it." Barnes got out his notebook and pencil. "Which she might because when Mrs. Stanway was screaming at Helena Rayburn, she made mention there had been gossip about her late husband. Are you thinking we need Mrs. Martell's corroboration about the affair to prove that Helena Rayburn had a motive to murder Filmore?"

"All we have now is Mrs. Stanway's insistence that the letters were written by Mrs. Rayburn to her late husband, but as there are no signatures on any of the correspondence, additional corroboration would be useful."

The doors opened and Isabelle Martell appeared. "My housekeeper says you wish to speak to me."

"We do, Mrs. Martell, and it's about a rather delicate matter," Witherspoon said.

She closed the doors, moved to the sofa, and gestured at the two wings chairs. "Please sit down," she instructed.

As they moved to their seats, Barnes flicked a quick glance at the inspector and could tell by Witherspoon's raised eyebrows that he, too, was surprised by Mrs. Martell's offering them a seat.

"Thank you." Witherspoon put his bowler on the side table and checked that the constable had his notebook at the ready. "Mrs. Martell, as I said, this is very delicate, but it's also very important that you tell us the truth."

"I'm not in the habit of lying, Inspector, but do get on with your questions. I don't have much time today as I'm taking the night train to Paris."

Witherspoon didn't like the sound of that. This case wasn't over as yet, and he didn't like the idea that any of the principals in the case would be leaving the country. But he had no grounds to stop her. "Paris? May I ask how long you'll be gone?"

"Long enough to pick up some new orchids." She smiled

faintly. "Now that I've had a good look in Helena's conservatory, I know exactly what I need to do to win first prize. I've a plant supplier in Paris who has some exquisite vandas as well as a nice collection of calanthes. I should be back in London within a day or so. Why? What does it matter to the police how long I'm gone?"

"You're a witness in a murder, ma'am," he explained. Didn't these women realize that a homicide investigation was more important than an orchid competition? "And your information could be of great value to us."

"I've already told you what I know, which is nothing. I don't see why you two keep darkening my door, but as you have, can you please ask your questions and be done with it."

"Did you know that Mrs. Rayburn was having an illicit relationship with Nigel Stanway?" he blurted out. He'd tried to think of a tactful way to phrase the question but hadn't been able to come up with anything.

Stunned, she gaped at him for a few seconds before she caught herself. "How on earth did you find out about that?"

"Then it's true, they were on intimate terms?"

"Oh dear, you misunderstood me, Inspector." She swallowed heavily. "I meant, how did you hear that old gossip?"

"I don't think that's what you meant at all," Barnes interjected. "And before you say anything else, you ought to know that a little while ago, Thea Stanway identified Mrs. Rayburn as the author of a number of romantic letters written to her late husband. We found those letters in Hiram Filmore's shop. We suspect he was using them to blackmail her."

"As you can imagine, Mrs. Stanway was most upset," Witherspoon added.

Isabelle closed her eyes and crossed her arms in a protective, hugging gesture. "What do you want from me? No matter what I say, I'll be betraying one of my friends."

"Just tell us the truth, Mrs. Martell. Hiram Filmore might not have been your friend, but he deserves justice."

"Really, Inspector? There are plenty of people who think he got precisely what he deserved."

"I didn't realize that Mrs. Attwater was one of your patrons." Ruth Cannonberry smiled at Jeannette Bourcier, her dressmaker. She had stopped in at the Bourcier shop after receiving a note from Octavia Wells. Octavia's note had been short and to the point.

"You and Chloe Attwater share the same dressmaker. Isn't it time you had a new dress?"

It hadn't taken much effort to get Jeannette talking. Even though she was someone who relied on repeat business, she had no hesitation in gossiping about her patrons. Perhaps she knew she could get away with it because she was so talented she could add a touch to an inexpensive day dress that made heads turn when one walked into a room, but her greatest talent was in fooling the observer's eye. Her outfits made even the portliest of matrons fashionable and svelt.

"She's been coming to us since she moved to London." Jeannette pulled a bolt of blue chiffon off the shelf and put it on the table. She was a slender, black-haired woman in her mid-forties, dressed in an elegant gray dress with huge muttonchop sleeves and a tight bodice of pale coral and gray stripes. "Like you, she prefers classical lines in her clothes. But as you're acquainted with her, I'm sure you know that. What do you think of this fabric? It's a bit heavy, but it would make a good gown that could be worn well into the autumn."

"I like it very much," Ruth said. "Shall we look at some dress patterns? I'm not really acquainted with Mrs. Attwater, but I'd like to be. Several of my friends have tried to interest her in our women's group, and she's been very supportive and donates to our great cause, but to date we've not been successful in getting her to join."

Jeannette moved the bolt of cloth to one side and waved at her apprentice. "Madeleine, please bring me the pattern book from the back, the new one that just arrived from Paris." She turned back to Ruth. "I'm surprised she has not joined your group. Like you, she is very much the egalitarian. She is English, but she has lived many years in the American West, but you know that, *n'est-ce pas?*" Jeannette was French and her English was excellent, but occasionally, she slipped into her native tongue.

"I've heard that, but as I said, I've never met the lady."

"She is like you, a lovely widow." Jeannette paused while Madeleine put the pattern book on the table. "I think there are designs in this section which would suit you very well." She flipped the pages until she found what she wanted and then pushed the book to Ruth.

"A lovely widow," Ruth repeated as she glanced down at the open page. "That's very kind of you. This dress is beautiful. I wonder if Gerald would like it?"

"It would look wonderful on you, and your Gerald will like it very much. He is your police inspector, *n'est-ce pas?*"

"He is." Ruth tried to think of a way to bring the conversation back to Chloe Attwater.

"Two lovely widows and such different men. You have the police inspector, and Madame Attwater, she has the advisor to the home secretary."

"Sir Jeremy Sanders?"

Jeannette made sure her apprentice was too far away to hear her and then she leaned close to Ruth. "I am glad you stopped by today. Otherwise, I thought of sending you a note. I know you pass along the tidbit to your inspector, *n'est-ce pas?* But I wasn't certain it was wise to repeat what I heard."

Taken aback, Ruth wasn't sure how to respond. Then she realized denying it would be insulting to both of them. "I do, madame, but you understand, I try to do it discreetly."

"But of course, the man must never know the woman is not just his equal, but his superior in intelligence." She reached across the table and patted Ruth's arm. "Do not look so worried, your secret is safe with me. You do not know it, but you and the inspector's household once saved a friend of mine, a very dear friend, from being arrested for a murder he did not commit."

"I'm glad our efforts were useful in keeping an innocent man from the gallows."

"He isn't that innocent," Jeannette replied, laughing, "but he was never guilty of murder."

Ruth was tempted to ask who it was but decided that as Jeannette hadn't volunteered the information, she might not want to share it. Ruth had heard stories that Jeannette wasn't overly concerned with her gentlemen callers' marital status. "What did you hear?"

"On Monday afternoon, I took a dress to the Attwater house, but the mistress had another visitor so I waited in the small sitting room next to the drawing room. There's a small connecting door between the two rooms and it was cracked open a tiny bit."

Ruth nodded in encouragement, though in truth, she'd bet her next hot dinner that Jeannette's foot had cracked it open even farther.

"That was when I heard about the murder," Jeannette said. "Mrs. Attwater was asking Sir Jeremy to use his influence with the home secretary to make sure that Inspector Witherspoon was given anything he needed to solve Hiram Filmore's murder."

Ruth pursed her lips. "Are you sure this was Monday?"

"*Mais oui*, of course. It was Monday afternoon."

"Do you remember what time you were there?" Ruth didn't understand it. The murder had only happened on Monday, and Chloe Attwater had only learned about the murder from the lad she'd paid to keep watch on the Rayburn home. How had she had time to get a message to the Home Office and then for Sir Jeremy Sanders to get to her house?

"It was four. I looked at the clock because I wondered why Sir Jeremy Sanders was at the Attwater house in the afternoon instead of at the Home Office. But even that question was answered. I overheard her apologizing. She said she hoped she'd not taken him away from anything important and that the home secretary wouldn't be annoyed. In other words, she'd sent for him and he'd come running. But then again, I've heard that both he and Lord Derring are in love with Mrs. Attwater."

Mrs. Goodge gave Hatchet a good frown as he dashed into the kitchen, whipping off his top hat as he headed for his seat. "I'm so sorry to be late, but I couldn't hurry my source along any faster."

"Phyllis and I were late, too," Ruth said. "We just arrived ourselves."

Mrs. Jeffries scanned the faces around the table. "I've a feeling there's a lot to report."

"So let's get on with it," the cook ordered. "Otherwise, we'll all still be sitting here when the inspector gets home. If no one objects, I'd like to go first as I need to make the puff pastry for the chicken pie." She paused for a moment, and when no one objected, she continued. "I had three sources come by today and two of them didn't even know there'd been a murder committed much less anything about either the victim or the suspects."

"You mean the ladies at the luncheon," Wiggins clarified.

"Who else? According to what Constable Barnes told us this morning, half a dozen constables have interviewed Filmore's neighbors, his customers, and the people working around his shop, and they've not found anyone else who wanted him dead."

"What about his competitors?" Smythe remembered what he'd found out from Blimpey. "My source says Lord Pennington's syndicate paid a street lad to keep an eye on Filmore."

"Most competitors don't actually murder their competition," the cook replied. "But can I get on with my report, please, that pastry isn't goin' to mix itself. Now my third source, she was useful and passed along some information about Isabelle Martell. Her nephew is a gardener and he used to work at number 10 Barrington Road in Bayswater,

right next door to Isabelle Martell. He was friendly with
the young man that Mrs. Martell had workin' in her greenhouse, and he run into him a while back and they got to
chattin'. Isabelle Martell used to buy all her orchids and
fancy flowers from a French plant collector in Paris. but
two years ago, she suddenly started giving some of her
business to Hiram Filmore."

"Two years ago?" Mrs. Jeffries said. "She told the
inspector she started using him five years ago when Helena Rayburn introduced him to her gardening club."

"That's not what my source heard, and what's more, she
says the Martell gardener told her nephew that he couldn't
figure out why Mrs. Martell bought any of her plants from
Filmore." She reached for the teapot and poured a second
cup. "He says the plant supplier in France gave her much
better specimens than Filmore ever did."

"Then why did she give Filmore any of her business?"
Mrs. Jeffries asked.

"She didn't know, but my own feelin' is that Isabelle
Martell just wanted to keep her hand in the game, so to
speak. Maybe she gave Filmore business to try and get
him to give her better plants than he was givin' the other
women." Mrs. Goodge scraped her chair back, got up,
and picked up her cup of tea. "I've got to get that pastry
sorted so talk loud enough for me to hear."

"Can I finish my bit now?" Smythe complained. He
told them the rest of what he'd learned from Blimpey
Groggins. "So it looks like there was at least two people
keepin' a close eye on Filmore. You'd think with so many
people watchin' the fellow, that someone would have seen
who killed 'im," he finished.

"This is very confusing," Mrs. Jeffries muttered. "I can understand why Filmore's competitors wanted to know what he might be up to at any given moment, but who on earth was the mystery woman watching him? I expect we'll be even more muddled before things become clear. Who would like to go next?"

"I'll have a go," Betsy said. "I didn't find out very much today, but the lad who clerks at the chemist's on the Kensington High Street told me that Thea Stanway has developed a nervous condition and has started buying laudanum again."

"Again?" Ruth repeated.

"Apparently the same thing happened about ten years ago when she was nursing her husband before he died. She took laudanum then, too." She cocked her head toward the cook's quarters, where Amanda was taking a nap, but must have heard nothing as she relaxed. "That's all I've got."

"Can I go now?" Luty whined. "I found out so much today I'm gonna bust if I don't tell it." She paused for half a second before telling them about her meeting with Sir Nathan Ramshaw. Luty forced herself to slow down as she spoke, making sure she left nothing out.

When she stopped to take a breath, Hatchet said, "Are you certain your information is correct?"

"Sir Nathan is old but he ain't senile," Luty retorted. "We spoke about it for a long time, and as we talked, he recalled more and more details. I got to thinkin' about everything he told me and I suspect that I know who killed Hiram Filmore."

"Tell us the rest of the details," Mrs. Jeffries said.

"As I told ya already, Anthony Treadwell was supposedly

accidentally killed by Malcolm Rayburn and his military buddies because he'd tried to force his attentions on Helena Blackburn as she was then. But when Treadwell's half brother, James Attwater, started raising a fuss and got a proper inquiry started, Sir Nathan remembered that when Attwater's lawyer tried to discredit Helena's story to clear his brother's name, one Isabelle Martell, the new wife of the Major Edward Martell, backed up her friend and claimed she'd witnessed the incident. Another witness to the supposed incident was none other than Hiram Filmore. They both claimed they'd seen Treadwell grab Helena and try to kiss her. Attwater knew they were all lying, but he couldn't prove it."

"So he took Chloe Camden and Kareema Dariwal with him and went home to America," Ruth murmured.

"That's about right," Luty said. "James Attwater fell in love with Chloe, too, and they got married soon after they reached San Francisco."

"You think that Mrs. Attwater murdered Hiram Filmore?" Mrs. Jeffries asked.

"I think she's startin' with him," Luty replied. "And I think she's fixed it so that Helena Rayburn is goin' to hang by making it look like she murdered Filmore. You know, killin' two birds with one stone."

"You think that Mrs. Attwater planned it to happen this way?" Hatchet stared at her incredulously.

"Don't look so surprised," Luty shot back. "I think she's a smart woman who carried on her husband's vendetta against the people who were responsible for Anthony Treadwell's death."

"Then why not kill all of 'em?" Smythe asked. "Malcolm Rayburn and Nigel Stanway are both dead, but you said there were four of 'em that were involved in Treadwell's death. Did she kill those two?"

"Sir Nathan wasn't sure, but he thought one of 'em might have died in India and he'd no idea what happened to the other one." Luty shrugged. "Now, I ain't sayin' Mrs. Attwater did it for sure, but I think we ought to keep a close eye on her. She had the motive and she's the one who left the luncheon. She could have slipped into the conservatory and plunged them shears in Filmore's chest before she went home."

"And Mrs. Clemments told the inspector she went into the conservatory because one of the maids had heard a noise," Mrs. Jeffries reminded them. "But nonetheless, let's find out more before we form any definite conclusions."

"I'll go next," Ruth offered. She told them about her visit to her dressmaker and Jeannette's trip to the Attwater home. "Which, of course, makes the whole situation even more confusing." She shook her head. "If Luty is right and the evidence could be pointing in that direction, then why would Mrs. Attwater involve a high-level government official to ensure that Gerald has every possible resource to solve the murder? He's solved more murders than anyone in the history of the Metropolitan Police."

"It would make more sense if she'd asked Sir Jeremy to take the inspector *off* the case," Phyllis mused.

"We don't know that Mrs. Attwater is our killer." Hatchet ignored Luty's glare and kept on speaking. "If Ruth is finished . . ." When she nodded, he continued. "I'll share what I learned today. My source didn't know anything about what happened years ago in India, but they did know that Isabelle Martell took two hundred pounds in cash out of her bank a week before Hiram Filmore was murdered. The money was in five- and ten-pound notes." Hatchet would die before he'd admit that he bribed half the bank clerks in London before he happened upon this tidbit of information.

"Isn't that the amount the inspector found in the envelope at Filmore's flat?" Mrs. Goodge pulled her rolling pin off the bottom shelf of her worktable and put it next to her mound of pastry.

"That sounds right." Mrs. Jeffries was desperately trying to keep up with all the information but was afraid she was going to forget something important.

Wiggins looked at Hatchet. "If you're done, I'd like to say my bit. It's gettin' late and I want everyone to hear this before the inspector comes home."

"I'm done." Hatchet smiled at Luty, who snorted in disgust.

"I met one of the housemaids from the Rayburn house today," Wiggins began. "And she told me somethin' right interesting." He repeated what he'd learned from Amy Broadhurst, and as the others had, he took his time with the telling, making certain he left nothing out.

"So Mrs. Rayburn got a letter before she went out," Betsy said. "That is interesting because the inspector found a letter in Filmore's shop supposedly from Mrs. Rayburn telling him to meet her in the conservatory. That doesn't make sense. Why would there be two letters?"

"Maybe one of 'em is a fake. Amy thinks the one that popped into the letter box is the reason Mrs. Rayburn went out," Wiggins argued. "She's sure of it, but it's only a feelin' she 'ad. Mrs. Rayburn didn't say as such to 'er."

"Thus far, we've a motive for Mrs. Attwater to murder the victim, some strange doings between Mrs. Martell and Filmore involving money, and Mrs. Rayburn might have been left that morning because of a letter she either sent or received." Mrs. Jeffries sighed. "I don't know what to make of any of this."

"And what I've got to contribute won't help much," Phyllis said. "The only thing I found out was that Susan, the Stanway maid, thinks the murder has distracted Mrs. Stanway from her usual cheap habits. Susan found one of Mrs. Stanway's expensive lace gloves on the floor, and when she asked the mistress where the other one was so she could launder it, Mrs. Stanway told her she'd left it on the omnibus. But this time, Mrs. Stanway didn't make her go halfway across town to retrieve it from the lost property office. Last time, Mrs. Stanway left her old carpetbag at Liverpool Station and made Susan go all the way there to get it."

Witherspoon was late getting home that day. "Do we have time for a glass of sherry before dinner?" He handed Mrs. Jeffries his bowler.

"It's chicken and ham pie, sir, and Mrs. Goodge only just took it out of the oven. She likes it to sit a half hour or so before it's served. There's also stewed lettuce, which isn't cooked as yet, and brown bread pudding. So we've plenty of time for a drink."

"Excellent. I've had the most peculiar day and it will be helpful to get a woman's point of view." He strode down the hall and into the study. Mrs. Jeffries hurried after him.

She poured their sherry and took her seat. "Goodness, sir, now you've aroused my curiosity. What happened today?"

"A substantial incident, well, actually, more than one." His brows drew together. "I think. To begin with, we went to speak to Mrs. Rayburn, and as expected, she denied writing the letter to Filmore instructing him to meet her in the conservatory. But before we left today, Constable Barnes showed it to Mrs. Clemments, and she confirmed the stationery was the same kind that Mrs. Rayburn uses."

"Did Mrs. Clemments confirm it was Mrs. Rayburn's handwriting?"

"She wasn't able to do that, more's the pity." He took a sip. "But then we asked Mrs. Rayburn about the love letters and that's where the day really got interesting." He told her about Helena's reaction when she saw them and how they'd been interrupted by Thea Stanway. "But for once, I was quite grateful for Mrs. Stanway's appearance. She confirmed that there were only two women at the army station with the first name 'Helena' and the other lady never went by her Christian name, but her middle name."

"So the letters had to be written by Helena Rayburn?" Again, something tugged at the back of Mrs. Jeffries' mind, but her head was so full of facts, gossip, and insinuation from today that she couldn't grab the idea and hang on to it.

"They were, indeed, not that she ever admitted it, but Thea Stanway had even more information that confirmed our suspicions." He tossed back the rest of his sherry and put his glass on the side table. "I imagine that poor woman now wishes she'd never set foot in the Rayburn house today."

"I take it she stopped in to see if Mrs. Rayburn was alright?"

"Indeed, and what she found out there will no doubt haunt her for the rest of her life. She didn't deserve what happened today and I do feel sorry for her."

"Let me get you another sherry, sir." Mrs. Jeffries got up, grabbed his glass, and poured him another one. She didn't want him skimping on the details now. "What happened, sir?"

"Thea Stanway found out the recipient of those letters was none other than her own husband, Nigel Stanway."

"Oh my goodness, that must have been dreadfully upsetting for her."

"It was." He took a quick drink and then told her the rest.

Mrs. Jeffries made no comment nor asked any questions as she listened to him. When he'd finished, she said, "Do you think Mrs. Stanway was entirely surprised to learn her husband had an affair?"

Taken aback, Witherspoon's mouth gaped open. "She appeared to be utterly stunned by the revelation. Her behavior certainly leads one to believe that she went into some sort of shock. She dashed about the drawing room, tossing letters willy-nilly even though she knew perfectly well they were evidence, then she kicked a rather expensive fire screen over and shattered it into pieces before she ran out, all the while accusing Mrs. Rayburn of murder and shouting threats that she'd see her hang for Filmore's death. Why did you ask? I mean, I'm astonished that you'd ask that particular question."

Mrs. Jeffries was rather amazed herself, but that's the one that had popped into her head. "Because, sir, most of the women I've known down through the years, even the stupid ones, generally have an inkling of suspicion when their spouses are unfaithful. I find it odd that she didn't, that's all."

Witherspoon thought for a moment. "That's why I wanted your opinion. You know more about women than I do. But on the other hand, Nigel Stanway has been dead for years, and when a loved one is dead and buried, people remember the best of their character and forget their faults."

"I doubt she'd have forgotten infidelity," Mrs. Jeffries said. "What's more, from what you've described as her character, she seems the sort of woman who . . ." She broke off as she tried to think of how best to phrase what she needed to say.

"Likes to mind other people's business," he finished. "Yes, Constable Barnes and I discussed that very thing afterward when we were on the way to interview Mrs. Martell. The constable pointed out that Mrs. Stanway's constant appearances at the Rayburn house was indicative of more than just being a 'concerned friend.' I believe he actually used the term 'nosey parker.'"

Mrs. Jeffries sent up a short, silent prayer of thanks that Barnes has said just the right thing to the inspector. As yet, she was still very confused about this case, but she had a feeling there was something right in front of them that none of them were seeing. "The constable is sometimes very blunt but usually correct." She laughed. "I'm not suggesting that Mrs. Stanway actually knew her husband was having an affair with Mrs. Rayburn, but I do think she had some idea he was being unfaithful."

"That's right, I forgot, that was one of the charges she hurled at Mrs. Rayburn." He frowned as he repeated Thea

Stanway's words. "How stupid of me, I should have remembered that. Of course she suspected her husband of straying from his vows."

"And apparently Helena Rayburn was the one who encouraged her not to listen to the gossip," Mrs. Jeffries murmured. "Why did you reinterview Mrs. Martell?"

"We needed her corroboration about the affair," he replied. "The letters between the lovers weren't signed, and so all we had was Mrs. Stanway's insistence that they were between her late husband and Helena Rayburn."

"What about the handwriting? Couldn't that be identified as Mrs. Rayburn's?"

"Possibly, but the Crown would put their witness on the stand saying it was her handwriting, and the defense counsel could easily call another witness, perhaps even an expert forger who might demonstrate to the court at large how easy it is to imitate handwriting. Mrs. Rayburn has resources, and I've no doubt that if she's arrested, she'll hire the best defense that money can buy."

"And a smart barrister will cast doubt on the authenticity of the letters, and without them, Mrs. Rayburn's motive would also be in doubt." Mrs. Jeffries nodded. "If she knew she hadn't written them, she wouldn't have been susceptible to blackmail."

"That's right, but Isabelle Martell was in Madras as the same time as everyone involved and perhaps in a position to know the truth. So we spoke with her again."

"What did she tell you?"

"At first she tried to pass it off as old gossip, but when I told her that Mrs. Stanway had identified both the writer and the recipient, she relented and admitted that Nigel

Stanway and Helena Rayburn were romantically involved. They met during the afternoons when Mrs. Stanway was at the infirmary and Colonel Rayburn was either at work or away on army business," he said. "I didn't mention the word 'blackmail.' Mrs. Martell brought it up on her own."

"She knew that Filmore had threatened to blackmail Mrs. Rayburn?"

"Not specifically, but she told us that she thought Filmore got exactly what he deserved, that there were rumors about him when he worked at the infirmary."

"What kind of rumors?" She wondered if Isabelle Martell had passed along the rumor that she herself had paid him off to lie about Colonel Martell's accidental death.

"That he was a thief, a liar, and a blackmailer." He put his empty glass down and stood up. "But she refused to say more than that. We're going to speak to Mrs. Attwater tomorrow and see if she can help us. Perhaps she'll remember something that might be useful."

"Are you going to arrest Mrs. Rayburn?" She got up, collected their empty glasses, and followed him out of the room. She still thought there was something right under their noses that none of them could see. But what was it?

He stopped at the door and glanced over his shoulder. "I don't see that I've any choice in the matter. The other ladies might not have liked Mr. Filmore, but the evidence against Mrs. Rayburn is overwhelming."

CHAPTER 10

Mrs. Jeffries checked that the back door was locked and then went upstairs. When she reached the front door, she opened it and stepped out into the warm summer evening. The household was quiet, everyone save her had gone to bed, but she knew it would be useless to try and sleep. Easing the door shut, she locked it, tucked the key in her pocket, and then crept down the stairs. The gas streetlamp across the road shone brightly, but there was no moon, so if she kept to the shadows, it was dark enough for her to feel safe.

She kept to her side of the street as she made her way to the corner. This case was quickly moving from simple confusion to hopelessly muddled, and before it reached that particular stage, she wanted to have a nice long think about it. Nightwalking, as she thought of it, cleared her mind and helped get her thoughts in order.

At the corner, she turned left onto Addison Road and hurried toward the Uxbridge Road, where she crossed and moved onto Royal Crescent. Here there was very little traffic and few pedestrians. She slowed her steps, breathed deeply, and let her thoughts wander.

Tomorrow the inspector would arrest Helena Rayburn, and logically, there was no reason why he shouldn't. She'd lied repeatedly when confronted with evidence that linked her to the crime, she was being blackmailed by the victim, and she had no alibi for the time of death. But if she'd hated and feared Filmore, why had she introduced him to her garden club and given him a substantial amount of business?

A hansom cab turned onto the street, and she quickly stepped back under the overhanging branches of a tree to avoid being seen. Whoever was in the cab was probably harmless, but as a lone woman walking at night, she was taking no chances. When the cab passed, she stepped out and continued her journey.

There were so many questions about this case. If Filmore was a blackmailer, was Helena Rayburn the only one he'd threatened? Had he approached Isabelle Martell? If she'd paid him to lie about her husband's suicide all those years ago, he could hardly claim the high road and threaten to expose her without exposing his own complicity. But he could start some nasty rumors, she thought, and Isabelle Martell, by her own admission, wanted to move into the highest reaches of society. But was that enough of a motive for murder? Would she kill to protect her social reputation?

Mrs. Jeffries reached the corner and turned onto Darnley Place, an even quieter street. Her mind leapt from one thought to another, and she didn't try to force any order to them; she merely let them come. What about Chloe Attwater? If what Luty had told them was true, Mrs. Attwater had the strongest motive of all for murdering Filmore. His testimony helped the men who'd murdered the man she loved avoid punishment. But surely, if she were the killer, she'd not have used her influence to keep Inspector Witherspoon on the case. On the other hand, she'd paid a young lad to keep an eye on Helena's house. Why?

Mrs. Jeffries reached the end of the street and stood there for a moment trying to decide whether to go left, which meant she'd have to walk past the The Queens Arms Pub to get home, or turn right, which was a quieter but longer route. She turned right. The Queens Road was busy, but there were plenty of spots along the way where she could step into the shadows and conceal herself if the need arose.

A hundred yards ahead, two men wearing evening dress came out of a house, so she slowed her pace until they were far enough away to be safely ignored. She went back to her thinking. Chloe Attwater wasn't the only one with prying eyes. Lord Pennington's syndicate had a boy watching Filmore, and Thea Stanway stood vigil at her old nanny's window so much that everyone in the neighborhood had spotted her. But the question was why? What did any of these snoops hope to gain? Lord Pennington's syndicate was the only one that made sense; they had a financial reason for wanting to know that Filmore was in London and not on a collecting trip. She wondered if the woman watching Filmore's shop was also one of Pennington's spies?

As she approached the corner of Addison Road North,

she moved as far away from the gas lamp as possible before turning and heading home. There wasn't much time left. Tomorrow, the inspector would probably arrest Helena Rayburn. There was ample evidence linking her to the crime but somehow it didn't feel right.

Mrs. Jeffries frowned and shook her head in disbelief. Right now her feelings weren't important. Everything they knew about this case was jumbled into a terrible muddle of old sins, innuendos, half-truths, and social-climbing widows trying to out do one another. What she needed was to remember the real reasons that people committed murder. As her late husband used to say, no matter how complicated the crime appears, when someone is killed, it's usually for one of three reasons: money, love, or vengeance.

Samson was curled on Mrs. Goodge's lap when she suddenly stopped stroking his fur and turned toward the back stairs. "Are you talking to me?" she asked as Mrs. Jeffries hurried into the kitchen. "I could hear you all the way down the stairs."

The cat head-butted the cook's arm in an attempt to get the petting restarted, but her attention was on the housekeeper.

"No, no." Mrs. Jeffries smiled sheepishly. "Unfortunately, you caught me talking to myself."

"You were havin' a right old chat with yourself. You kept goin' on and on about some letters. There's so many notes and letters with this murder that I can't keep them straight in my head. So which ones are they?" She resumed stroking the cat.

"The only ones that matter." Mrs. Jeffries came to the table and poured a cup of tea. "The ones that I hope will prove Helena Rayburn is innocent. I do hope that Constable Barnes is early today; there's something he must do. I heard the inspector up and about when I came down, so he'll be wanting his breakfast quickly."

"It's in the warming oven. But you've sussed it out, haven't you." Mrs. Goodge grinned broadly. "I knew you would."

"I haven't, I've just got an idea, but there is a very good chance that all my assumptions about this case are dead wrong." She helped herself to a lump of sugar, gave her tea a stir, and had started to pull out her chair when there was a light knock on the back door. "Thank goodness, he's early today."

A few moments later, Samson had given the visitor a good hiss, Mrs. Goodge had handed off the inspector's breakfast tray to Phyllis, and the two senior members of the household were huddled at the end of the table with the constable.

Barnes looked at Mrs. Jeffries as he reached for his mug. "I'm sure the inspector gave you a full report about yesterday's activities."

"He did," Mrs. Jeffries said. "Constable, he also said that Helena Rayburn might be arrested today."

"The evidence against her is strong," he hesitated.

"But you don't believe she's guilty," Mrs. Jeffries charged.

"And neither does Hepzibah," Mrs. Goodge interjected. "And she's usually right."

"That's true," Barnes agreed. "But none of the evidence points to anyone else."

"Not yet," Mrs. Jeffries said. "But I think there might be a way to prove she didn't do it and to catch the person who did."

The constable eyed her speculatively. "What do you want me to do?"

"It's very simple, and once you find out these few facts, if you come to the same conclusion as I have, then I know we'll be right."

By the time she'd finished and Phyllis arrived with the inspector's dirty dishes, Barnes was fully apprised of what needed to be done. He got to his feet, and just then, there was a knock on the back door.

"I'll get it." Phyllis popped the tray on the worktable and disappeared down the corridor. "Why, Constable Griffiths, this is a surprise."

"I need to speak to Constable Barnes or the inspector," he said.

"Come in, then."

A moment later, they entered the kitchen. Griffiths nodded smartly to the two women and then addressed Barnes. "Sorry to interrupt your day, but I've got a message from the duty sergeant. He wants you and the inspector to come to the station before you go anywhere else."

"Why, what's wrong? Someone confess?"

"That would be good, sir, but no." Griffiths grinned. "There's a man at the station the inspector needs to interview about the Filmore murder. The constable at Filmore's shop sent him along to us, sir. He's demanding to see Inspector Witherspoon. He claims he needs to get into the shop because Filmore sold him all the fixtures and fittings. He's got a legitimate bill of sale. He says Filmore was supposed to meet him at the shop at seven this morning."

"He didn't know Filmore was dead?" Barnes raised his eyebrows. "Ye gods, it's been in all the papers."

"He didn't know. He said he just arrived this morning on the night train from Liverpool. He's in a bit of a hurry, sir. He's rented a wagon and hired three workers."

Mrs. Jeffries was itching to ask questions but knew that she couldn't.

"Did he say why Filmore was selling his fixtures and fittings?" Barnes asked.

"Oh yes, sir, he claimed Filmore was selling the shop and going out to the East to do some orchid hunting."

"This is the first we've heard of this," Barnes said.

Mrs. Jeffries was very grateful. He was asking just the right questions.

"That's what the duty officer told Mr. Tinworth, sir, that's the gentleman's name. He said Mr. Filmore had told him everything had to be kept confidential because he didn't want his competitors to know his business," Griffiths replied. "What should I do, sir?"

"We'll come to the station, Constable," Barnes said. "You go back and tell them we'll be there in a few minutes. Give this Mr. Tinworth a cup of tea and have him hold his horses."

As soon as Griffiths disappeared with Phyllis down the corridor, Mrs. Jeffries said, "Thank you, Constable. I know you kept Constable Griffiths talking longer than necessary so we could hear the latest information."

"I hope it was useful."

"It was very useful. I know that the interview with Mr.

Tinworth is important and that has to be your top priority."

"We'll get to your task as soon as we're done," he assured her. "Don't worry, I'll make sure no one is arrested just yet."

As soon as the two policemen had left, the household took care of the chores and got the kitchen ready for their morning meeting.

Smythe, Betsy, and Amanda arrived first. "Thank goodness," Mrs. Jeffries exclaimed when the three of them entered the kitchen. "I'm so glad you're here." She looked at Smythe. "I need you to do something."

"You've sussed it out." He laughed and looked at Betsy. "You owe me half a guinea. I told you she'd 'ave the answer today."

Amanda held out her arms and started gurgling happily when she saw Mrs. Goodge. Betsy plopped the child into the cook's lap. "You've not won yet," she told her husband. "It might still be tomorrow before she does it."

Mrs. Jeffries didn't know whether to laugh or cry. "Flattering as your faith in me might be, we've much to do today and little time to do it in." She heard the back door open again.

"Figured it out, have ya," Luty cried as she and Hatchet entered. "It's about time, too."

"She's got it," Wiggins said as he took his seat. "Phyllis said she's got that look in her eyes now."

"There is no look," Mrs. Jeffries began only to be interrupted by the maid.

"Oh, but there is, you've had it all morning." She took her spot at the table. "So what is it you need us to do?"

Half an hour later, she'd given them a concise but thorough report on what she'd learned from the inspector and Barnes before sending Smythe, Wiggins, and Phyllis off to learn some very specific information.

When they'd gone, Luty looked at Mrs. Jeffries. "Is there anything I can do?"

"Yes, you can use your resources in the financial community and see if you can find out how much money Chloe Attwater, Isabelle Martell, and Thea Stanway have at the moment. Is that possible?"

Luty grinned. "I'll have to call in a lot of favors, but there's a boatload of bankers in this town that owe me a few."

"What, if anything, should I try to learn?" Hatchet asked.

"We need to find out what Isabelle Martell and Chloe Attwater did after they left the Rayburn home on the day of the murder," she said. "I don't know if that's possible, but do you think you can try?"

"Let me take Isabelle Martell," Ruth suggested with an apologetic smile at Hatchet. "I don't mean to intrude on your task—"

"It's quite alright," he interrupted. "It might take me hours to find out what even one of those women were doing later that day so I'm glad for the help."

Smythe banged on the back door of the Dirty Duck. It was too early for opening but he hoped that Blimpey would be inside having a cup of tea.

The door opened and Eldon, Blimpey's man-of-all-work, stuck his head out. "Hello, Smythe, you wantin' to see the guv?"

"It's right important, Eldon. Is 'e here?"

Eldon ushered him inside. "Come on in, his nibs is having a cuppa. He's in a good mood, too. Should I bring you somethin' to drink?"

"No, I'm fine, but thanks."

Blimpey looked up from the paper he was reading. "Bloomin' Ada, you're early."

"I need your 'elp." Smythe took the stool across from him. "You said that lad that was keepin' an eye on Filmore's place was workin' for you now?"

"That's right."

"Can we find 'im right quick? I need to ask 'im somethin'."

"Mrs. Jeffries has figured it out, has she." Blimpey lifted his heavy ceramic mug and drained it. "Took 'er long enough."

"Blast a Spaniard." Smythe felt obligated to defend Mrs. Jeffries' honor. "It's only been a few days since Filmore got killed."

"Don't get your bowels in an uproar." Blimpey got up. "I was havin' a go at ya and ya fell for it. Come on, then, let's get to movin' if we want to find that young lad before he gets out an' about."

"I am sorry Mr. Tinworth has been inconvenienced." The inspector opened the door of the hansom and stepped onto the pavement. "But it isn't our fault he was unaware of Mr. Filmore's murder."

"He's a businessman, sir, and all he has to do is wait until the local magistrate verifies his bill of sale. Then he can take the fixtures and fittings anywhere he likes."

Barnes paid the driver. "What did you think of his information, sir?"

"It was most interesting. Apparently, Mr. Filmore knew that he was being watched by his competition and went to great lengths to keep his plans a secret. But I am surprised we didn't find any documents relating to the sale in his flat or shop." Witherspoon started for the front door and then stopped. "Let's go to the back door, Constable. You did say it was Miss Pooley you wanted to interview?"

"That's right, sir, it was something you said that got me to thinking." He raced for the servants' entrance, hoping that Witherspoon wouldn't pester him to reveal exactly what it was that had sent them here. He knocked softly on the side door and felt a surge of relief when Peggy Pooley opened it herself.

"Constable Barnes and Inspector Witherspoon." She gave them a welcoming smile and opened the door wider. "The mistress has gone out, but I can get the housekeeper for you."

"That won't be necessary, Peggy," Barnes said. "We don't need to speak to either of them. It's you we're here to see."

"Really, you want to talk to me again? But I've told you everything I know about that day."

"We'd like to ask you some additional questions," Witherspoon said.

"Is it about that ruckus yesterday?" She led them down the hall, pausing only long enough to stick her head in the kitchen. "The police are here again, Mrs. Wickham, and they want to speak to me. I'm taking them into the old butler's pantry."

"Do they want tea?" Mrs. Wickham called.

Barnes shook his head for the both of them.

"They said no," Peggy yelled. She continued down the hall. Opening the door to the pantry, she waited until Barnes and the inspector were seated at the rickety table before she joined them. "What do you want to ask me, sir?" she asked the constable.

"Miss Pooley, you told us that you used to work for Mrs. Stanway, right?"

"That's right, sir, Cook and I both came here at the same time. Mrs. Stanway wasn't an easy mistress and she had a bit of a temper, but she never had a fit like the one she had yesterday."

Barnes had picked Peggy rather than Mrs. Wickham because she liked to talk and he also had a suspicion that she was more inclined to have a bit of a snoop now and then when the mistress wasn't around.

"That must have been very frightening for all the staff." Witherspoon gave her a sympathetic smile.

"It was, sir, but like I say, Mrs. Stanway wasn't easy to work for, and I don't mind sayin' that both Aunt and I were glad to get out of her house."

"Can you be more specific?" Barnes asked.

"It was little things." She tapped a finger against her chin. "It's hard to put it into words, but when she went out, she'd never tell us when she was comin' home, and that made it hard for Auntie to get meals cooked properly. Dinner wasn't a problem, it was served at half seven unless she told us different, but my poor auntie never knew if Mrs. Stanway'd be in for the noon meal, and if she was and it was late or too early, she'd get angry. Plus, she was always lockin' doors."

"You mean the outside door?" Witherspoon asked.

"Not them, I'm talking about the rooms in the house. She had keys to all of them and she carried them in her skirt pockets. She'd go out for hours, and when she'd come home, she'd go to her room or the drawing room, lock the door, and be inside for hours. I know it sounds silly, but after a while it just made you want to leave. I was ever so glad when Auntie got a position here and took me with her."

"What a pity that you never had a chance to see what she was doing behind those locked doors." Barnes shrugged. "It might have been a great help to us."

She glanced at the closed pantry door. "Well, I wouldn't say I never saw what she was up to." She giggled. "Don't say anything to Auntie, she's a Congregationalist and they're right strict about snoopin' and such, but I did see something, twice in fact. Both times Mrs. Stanway was in her bedroom. The first time was an accident. Auntie had sent me upstairs to ask her about something, I can't remember what it was, but when I got there, her bedroom door was open an inch or so. Which was odd because she was so careful about keeping it closed and locked, but the latch was loose and it hadn't stayed shut. Mrs. Stanway was cheap and Mr. Layton, the usual man that did repairs for her, was in Manchester and she wouldn't spend the money to have it fixed by anyone else."

"What did you see?"

"She had a wooden box on her bed, a fancy one with a carved lid, and she was putting something inside it. I couldn't see what it was. She locked it and put the key on the top of the wardrobe ledge. I remember that because she's so short she had to use her footstool to reach it."

Barnes stopped writing and looked at her. "What did you see the second time? Please, Miss Pooley, this could be very important. Your information could help us catch a killer."

"Well, I'd not like you to think I make a habit of doing this, but the second time was the next day. Mrs. Stanway come and hurried upstairs, but it was my afternoon out so I went up to get ready to leave. Just like before, the door was open a bit, so I had a look. Only this time, she'd taken things out of the box and spread them on her bed."

"What things?" Witherspoon asked.

"A small black lacquer box—it was really lovely, it had a mother-of-pearl inlay—and a stack of letters tied up with a blue ribbon; a pouch of some kind, but of course I couldn't see what was in it; and a small brown bottle, you know, the kind you get at the chemist's shop."

"What are you doin' here?" Susan Sawyer looked over her shoulder toward the kitchen.

Phyllis was at the servants' door of the Stanway house, and she was glad that the previous time she'd met the housemaid, she'd pretended to work for a private inquiry agent. "I need to ask you something. Can you slip out for a minute or two?"

"You're lucky the mistress is out," Susan whispered. "Cook's doing next week's menu so I've got a couple of minutes, but that's all." She stepped outside and eased the door shut. "I may not like it here, but I need my position."

"Last Monday, when Mr. Filmore was murdered, what time did Mrs. Stanway come home?"

"She didn't," Susan said. "She didn't get home on Monday till late in the evening. The only reason Cook and I didn't get upset is because she often comes and goes at odd times. I've told you that before."

"What time on Monday evening?" Phyllis pressed. She didn't understand why Mrs. Jeffries wanted to know about Thea Stanway's movements after the murder, but Phyllis knew it must be important.

"Sawyer, Sawyer," a voice called from inside the house. "Where are you? These potatoes need peeling."

"I've got to go." She opened the door and stepped inside. "Coming, ma'am, I just stepped out to get a breath of air." She started to close the door but Phyllis shoved her foot in the opening.

"Please, it's important. What time did she get home that night?"

"It was after ten," Susan hissed. "I know because I was up past eleven cleaning up after she ate her dinner! Now go away before I get the sack."

"Cor blimey, it's taken me half the day to find you," Wiggins said to Kevin Nelson. He'd finally found the lad coming out of St. Michael's churchyard. "You weren't on your patch."

Kevin didn't stop walking. "I'm too busy to hang about the station now. Mrs. Attwater's still got me keepin' watch on the Rayburn house, only she wants me to nip back to her place three times a day. She's payin' me a shillin' a day, can you believe it, a whole shillin'."

Wiggins increased his pace to keep up with the lad. "Can I ask ya something? On the mornin' of the murder, was you keepin' watch on the Rayburn house then?"

"Some of the time, but I nipped back to the station when it started to rain hard." He turned the corner and crossed the busy road, dodging between a delivery van and an omnibus.

Wiggins let the van pass and then ran to catch up with Kevin. "Did you see anyone hangin' about the place before it started to rain?"

"Lots of people, but I don't know 'em by name . . . Wait a minute, I tell a lie, I saw Mrs. Stanway."

"You know who she is?" Wiggins pressed.

"'Course I do. Mrs. Attwater pointed her and another lady named Mrs. Martell out when they were comin' from the Rayburn house. She told me their names and said it was real important I tell her every time one of them went to visit Mrs. Rayburn or when Mrs. Stanway came to see her old nanny. That's where I'm headed now. I've got to tell Mrs. Attwater that Mrs. Stanway is here again."

"Is that where you saw her on Monday, going to her nanny's?"

"She was comin' from the old lady's flat on Monday." Kevin moved sharply right and Wiggins angled to his left to avoid a black-suited businessman racing toward Kensington Station.

"Funny thing is," Kevin continued, "she was wearin' a big hat that hid her face and an overcoat that dragged along the ground. The only reason I recognized her was because she stumbled and lost her grip on the carpetbag and the hat went to one side so I could see who she was."

"The ramifications of Miss Pooley's statement could be enormous." Witherspoon grabbed the handhold as the hansom careened around the corner onto Webster Crescent. "If, of course, the letters she saw from Thea Stanway's box are the same ones that we found in Hiram Filmore's shop."

Barnes thought before he spoke. Mrs. Jeffries and Mrs. Goodge had given him so much information this morning that he was worried he'd accidentally blurt out a fact the inspector would know hadn't come from the police investigation. It had been difficult enough steering him to the Rayburn home to speak to Peggy Pooley, but Barnes had managed it by pointing out that Miss Pooley had worked for two of the three ladies and therefore might know more than she thought she did. He'd only gone there because Mrs. Jeffries had said they needed to know more about Thea Stanway's character and hoped that her former servants could give them more insight. It was only luck that had led to them finding out about the contents of the rosewood box. "She did say that the letters were tied with a blue ribbon and the ones we found at Filmore's shop were bound in the same manner."

The hansom pulled up in front of the Attwater home and the constable silently prayed the hints he'd dropped while they'd discussed the case on the ride here had hit the mark. Mrs. Jeffries had been very specific in what she needed to know, and she'd been sure that as the day progressed, the inquiries she wanted the constable to spearhead would lead both him and the inspector to what she hoped was the right conclusion. At the moment, his only wish was that she hadn't made a mess of things.

"It was good of you to suggest we speak to the girl again." Witherspoon opened the door and stepped out. "Excellent work, Constable."

The front door opened as they climbed the stairs. Kareema smiled politely. "Good day, gentlemen."

"Good day, ma'am." Witherspoon nodded politely and whipped off his bowler. "Is Mrs. Attwater at home? We'd like to speak with her."

She motioned for them to come inside. "She is. If you'll wait in the drawing room, I'll get her."

Mrs. Attwater didn't keep them waiting long; she swept into the drawing room with a welcoming smile. "Inspector, Constable, how nice to see you again. Would you like tea?"

"No, ma'am, we're not staying long. But we do have a few questions for you."

She took a chair opposite them. "Ask me anything. I want to see Hiram Filmore's killer caught."

Witherspoon opened his mouth but Barnes interrupted before he could get the words out. "May we ask why, Mrs. Attwater? From what we understand, Hiram Filmore's testimony ensured that the English officers who killed your fiancé were never punished."

She said nothing for a moment. "You know about that. I'm not surprised. Evil always leaves a trail. There were many people involved in covering up what was essentially the murder of an innocent man. All of them were guilty." She smiled proudly. "And that's why I wanted Filmore's killer caught. I knew the murderer had to be one of those women, and once you make an arrest, all of this, all of what they did, will come out at the trial. The killer will hang and the others will be ruined socially."

"By those women, I take it you mean—"

She interrupted him. "Helena Rayburn, Isabelle

Martell, and Thea Stanway. One of them did it. I'm sure of it. Filmore was out of money, his business wasn't doing well, and old habits die hard. He got the seed money for his business by being a paid liar and blackmailer. He needed cash to fund another trip out to the tropics."

"You're implying he was blackmailing one of these women?" Witherspoon said.

"I'm certain of it. But all of them had something to hide, so as to which one was going to be his current victim"— she shrugged—"I don't know. But I've every faith in you and Constable Barnes. Your record for solving murders is remarkable so I'm sure you'll arrest the right one."

Everyone, except Wiggins, was back in the kitchen well before the usual time of their afternoon meeting.

"You'll have to wait till the kettle boils before we can have tea," the cook warned as they took their places at the table. "And all I've got to go with it is half a seed cake and a loaf of brown bread."

"That will be plenty." Mrs. Jeffries put the cake on the table next to the cake knife and the stack of plates. "Should we wait for Wiggins? No, that won't do, let's get on with it and I can catch him up when he arrives. Phyllis, were you successful?"

"I was. Susan wasn't thrilled to see me, but lucky for her, Mrs. Stanway wasn't home," Phyllis said. "She said that on Monday, Thea Stanway didn't get home till past ten o'clock that night."

"Excellent, Phyllis." Mrs. Jeffries nodded, relieved that her theory now had a few facts to back it up. "Smythe, how did you fare?"

"Pennington's lad was watching Filmore for the past month. A week before the murder, he followed him to Hammersmith Cemetery. The boy hid behind a headstone and kept watch. Filmore met a woman there and she gave him something."

"Did the lad see what it was?" Mrs. Jeffries asked.

"He wasn't sure, but he thinks it was a letter." Smythe moved slightly so Mrs. Goodge could put the teapot on the table. "But I asked if he could identify her if he saw her again. He says he got a good look at her face."

"Can we get him here quickly if we need him?" Mrs. Jeffries reached for the teapot and poured it into the waiting ring of cups.

"He wasn't keen on that, but I think I convinced the boy to do 'is duty." He gave the housekeeper a knowing smile that she acknowledged with a barely imperceptible nod of her head. Smythe had crossed his palm with enough silver to ensure the boy would tell the truth. "Good, this case is coming together for us." She passed the tea down the table.

"I'm glad everyone else has done well." Ruth's expression was forlorn. "All I found out was that Isabelle Martell was supposed to be at the Stanfields' dinner party Monday night but she didn't show. Hilda Stanfield was furious about it, too. Isabelle's excuse was that she was suddenly taken ill that evening."

"Don't look so disappointed, you've done better than I have," Hatchet complained. "I couldn't find any source that knew anything about Mrs. Attwater's whereabouts after she met with Sir Jeremy Sanders that afternoon."

"So we don't know if she stayed in or went out?" Mrs.

Jeffries pursed her lips. "That's unfortunate, but it'll need to suffice. Luty, what did you find out?"

"I didn't have a lot of time, but I found out that Chloe Attwater is as rich as we thought—she's got plenty. Isabelle Martell is doin' alright, too, but it wasn't inherited cash. She spent most of the inheritance from her husband on that fancy house she lives in, but she invested the rest and built up a tidy sum. The lady has a good head for business and doesn't use an advisor or broker. She takes care of her own investin'."

"Helena Rayburn?"

"She's almost broke." Luty put a lump of sugar in her tea. "All she's got is her late husband's pension. There used to be some income from investments, but it's dried up, and Thea Stanway doesn't have much, either. Her husband's family has money, but he died years before his siblings so all the Stanway family cash went to them. I heard somethin' else funny about her—the banker I was chattin' with mentioned that his brother-in-law was Nigel Stanway's doctor, and he thought Stanway was on the mend then the feller up and died. Stanway was supposed to have had some kind of tropical fever, but there was somethin' about his death that hit the doctor wrong. There wasn't anything he could do about it, the man had been ill a long time, so it wasn't considered a suspicious death."

"There was no evidence of poisoning?" Mrs. Jeffries asked.

"Our conversation didn't get that detailed," Luty replied.

Just then they heard the back door open, slam shut, and footsteps racing up the corridor. Fred, who'd been asleep on his rug, jumped up and rushed to greet his best friend. "Cor blimey, Fred, get down, I've only been gone a few hours." Wiggins hurried into the kitchen with the dog trotting at his heels. "Sorry to be late, but I 'ad my reasons." He pulled out his chair and flopped down. "I don't mean to be rude, but you've got to 'ear what I 'ave to say. Somethin' is getting ready to 'appen at the Rayburn place."

"What?" Mrs. Jeffries demanded. Smythe and Hatchet were already on their feet.

"The lad I spoke with today saw someone goin' into the mews on the morning of the murder and it wasn't Mrs. Rayburn."

"Who was it?" Mrs. Jeffries' hands balled into fists.

"It was Mrs. Stanway, but that's not important now," Wiggins cried. "I did what you said and 'ad a word with the boy Mrs. Attwater paid to keep an eye on the Rayburn house, and we need for the inspector to 'ear what he's got to say. We went to the Attwater house 'cause Kevin had to tell Mrs. Attwater that he'd seen Mrs. Stanway goin' into her old nanny's house today. But when Kevin and I got there, the inspector and Constable Barnes come out, and before the lad and I could get round the back and tell Mrs. Attwater what he'd seen, as soon as we'd got shut of them, a carriage drew up and Mrs. Attwater raced out the front door and got into it. That's why I'm so late, I told Kevin to come 'ere while I followed the carriage. He's outside now waitin' for me. It's a good thing I know this part of London like the back of my hand; otherwise I'd never 'ave kept up."

"Where did the carriage go?" A frisson of alarm climbed the housekeeper's spine.

"To the Rayburn house." Wiggins looked worried. "And what's more, I saw Mrs. Martell get out and practically drag Mrs. Attwater into the house. I don't know what's goin' on—that's why I raced back 'ere. What should we do?"

"Should we go?" Smythe was already on his feet and Hatchet got up as well. They both knew what was expected. Wiggins pushed his chair back and joined them.

"Let us know what's going on," Mrs. Jeffries ordered.

"You be careful," Betsy called to her husband, who stopped long enough to blow her a kiss.

Luty got up. "Maybe I ought to go, too. My Peacemaker might come in handy."

Hatchet skidded to a stop and turned. "That won't be necessary, madam." He patted his coat pocket. "I'm equipped to handle any emergencies."

"Still, I might come in useful," Luty called. But Hatchet merely gave her a good frown and hurried to join the others.

"Nell's bells, they never want me to have any fun," Luty muttered as she flopped back into her chair.

Ruth waited until the door slammed before she turned her attention to Mrs. Jeffries. "I don't understand what is going on, but is Gerald safe?"

Mrs. Jeffries hesitated and it was Luty who answered. "Don't worry, Ruth, the men will make sure nothin' happens to him." She turned to Mrs. Jeffries. "Can you tell us what's goin' on now?"

A knot of dread coiled in Mrs. Jeffries' stomach but she dared not show her true feelings. If she was wrong, it could be disastrous for all of them. "I'm not certain," she began.

"Not certain," Ruth interrupted, her eyes pooling with tears. "Hepzibah, I almost lost Gerald on our last case. Please tell me you know what's going to happen."

Mrs. Jeffries thought she knew what was happening, but she wasn't a hundred percent positive. There was always a chance she was wrong and that her evaluation of what she assumed were the facts in the case was completely wrong. "No one knows every detail of the future, but I've a feeling that, by now, our inspector has determined that Helena Rayburn had nothing to do with Filmore's death. What's more, I think it is certain that he's realized there has been a deliberate attempt to manipulate the evidence in such a way as to ensure that the wrong person is arrested for Filmore's murder."

"You mean Helena Rayburn," Betsy guessed. "She's the wrong person?"

"That's right and the person who did kill Hiram Filmore has hated her for a long, long time."

CHAPTER 11

———

"That was very clever of you, Constable," Witherspoon remarked as he and Constable Barnes turned the corner onto the High Street. "I've no idea what made you ask that particular question of Mrs. Attwater, but it most certainly set the cat amongst the pigeons."

Barnes was ready with an answer. "I'm embarrassed to tell you, sir, but my wife heard some gossip from one of our neighbors and I took a chance that what she passed along to me might have a grain of truth in it. Sorry, sir, I know you don't like me discussing our cases . . ." He let his voice trail off.

The inspector waved at a hansom cab dropping a fare two houses down. "Don't be ridiculous, Constable, of course you must talk to your wife. I'm not married, but I discuss our investigations with Mrs. Jeffries and Lady Cannonberry. In our sort of work, it helps to be able to talk about it with a sympathetic ear." The cab pulled up at the curb and he climbed inside as Barnes gave the driver the address.

"I'm please you understand, sir," the constable said as he settled into his seat. "My wife does love hearing about our cases. She's a great admirer of yours, as apparently is Mrs. Attwater."

Witherspoon smiled self-consciously. "Really, Constable, your name was mentioned as well, but we mustn't get our heads turned by flattery. We must keep digging on this case."

"What are you going to ask Mrs. Gilchrist?" Barnes relaxed a bit. He'd been walking on thin ice all day, and at his age, the stress was telling. But now it seemed as if the inspector had turned his sights away from Helena Rayburn and onto the real target.

Witherspoon grabbed the handhold as the hansom hit a pothole. "I want her to verify that Mrs. Stanway was in her flat from the time Mr. Tufts, the Rayburn gardener, was in the conservatory, until she went to the luncheon. It ought to be simple enough."

They discussed the case as the cab traversed the short distance to Bellwood Place. Barnes paid the driver and then glanced across the road to the Rayburn home. "Your instincts are sound, sir," he said as they headed for the front door. "I don't think Helena Rayburn did it, either."

"Yes, we both know who we think killed Filmore, but we'll have a devil of a time proving it."

A few moments later, they were knocking on the front door of Mrs. Gilchrist's flat. When the door opened, Witherspoon's heart sank. The woman standing in front of them was old and her eyes were covered with cataracts. "Who is it?" she asked.

"It's the police, ma'am," Barnes said. "May I take your hand so you can run your fingers over my badge?"

"That won't be necessary, my eyesight isn't very good, but I can see enough to know you're the police." She held the door open. "Please come in. Is this about that awful murder across the street?"

"Yes, ma'am," Witherspoon said as he and Barnes stepped inside. "I'm Inspector Gerald Witherspoon and this is my colleague, Constable Barnes. You are Mrs. Gilchrist?"

"I am." She waited for them to cross the threshold and then closed the door. "Please, come in," she shuffled past them into the drawing room.

The flat was neat and tidy, a three-piece suite of muddy brown horsehair was arranged in front of the sitting room windows, a small dining alcove with a table and four chairs was visible in the little kitchen, and an open door on the far side of the room revealed a bedroom with a single brass bedstead covered with a cream-colored chenille spread. The walls were painted a pale yellow and decorated with needlepoint of biblical homilies, birds, butterflies, and woodland animals in square and oval frames.

She made her way to one of the armchairs by the window and sat down. "I'm quite happy to answer your questions, but I must tell you that I didn't see anything." She lifted her hand and gestured at her eyes. "Cataracts, Inspector, I can't see that far."

"That's quite all right, ma'am." Witherspoon put his bowler on the arm of the overstuffed chair. "As you're aware, there's been a murder across the street. It was a man named Hiram Filmore."

"I know who he was, Inspector. I'm half-blind, not senile. He was killed in Helena Rayburn's greenhouse either before, during, or after a luncheon for her lady friends."

"Of course, ma'am, I didn't mean to imply your faculties were wanting," the inspector said. He glanced toward the constable and noticed that Barnes was moving slowly backward to the coat cupboard.

"I'm sure you didn't. Would you and your constable like to sit down?" She waved her hand toward the chairs. "You'll be more comfortable."

"Thank you, ma'am," Witherspoon sat down.

"I'd prefer to stand, ma'am," Barnes said quickly. "My hip bothers me if I sit too much."

"Of course." She nodded in his direction and then turned her half-blind gaze to Witherspoon and waited expectantly.

"As you know, Mrs. Stanway was one of the guests at Monday's luncheon." Witherspoon tried to think of a tactful way to phrase the question. "As a police officer, it's my duty to confirm witness statements, and Mrs. Stanway has stated she was here with you until she went to the luncheon. Is that correct?" From the corner of his eye, he saw Barnes move. He flicked a quick glance at the constable and saw he was now directly in front of the closet.

Mrs. Gilchrist bobbed her head. "She was here that day. My Thea grew into a very thoughtful and generous woman. She comes to visit me almost every day. As a matter of fact, she was here today."

"What time did she arrive on Monday?"

"She usually comes between ten and half past. I don't know the exact time she arrived on Monday but it was probably close to a quarter past the hour." She grinned broadly, revealing a mouthful of surprisingly white teeth. "She'd bought me my birthday present. When you get to be my age, Inspector, having another birthday means you've beaten the grim reaper one more time." She cackled at her own wit.

"Yes, ma'am, I'm sure that's true." He glanced at Barnes again and saw the constable staring down at the floor. "What time did Mrs. Stanway leave to go to the luncheon?"

"It was probably close to half past twelve, yes, that's right. I remember now, she woke me up. I'd fallen asleep, you see. Too much indulgence in my birthday present, and she had to shake me awake. She said, 'Nanny, I've got to go, it's almost half twelve.'"

"So you were asleep for some of the time she was here with you?" Witherspoon leaned closer to her.

She smiled sheepishly. "I'm ashamed to admit it, because I do so look forward to her visits, but I fell asleep within minutes of drinking my whiskey."

"Whiskey?"

"That was my birthday present from her, a lovely bottle of Laphroaig. It's expensive so I don't get it often, but she'd brought me one and insisted I have a drink with her. Who could resist? It's a great treat, Inspector, and when you get to be my age, you take a nice treat whenever one is offered."

"I understand," he said. "So you were asleep by when? A quarter to eleven? Would that be correct?"

"Yes, I expect it was about then that I nodded off." Her brows drew together in a frown. "Whiskey doesn't usually put me to sleep. But I expect the Laphroaig was a better quality than the bottle Mr. Crannock sends me every Friday."

"You drink a bottle a week?"

"I'm an old lady, Inspector," she retorted with a smile. "And I have few pleasures left in life. But I do like my drink. I've an account with the pub around the corner. He sends me a bottle of whiskey every Friday and I make it last the whole week."

Witherspoon was no expert on spirits, he knew that the quality could vary greatly from one brand to another, but he thought the actual alcohol content was standard. As a matter of fact, he knew it was, since it was determined by statute. "But the drink you had on Monday made you fall asleep? Did Mrs. Stanway pour you a larger than usual glass?"

"No, it was the same amount I usually drink." She gave him a sharp, hard stare and fixed her clouded gaze on him. "What are you implying, Inspector?"

"I'm not implying anything," he protested. "I'm just asking questions."

"You're trying to say that while I was asleep, she might have slipped across the road and murdered that man?"

"We're just trying to get at the facts, ma'am."

"No, you want me to say she wasn't here at that time, but she was here." She slapped her hands against the chair arms. "Now I'll thank you to leave. You'll not get me to say another word against her."

"If you want to prove that she's innocent, let us have

a look around your flat, Mrs. Gilchrist." Barnes had left his spot by the coat closet and come up behind her chair.

She twisted in her seat. "I don't need proof she's innocent. I know she wouldn't do something as awful as murder."

"Then let us have a look around." He kept his voice level, as though the matter were of no importance. "Unless, of course, you'd rather we come back with a warrant? You do understand this is a murder investigation, and we do have the legal right to search any premises that we suspect has evidence of the crime."

"There is no evidence," she cried. "But go ahead, then, search to your heart's content and then I may or may not accept your apology."

Witherspoon wasn't sure what Barnes was trying to accomplish, but he trusted the constable to know what he was doing. He got up. "Thank you, Mrs. Gilchrist, I assure you we'll be as quick as possible and we'll put everything back in the proper place."

Barnes was already at the coat closet. He yanked open the door, scanned the inside, and then dragged out an old carpetbag. It had once been a brilliant red decorated with blue medallions and gold fleurs-de-lis but was now faded and bare in spots. The leather handle was frayed and the clasp was loose. Barnes picked it up carefully and carried it to the chair Witherspoon had just vacated. He put it down on the seat, opened it, and looked inside. "It's lined with oilcloth."

"What is it? What are you doing?" She focused her gaze on the chair. "Is that my carpetbag?"

"Yes, ma'am." The constable kept on rummaging through the contents.

"It can't be, my bag isn't lined with oilcloth."

"It's not sewn in, ma'am." Barnes pulled out a square brown box and handed it to Witherspoon.

He opened it and took out three sheets of folded paper—two of them were fancy cream-colored stationery and one was plain notepaper of the kind one used in a busy household or office.

Barnes gave them a quick glance and went back to digging through the bag. "The cream-colored paper matches the stationery Helena Rayburn uses."

"Let's start with the plain notepaper first." Witherspoon unfolded the top one, stared at it for a moment, and then said, "Constable, look at this." He handed it to Barnes. "It's a list of dates, and there's a small, personal item by each date and next to that a name. The same name all the way down to the bottom of the page."

The constable scanned the contents then glanced at Mrs. Gilchrist, who was watching them with squinted eyes, trying to see what was happening. He put the list down next to the open carpetbag. "What's on the stationery?"

Witherspoon unfolded it and took a look. He handed it to the constable. "It appears she was practicing." He flicked open the last piece of stationery. "Same with this one. She's apparently practiced not just the signature, but the lady's handwriting. There's probably a sample somewhere in that bag."

Barnes dug farther into the bag until his fingers brushed against a hard, rounded object. He pulled out a small, brown bottle and held it close enough for the inspector to read the label. "I think this explains why Mrs. Gilchrist fell asleep, sir."

"What explains it?" she cried. "Tell me what you're doing. This is my house, I have a right to know."

"We're taking your carpetbag into evidence, Mrs. Gilchrist," Witherspoon said gently. "And it appears that the reason you slept so soundly on Monday was because there was laudanum in your whiskey."

Across the street, Helena Rayburn had no idea that an unwelcome visitor had come through her conservatory and into the house. The servants, the only people who would have been able to stop this intrusion, were in the butler's pantry enjoying a very lavish afternoon tea that the mistress had surprised them with earlier today. All of them were stuffing cream cakes, shortbread biscuits, and gooseberry tarts into their mouths as fast as possible.

"But surely you see that your reputation is at risk as well," Helena said to her guest.

"I agreed to come here because Isabelle begged me to listen to what you had to say." Chloe Attwater gave Isabelle Martell a quick, stern glance. "But so far, you've said nothing worth hearing."

Helena stepped away from the fireplace and stopped next to a wingchair. "You're being deliberately obtuse. You know perfectly well that none of our reputations will be enhanced by a scandal, and I might remind you that you've been gone from England for years. Isabelle and I have been right here, and socially, our word will carry far more weight than yours. So if you want a decent place in society, a place where your money won't have any influence, you'll do what I say."

"And what precisely is that?" Chloe leaned forward in

her chair, balancing herself on her parasol. She was enjoying herself immensely.

"We've already told you. We want you to speak to Thea Stanway and make sure she doesn't spread gossip all over town."

"Why would she listen to me?" Chloe interrupted. "I've no influence over the woman."

"You've more influence than we do at the moment," Isabelle muttered.

Helena ignored both their comments. "Secondly, stop telling the police every little detail about what happened all those years ago in India. That matter does none of us any credit. It's ancient history."

"What happens if I don't do as you say?" Chloe picked up her parasol and placed it neatly on her lap.

Helena lifted her chin. "Then I'll have no choice but to speak to a few of my friends about you. I'm sure everyone is dying to hear about your relationship with Sir Jeremy Sanders or Lord Derring. I could say anything I want; it would be my word against yours."

Chloe stared at her for a moment and then burst out laughing. "You're wasting all our time. I don't intend to do one thing to save your reputation, and frankly, I don't care what happens to mine. I'm a widow and both those gentlemen are unattached, so I hardly think they'll be unduly upset about any gossip you spread. But go ahead, do your worst."

"I certainly intend to," Helena snapped.

"Good, because I'll be cooperating fully with the police, and once this case comes to trial, I'm going to be a witness for the prosecution."

"But you don't know anything!" Helena shouted. "How could you? You were gone by the time the body was discovered so what could you possibly say?"

Chloe laughed again. "You really are a fool, aren't you, Helena. Do you think the prosecution is going to bother asking me questions about this most recent murder? No, no, no, once they hear what I've got to say, the entire case will rest on the reason Filmore was killed." Her smile disappeared. "And we all know that the motive for his death started years ago in India. Those murders are the ones I'm going to talk about. I'm going to tell them how your lie to Malcolm Rayburn got an innocent man killed. Was it worth it, Helena? Did two people have to die so you could manipulate Rayburn into marrying you?"

"Stop it, that's not true. He wanted to marry me."

"No, he didn't. His eye had already started roving, and once you realized that, you came up with that disgusting story about Anthony so Malcolm would protect your so-called honor. Then he had no choice but to marry you. But was it worth it? I don't think so."

"You're being cruel," Isabelle cried.

Chloe turned on her. "Cruel? Don't make me laugh. You don't give a tinker's dam about cruelty. You backed up Helena's lies because she was your friend and you didn't care that other people suffered."

"We were young and foolish," Isabelle sputtered. "Listen to reason, this story getting out will hurt all of us."

"It won't hurt me," Chloe yelled gleefully. "Once the court hears what the three of you did to Anthony and Jairaj, one of you will hang and the other two will be completely ruined." She locked gazes with Helena, who'd now gone so pale her skin was almost green. "Once I've testified in court, your chances of getting on the Narcissus Committee will be about one in a million."

"That's absurd," Isabelle interjected. "You've no idea what will or won't be asked in a court case."

"I most certainly do," she snapped. "I'm not the poor nobody I was back then. I've got money and power. I'm going to make sure the truth comes out."

Isabelle's hands balled into fists. "What does that mean? What truth? The fact that your former fiancé tried to rape Helena, or the fact that you acted the tart and married his half brother the moment the ship docked in America? You see, Chloe, you're not the only one who can smear a reputation with half-truths from the past."

Chloe's eyes narrowed and she rose to her feet. "Those are lies and you know it."

"So what?" Isabelle looked smug. "It'll be my word against yours, and people here have known me longer than they have you."

"Try it, Isabelle, and we'll see who comes out the winner."

Across the street, Witherspoon and Barnes came out of the house and stopped on the pavement. Not trusting the old handle, the constable carried the carpetbag under his arm as he glanced up and down the road, hoping to see a hansom cab. Witherspoon was staring at the front door of the Rayburn house.

There was a flash of movement at the entrance to the mews, just enough to catch Barnes' gaze. He stared at the location and Wiggins suddenly popped into view. He stood there for a brief second, making sure the constable had spotted him and then gestured frantically toward the Rayburn house.

"Why don't we go and have a word with Mrs. Rayburn," Barnes suggested. "Let's see if she can identify this stationery as hers." He was thinking fast; he knew that Wiggins wouldn't have risked showing himself if it wasn't urgent. He hoped the inspector wouldn't insist on taking the carpetbag and its contents into evidence immediately. "And we can also see if she can identify that page we found crumpled in the bottom of the bag, the one we think was used as a sample for Mrs. Rayburn's handwriting."

"That's an excellent idea," Witherspoon said.

Inside the house, the three women stood in a semicircle, Chloe leaning on her parasol, Isabelle with her hands on her hips, while Helena clutched a handkerchief in her hand.

Unexpectedly, the door opened. Thea Stanway smiled at them. "May I join you?" She didn't wait for a reply; she just stepped inside and pulled the door shut behind her. "You really ought to keep your voices down, the servants will hear you."

"They're in the butler's pantry." Helena watched Thea warily.

"I know." Thea smiled sweetly. "You provided them with a very elaborate tea so they'd be downstairs while you had your little chat with Mrs. Attwater."

Helena swallowed heavily. "What do you want? Why are you here? How'd you get in?"

Thea reached in her pocket and took out the keys to the conservatory. "You really should have had the lock changed," she chided her. "But you had the locksmith make you a new key to the old one because he still had the mold. Honestly, Helena, stop being so cheap. How much more would it have cost you to get a brand-new one installed?"

"What do you want?" Helena repeated. "Say whatever it is and then get out."

"Why, Helena, I'm hurt. Are you saying I'm not welcome?"

Helena straightened and got some of the starch back in her spine. "After your behavior yesterday, I'm surprised you'd want to come here."

"Why? Just because you made a fool of me by having an affair with my husband?" She moved a few steps farther into the room and stopped. "That wasn't very nice of you, Helena."

"She isn't a nice person." Chloe straightened but kept a tight hold on the end of her parasol. "But then again, you know that. You're not a nice person, either, and neither is Isabelle. They're liars and cheats, but they haven't actually stuck a pair of gardening shears in a man's chest." She gave them a quick, disgusted glance. "They kill with words. At least you used a weapon on Filmore. That's a bit more honest, I suppose."

"Did that inspector tell you he thought it was me?" Thea asked.

"He didn't need to. By the questions he asked, it was obvious they think you're the most likely person to have murdered Filmore."

"That's unfortunate." She pulled a gun out of her other pocket. It was a small derringer. "I don't mind them putting me in their sights, but I did want Helena to suffer a bit longer. She's like Nigel was when he confessed what he'd done and showed me the letters. He thought I'd forgive him. He was so sick, so weak, and it was so easy to hold that pillow over his face until he was dead."

Helena choked out a sob, Isabelle gasped, and even Chloe raised an eyebrow.

Thea looked at their expressions and understood immediately what they thought. "Don't look at me like that. I'm not insane, I'm vengeful. There's a difference. No matter how long it takes, I eventually get back at those that wrong me. Just ask Nanny Gilchrist. I've always been this way. I like holding grudges." She waved the gun at Chloe. "But I don't have anything against you, so you can go."

Chloe didn't wait. She raced across the room and yanked open the door. Witherspoon and Barnes crashed through and into the room. Helena and Isabelle screamed as Thea whirled around just in time for Chloe's parasol to whack her on the arm. "Well, damn," she cried as the derringer fell out of her grip. A loud bang rang out as it hit the floor; ignoring the danger, Thea dived for the gun. But she wasn't fast enough and the inspector, who'd landed hard on his knees, grabbed it and rolled away.

Thea crossed her arms over her chest and stared at him as he caught his breath. "I suppose you're going to arrest me."

The inspector climbed to his feet and did a quick check to make sure everyone was in one piece. "Yes, ma'am, you're under arrest for the murder of Hiram Filmore and the attempted murder of . . . of . . . those two." He waved at Helena and Isabelle.

"And Nigel Stanway," Chloe added. "She just admitted to us she killed him, too."

"Right, then, Nigel Stanway as well."

Wiggins, Smythe, and Hatchet raced back to Upper Edmonton Gardens as soon as they knew the inspector and Barnes weren't dead and that Thea Stanway was under arrest.

"I don't mind tellin' ya, when I 'eard that gunshot, I liked to nearly died. That's twice now there's been a lunatic with a gun the inspector's 'ad to arrest," Wiggins said to the others.

"I don't think she was a lunatic," Smythe commented. "She sounded sane to me when they was leadin' her off to the station."

"Did anyone see you there?" Mrs. Jeffries asked.

"No, Mrs. Jeffries," Hatchet assured her. "A crowd had formed and we managed to stay out of sight."

They were gathered at the table, but this time, Mrs. Goodge had broken out a bottle of sherry. "You were right," she said to Mrs. Jeffries. The women had been talking about the murder since the men had gone. "What made you realize that it was Thea Stanway who killed Filmore?"

"It was the letters," Mrs. Jeffries explained. "What bothered me all along was that we had too many suspects and too many reasons for all of them to want Filmore dead. But those reasons didn't make sense when one thought about it logically." She paused and took a quick drink. "Filmore had been supplying Helena Rayburn and Isabelle Martell with orchids for years. So why kill him now, right before a flower competition that both of them desperately wanted to win?

Why kill the one man who might be able to get you the winning orchid? As for their motives, Helena and Isabelle were both under the impression that the lies Filmore had told on their behalf were well in the past. Why would he blackmail them now? He certainly wouldn't admit to lying at the civilian inquest for Anthony Treadwell."

"You mean he'd not admit to committing perjury," Phyllis said.

"Correct." Mrs. Jeffries nodded approvingly. "When we found out about the love letters between Helena and Nigel, it looked very much like Filmore had decided to use them to blackmail Helena, and that, of course, would give her a motive for killing him. But then I got to wondering, how on earth did Filmore get those letters?"

"Maybe he stole them while the Stanways were still in India?" Luty suggested. "He coulda done that."

Mrs. Jeffries shook her head. "I thought of that, then I remembered that Mrs. Stanway was at the infirmary every day and that her brother was a doctor."

"And someone said that her skills were as good as her brother's," Ruth said.

"Right." Mrs. Jeffries smiled. "So her husband wouldn't have been in the infirmary. He was diagnosed with a fever, not a wound. They wouldn't have used an infirmary bed when she could give him better nursing care at home."

"So Filmore couldn't have had access to the letters when he was in India," Phyllis concluded.

"That was my thinking," Mrs. Jeffries said. "And remember, the Stanways returned from India years before the others. I expect that he had the letters hidden away and she found them after he'd died. But that wasn't the only thing that pointed to her. Remember that Dr. Bosworth said he was certain that Filmore had been stunned with blows from a police truncheon before the killer stabbed him. Thea Stanway was the only person who might have had access to such a weapon."

"How would she have had something like that?" Luty demanded.

"Her old nanny bought a flat that had been owned by a policeman's widow," she reminded them. "A truncheon could easily have been left behind, especially if it had been shoved in the back of a dark closet or cupboard."

"And my source said that Thea Stanway insisted on helping her old nanny find a flat and that the one she encouraged Mrs. Gilchrist to buy was the most unsuitable of the lot," Mrs. Goodge said.

"But she did it 'cause she wanted to keep an eye on the Rayburn home. She made her poor old nanny climb four flights of stairs just so she could spy on Helena Rayburn. That's right mean if you ask me," Wiggins shook his head in disgust.

"And as a bonus, she must have found the truncheon she used to bash Filmore's head with," Phyllis mused.

"That's the only explanation that made sense to me," Mrs. Jeffries agreed.

"But why kill Filmore?" Hatchet asked. "Why not kill Helena Rayburn?"

Mrs. Jeffries thought back to everything they'd learned from Constable Barnes. "Filmore was closing up his shop to go on another orchid hunt. That takes a lot of money. I suspect he was trying to blackmail Thea Stanway to raise some additional cash."

"But what could he know about her?" Phyllis asked.

"That she was the person stealing dead soldiers' personal effects." She looked at Smythe. "Your source said that on several occasions when things went missing, Filmore wasn't at that infirmary. So it couldn't have been him who was the thief. The only other person who was there frequently was Thea Stanway. Not only that, but one of her tasks was to help write the letters that accompanied the personal items back to England, so we know she had access to the items. When she discovered Filmore was going to leave England, she knew she had to act." She looked at Smythe. "Was your lad there when the police took her away?"

"'E was, and he said it was the lady who met Filmore in the churchyard," he replied, "the one who gave him what the boy thought was a letter."

"And I suspect that Thea Stanway gave that letter to Filmore in order to convince him there was a much bigger catch in the pond. Namely, Helena Rayburn."

"That was clever of her," Betsy said. "Thea didn't have much money, but everyone thought Mrs. Rayburn had plenty, and if he had something to blackmail her with, he'd get more money than if he blackmailed Mrs. Stanway. But wouldn't she be upset that everyone would know her husband betrayed her?"

"It might have been the lesser of two evils," Mrs. Jeffries replied. "I suspect she was more concerned with vengeance than with her pride. Murdering Hiram Filmore was useful on two levels—it got rid of a blackmailer and it made the woman who'd stolen her husband's love suffer."

"But why wait so long?" Phyllis asked. "Filmore and Mrs. Rayburn have been in London for years."

"There were two reasons she acted. One, Filmore was getting ready to leave, and two, she realized she could use Filmore's murder to frame Helena Rayburn."

"That lady holds a nasty grudge," Wiggins muttered.

"Indeed she does," Mrs. Jeffries agreed. She glanced at Betsy. "Remember what her maid saw her doing? She destroyed a letter to the housemaid that had left her to go work at the Rayburn house to get back at her, and she was also overheard saying that the two servants who'd left her had better plan on staying at Helena's for a long time as they'd never get a reference from her."

"But holding a grudge for ten years." Betsy shook her head. "That must take a lot of energy."

"Another thing that bothered me was the notes."

"Which ones?" Mrs. Goodge complained. "We've had so many of 'em in this case, I can't keep track of which is which."

"Both of them," Mrs. Jeffries smiled. "The inspector found a note from Mrs. Rayburn instructing Filmore to meet her in the conservatory and to bring her another plant . . ."

"She denied writing it," Mrs. Goodge put in.

"That's because she hadn't written it. Thea Stanway did. But I'm getting ahead of myself. Amy Broadhurst, the Rayburn housemaid, told Wiggins a letter came through the mail slot on the morning of the murder and she was positive that's what sent Mrs. Rayburn out into the rain. Helena admitted to the inspector that she got such a letter but she denied writing the first note. That was one of the reasons I realized that Helena was innocent. Why admit to one letter—a letter that destroys any hope of an alibi—but deny the other? I knew there could only be one reason. Helena never wrote the first note, the one telling Filmore to come to the conservatory."

"But it was found in his things," Mrs. Goodge protested.

"It was put there by the killer," Mrs. Jeffries said. "Let's think back. It took the inspector and Constable Barnes two days before they could search the victim's flat and place of business. Plus, Filmore's keys were missing when his body was searched."

"Thea Stanway took them," Phyllis said. "And she used the keys to break into his flat and home to plant evidence against Mrs. Rayburn."

Mrs. Jeffries beamed proudly. "That's my conclusion. I asked myself, who benefited from the delay in searching? The killer. It gave her time to plant evidence and to muddy the waters."

"Is that why you wanted us to find out what the ladies were doing Monday after the body was found?" Ruth asked.

"Yes, and the only person who we know for certain was out until past ten o'clock that night was Thea Stanway."

"But Isabelle Martell didn't go to the dinner party that night, either," Hatchet reminded her. "And we don't know what Mrs. Attwater did after Sir Jeremy left that day."

"That's true, but Filmore couldn't blackmail Isabelle Martell without incriminating himself. The only thing he really had on her was that she, along with him, had committed perjury during Anthony Treadwell's murder inquiry. He had nothing on Mrs. Attwater. From what we know of her character, if he'd tried to blackmail her, she'd have laughed in his face and told him to do his worst."

"That's true." Ruth giggled. "I like her and I'm hoping that once this is over and done with, she'll join our women's group."

"Furthermore, I suspect Thea was the one that shoved the free return ticket through his landlady's front door. She wanted her gone so the search would be delayed and/or to plant evidence."

"And Kevin did identify her coming out of the nanny's flat and heading into the mews right before the murder," Wiggins said.

"My lad said she was also the one that was keepin' watch on Filmore's shop all those weeks before he died," Smythe added. "Bloomin' Ada, that woman spent 'ours concoctin' this plan. She musta 'ated Filmore's guts."

"She hated Helena Rayburn more," Betsy murmured. "That's the reason she made it look like Helena was the killer. She wanted to see her hang." She looked at Mrs. Jeffries. "She must have stolen the keys to the conservatory."

"She wanted to make sure it remained unlocked," Mrs. Jeffries agreed.

"And I'll bet she loosened those boards at the end of the garden." Luty tossed back the rest of her drink. "She thought of everything."

"Not quite, we all figured it out," Mrs. Jeffries said. "Now we've just got to wait for the inspector to find out the rest of the details. What say we meet here tomorrow afternoon for the final report?"

Everyone agreed that was a fine idea.

The inspector got home quite late that night, but as per usual, Mrs. Jeffries was at the front door waiting for him.

"You look exhausted, sir, and Mrs. Goodge wanted me to let you know how grateful she was that you sent a constable to let us know you'd not be home for dinner. He said you'd made an arrest."

"We arrested Thea Stanway." He handed her his bowler. "At first, we thought she was insane, but she's not. Oh, I know it's late and you must be exhausted, Mrs. Jeffries, but do lets have a glass of sherry. I must talk this out or I'll not get a wink of sleep tonight." He headed to his study.

She hung up his hat and hurried after him. Neither of them spoke until she'd poured him a sherry and taken her seat. "Now, sir, tell me what happened. How did you determine Mrs. Stanway was the murderer?"

"I began to have my doubts this morning." He took a drink. "Actually, I began to doubt that Mrs. Rayburn was guilty several days ago. But I couldn't figure out who else it might be. Then some remark I'd made to Constable Barnes got him to thinking, I can't recall exactly what it was, but he wanted us to go back to the Rayburn home and have a word with one of the maids." He told her about their meeting with Peggy Pooley. "Of course, that information got my 'inner voice' as you describe it thinking that perhaps we ought to have a word with Mrs. Attwater."

"Mrs. Attwater? Why?"

"Well, we originally went to see her to ask her to account for her movements on the Monday afternoon after the body was found, but Constable Barnes had heard some gossip from his wife and he blurted out the most extraordinary question."

"Really, sir?"

He told her about Chloe Attwater's accusations and

how she wanted the killer caught so their past crimes could be brought to light. "Once she found out that Filmore was dead, she used her telephone to contact Sir Jeremy Sanders. Can you believe it, she used that instrument to contact him. I tell you, Mrs. Jeffries, in the future, everyone will have one of those contraptions. Now that I know how useful they can be, I'm thinking of getting one for us. Perhaps I can talk Lady Cannonberry into getting one installed as well. It would save us walking across the garden when it's wet out."

"That's a wonderful idea, sir, but what happened next?" she prompted. Witherspoon loved gadgets, but it was getting late and she wanted him to tell her the rest before he collapsed from exhaustion.

He told her about their discoveries in Mrs. Gilchrist's flat. "Mind you, by the time we reached Mrs. Gilchrist, I was leaning toward Mrs. Stanway as the guilty party, and of course, what we found in the carpetbag confirmed my suspicions. The white note paper was a list of items that had been stolen from dying soldiers."

"And Mrs. Stanway was the only person who was the common factor?"

"That's right. After we arrested her, we confronted her with the list. She admitted she'd taken the items, and she'd sold them and had quite a tidy sum saved. She claimed she deserved them, that she'd spent hours nursing a pack of disgusting men who couldn't be bothered to say a proper 'thank you.' But then Filmore got suspicious and blackmailed her. That's where he got the seed money for his first orchid hunt. From Thea Stanway's thefts."

Mrs. Jeffries felt a rush of relief. She'd been guessing

earlier that Thea was one of Filmore's blackmail victim's. She had deduced it had to be because Filmore realized if he wasn't the thief, it had to be her. It was so good to be proved right. "Then you went to Mrs. Stanway's and made the arrest?" She knew that wasn't true, of course, but she had to pretend ignorance.

"No, we went across the street, to the Rayburn house. I tell you, Mrs. Jeffries, it was extraordinary. I don't think I'll ever understand women. Who would have thought that Thea Stanway would set foot in Helena Rayburn's home after the way she behaved just yesterday?"

She listened carefully as he told her everything that had transpired. "Gracious, sir, that's amazing. What was she going to do with the gun, murder Helena Rayburn?"

"She never actually admitted to that," he replied. "But I expect that's exactly what she had in mind. She told us she'd come to Mrs. Rayburn's today because she'd over-heard a police constable saying that with the evidence we had against Mrs. Rayburn, there was a good chance she'd not be convicted. Mrs. Stanway said she couldn't take that risk, that Helena had to pay for her crimes."

"But what about the crimes Mrs. Stanway commit-ted?" Mrs. Jeffries pointed out. "Surely she doesn't think everyone will turn a blind eye to her murder of both her husband and Hiram Filmore."

He grew thoughtful. "For some odd reason, she thinks her case will never come to trial."

"Why would she think that, sir?" Mrs. Jeffries finished her sherry.

"When we were questioning her, she kept saying that she was the sort of woman who'd spent her whole life watching and listening. That everyone had secrets, too, even very important people."

"What does that mean?"

"She said that when she was working in the infirmary, that as the men lay dying, they often confided in her. Not just the soldiers, but the officers as well. She said they confessed all manner of sins they didn't want on their consciences as they went to meet their Maker. She wrote everything down, and she said that when she gets to court, there will be a lot of important men, powerful and wealthy men, who won't want the world to hear what she's got to say."

"But surely that's nonsense. Surely she can't possibly believe that justice won't be done because she might embarrass a politician or an aristocrat." But as the words left her mouth, Mrs. Jeffries was uneasy. She didn't like to think that in this modern world justice could be so easily perverted. But she wasn't sure.

They discussed the case for a few more minutes and then the inspector retired. Mrs. Jeffries locked up the house and went upstairs. But despite the fact that the crime was solved and the killer caught, she didn't sleep well that night.

Over the next few days, she pushed the case to the back of her mind. But it was brought sharply back into focus one afternoon as she went down the front hall toward the drawing room. She heard someone coming up the front stairs so she went to the door and opened it.

A young man in footman's livery stood there holding a flower with beautiful red blooms. "Are you Mrs. Jeffries?" he asked.

"I am." She couldn't think of anyone who'd send her a potted plant.

"This is for you, then." He put it in her hands, nodded respectfully, and left. The plant was heavy so she shoved the door shut with her foot and took it downstairs. Mrs. Goodge was at her worktable slicing strawberries and Phyllis was cleaning the cooker. Both of them stopped what they were doing and gaped at the gorgeous blooms.

"Goodness, Mrs. Jeffries, those are lovely." Phyllis draped her cleaning rag over the cooker handle.

"Maybe you've an admirer." Mrs. Goodge grinned as she wiped her hands on a tea towel and came to have a closer look.

"I've no idea who sent it." Mrs. Jeffries lowered the heavy terra-cotta pot to the table.

Phyllis pointed to a white envelope propped in the soil. "That should tell you."

Mrs. Jeffries pulled it out, opened the flap, and read the note. She laughed. "It seems I'm not the only one with an admirer. This is for all of us to enjoy."

"Read it then," Mrs. Goodge demanded.

Mrs. Jeffries cleared her throat importantly and began to read.

Dear Mrs. Jeffries and the others at Upper Edmonton Gardens,

Thank you for your help in bringing to light a terrible miscarriage of justice. Don't worry, your secret is safe with me and I know how to hold my tongue.

Please accept this small token of my gratitude and esteem. It is a prize-winning orchid, but as I am no longer a member of the Mayfair Orchid and Exotic Plant Society, I would like you and your friends to enjoy its beauty.

By the way, I'll see to it that no matter how many secrets Thea Stanway threatens to share with the world, she will stand trial and pay for her crimes. So will the others.

Regards,
Chloe Attwater

"I don't know what to think about this," Mrs. Jeffries said when she'd finished.

"What it means, Hepzibah," Mrs. Goodge announced, "is that you've won the prize."